# ONE MORE TOMORROW

## S.A. Martin

Paranormal Romance

New Concepts                    Georgia

One More Tomorrow is an original publication of NCP. This work has never before appeared in book form. This work is a novel. Any similarity to actual persons or events is purely coincidental.

New Concepts Publishing
5202 Humphreys Rd.
Lake Park, GA 31636

ISBN 1-58608-676-6
© copyright Shirley Martin
Cover art by Eliza Black, © copyright 2003

NCP books are available at special quantity discounts for bulk purchases for sales promotions, premiums, fund raising, or educational use. For details, write, email, or phone New Concepts Publishing, 5202Humphreys Rd., Lake Park, GA 31636, ncp@newconceptspublishing.com, Ph. 229-257-0367, Fax 229-219-1097.

First NCP Trade Paperback Printing: 2004

Printed in the United States of America

Other Titles from NCP by S.A. Martin:

Dream Weaver
Night Secrets
The Sacrifice (In the Witching Hour anthology)

Chapter One

*Present day*

Galan lurked in the shadows, a solitary figure intent on finding his prey. Hunger raged inside him, a fiery, agonizing torment. In silence, he bided his time, certain his perseverance would find its reward.

He cursed the darkness, hating what he'd become.

Wishing he were mortal again.

\* \* \* \*

After a long and busy day, Stephanie Novak locked the door of The Bookworm's Delight in downtown Miami and headed for the bus stop. A cool November breeze blew across the deserted streets, making her shiver. Thunder rumbled in the distance, and dark clouds hid the moon. She should have left earlier, but she'd stayed late to stock new inventory and lock up.

As she hurried along, her gaze covered both sides of the street, where the lights of cheap electronic and sporting goods stores glowed behind their barred windows. She didn't like being downtown so late, walking the empty streets, never knowing who or what might be prowling these same avenues, but--

A man sprang out from behind a dumpster. "Hold it there, lady." He held a gun, leveled at her heart. Young and sloppy with clumps of stringy hair hanging past his shoulders, he reeked of alcohol.

Chills raced across her arms and legs. Her mouth went as dry as the Sahara at high noon, but she would not reveal her fright.

The mugger pointed to her wrist. "I like your Rolex. Hand it over."

She took a deep breath. "It's a Seiko, but you can have it," she said as she undid the clasp.

"Whatever. Gimme your purse, too."

A quick movement out of the corner of her eye jerked Stephanie's attention from the mugger. A flash of white and black dashed in her direction.

In a split second, the gun flew out of the man's hand and slid across the sidewalk, clattering onto the street. The thief stared at his hand, then at the pistol lying on the street, like a discarded toy. "Wh--what?"

The tall stranger in a white long-sleeved shirt and black pants darted behind the man and whacked him at the base of his neck.

"Ahhh." The jerk crumpled to the ground with a thud.

"Thank--" Her gaze switched to the criminal, a chill racing along her spine. "You killed him!"

"Nonsense, only put him out of commission for a while ... for a very long while. Don't worry, he won't bother you again."

She gave her assailant a sideways glance. "Shouldn't we call the police? We can't just leave him here to rob someone else when he recovers."

"Yes, of course. Only wait whilst I fetch the gun," he said as he turned away from her.

She stared at his retreating back. Whilst?

The stranger headed for the street to retrieve the weapon, his step lithe and purposeful. He radiated raw, restless energy, as if he'd been imprisoned for a long time, then set free. An air of mystery surrounded him ... mystery and danger, like a hungry cobra. Her fanciful imagination must be getting the best of her, she thought, her steady gaze on him. Besides, he'd just saved her from a very dangerous situation.

With a look of calm assurance, he strode toward her again, giving her a chance to study him. Thick, heavy eyebrows topped eyes that shone like onyx, eyes with a hypnotic, sensuous quality. Sharp, angular features and high cheekbones imparted a harsh cast to his face, as though it had been chiseled from the finest alabaster. His curly black hair was cropped short at the neck, a stiff breeze ruffling the locks on his forehead. He was really handsome, but even by the streetlight several yards away, she thought he could use a slight tan. Just the same, his was an intriguing face, one she'd never forget. A man she would never forget.

Pistol in hand, he joined her. "Nasty things, handguns. Can cause a lot of trouble." Lightly, he touched her arm, nodding toward the criminal. "Here, let's move away from the scoundrel, so you don't have to look at him."

"The police," she reminded him after they moved next to a newspaper dispensing machine.

"Yes." He dug in his pocket and handed her his car keys, indicating a Mercedes parked across the Boulevard. "Whilst I hold the gun on this criminal, please go unlock my car and fetch my cell phone. You must forgive me for asking you to brave the traffic, but better that than to leave you alone with this thug."

"Hey, no problem."

The rush of oncoming cars kept her on the curb for precious minutes, but after an old pickup truck rattled past, she saw a break in the traffic and hurried across the wide Boulevard. Within a couple of minutes, she retrieved the phone, then with another break in the traffic, returned and handed it to him. After he called the police, he pocketed the phone and smiled, turning the full force of his considerable charm on her.

Despite her agitation, she returned his smile. He had that effect on her.

As they waited for the cops, she searched for the right words to thank her rescuer. He'd saved her from a robbery and maybe even--she shuddered to think about it--he'd saved her life. But how had he knocked the gun from the man's hand? It had happened so quickly.

Her gaze roved over the stranger again, this man with a gentle voice but a face comprised of sharp lines and angles. Here was a man who'd just rescued her from a dangerous encounter, one whose smile could make her forget she'd ever been in danger.

Across the street, the #3 MTA bus rumbled past on Biscayne Boulevard. "There goes my bus," she groaned, "and who knows when the police will arrive!"

Lightning scorched the southern sky, one burst after another, followed by loud claps of thunder. A gust of wind whipped strands of hair across her face, and she tucked the locks behind her ears. The temperature dropped several degrees, and now, a rainstorm would catch her for sure.

He inclined his head. "You must let me drive you home, Miss...?"

"Stephanie Nov--everyone calls me Stevie, which I prefer." Her teeth chattered. She didn't even know if she made sense, her narrow escape still gnawing at her nerves. "Thanks for your offer, but I can't expect you to drive me home." What was she doing with this stranger in downtown Miami--at night? "I sure want to thank you for ... for what you did. If you hadn't come along ... well, I--I don't know what I would've done, Mr. ... uh?"

"Galan Kent." He grinned, revealing even white teeth. "It would be my pleasure to drive you home." Richly sensual, his voice slid over her like a Persian kitten. His eyes were dark and mysterious, his gaze quite the most compelling she'd ever seen.

Stevie waved her hand dismissively. "Thanks, but I can take a taxi, Mr. Kent." She wished she could ride home with him, this fascinating man with his ebony eyes and deep voice.

"Galan," he murmured.

"Galan. I can't thank you enough for the way you saved me from this--" she looked toward the man who still lay prone on the sidewalk-- "this jerk, but I can't expect you to do any more for me."

"Why go to the trouble and expense of a taxi when I can take you home?"

"Well...."

Galan folded his arms across his chest. "Don't tell me, let me guess. Now that I've saved you from robbery and quite possibly murder, you fear a fate worse than death." He looked at her closely, a hint of a smile on his face. "Am I correct?"

In spite of her shattered nerves, Stevie smiled. "Like I said, I appreciate what you did for me, but I don't know you from Adam."

In a burst of theatrics, he placed his hand over his heart. "Madam, I assure you I have nothing but honorable intentions." He paused. "Here, permit me to show you something," he said as he dug a wallet from his back pocket and flipped through it.

Stevie liked his hands, strong, masculine hands, the fingers long and expressive. Something told her those hands could be gentle, too. Where had that idea come from?

"I believe you can see well enough by the streetlight." He held his wallet in front of her, showing a laminated card that revealed he belonged to the Police Auxiliary. "I help the police catch criminals," he said in his resolute voice.

How did she know he told the truth? She really couldn't see his photo well by the streetlight. "So? I still don't know you." But she sure would like to.

He smiled, a slow, potent smile that made her want to believe anything he said, no matter how outrageous. "Ah, but--"

Lights flashing, the police car arrived. Two blue uniformed policemen--one tall and the other with a medium build--approached.

The tall cop greeted Galan. "Why, Mr. Kent, they didn't tell me it was your call."

"Indeed." Galan gestured toward the unconscious man. "Bit of trouble here."

Stevie's gaze flew from the policeman to Galan. Apparently her rescuer had told the truth about his membership in the Police Auxiliary, so maybe it was safe to ride home with him. The prospect sent her imagination skittering in a hundred different directions, each one more exciting than the last.

The tall officer focused his attention on Stevie. "You're the young woman who was assaulted?"

"Yes." Loud claps of thunder in the distance made her wince. All she wanted was to go home, forget the damn mugger.

Stepping over the unconscious man, Galan handed the gun to the shorter officer who knelt by the criminal and felt for a pulse.

"This perp's out cold," the officer said to his partner. "I'll call for an ambulance." While he radioed in the request, the other one turned to Galan and Stevie.

"We'll need statements from both of you tomorrow, but you can leave as soon as I get some initial information from you."

"I'll give a statement later tonight," Galan said.

"Fine, Mr. Kent."

Minutes later, the officers gave them permission to leave.

Another clap of thunder boomed, then raindrops poured from a leaden sky, thick, heavy drops that splattered on the sidewalk and dampened her hair and clothes.

Galan tapped her arm. "You don't want to get wet. Permit me to take you home now."

He's a nice enough guy, she thought as she wiped the raindrops from her eyes. Talked funny, though. Where'd he come from, the Dark Ages?

"Okay." Chilled from the rain and convinced she could trust him, Stevie rushed with Galan to his sleek Mercedes. He opened the passenger door for her, then hurried around to the other side and slid into the driver's seat.

"Now tell me where you live," he said as he turned onto S.E. First Street.

"Miami Shores. Just go north on the Boulevard."

"I know where Miami Shores is, in fact, it's not too far from where I live." After the light turned green, he headed north. "You live in a nice area," he said with a quick smile in her direction. "I often pass through there."

"I don't live in one of the big houses. Just rent a small apartment connected to a mansion. Guess it was the maid's quarters at one time."

"You don't live with your parents?" he asked with another glance her way.

"Uh, uh, they live up north." She paused, trying to forget tonight's scumbag as well as family worries. "What about your family?"

He shook his head, sorrow in every line of his face. "They have all been dead for a long time."

"Oh, I'm sorry." He looked so alone with such a deep sadness in his eyes, and she wished she could reach over to touch him, comfort him. She wondered what kind of job he had, or if he had any. Maybe he was a playboy with money to burn; plenty of them in Miami. "You work downtown?"

"No, I had business to attend to this evening."

"Kinda late, don't you think? It's after ten."

"Only time possible."

"Well, where do you work?"

He chuckled. "Maybe I don't work at all." He spoke quickly, sending a faint smile her way. "Mind if I ask why you were downtown so late?"

What a voice, as hypnotic as his eyes, as smooth as black velvet. With a voice like that, she could ride to Los Angeles and back with him and never tire of the trip. The smell of new leather mingled with the faint scent of sandalwood, an unbeatable combination that added to his attraction.

"Madam?"

"Oh!" She licked dry lips. "I'm a manager at a bookstore, and I still had a few things to do after the store closed. It's a temporary job," she added, wondering why she felt the need to explain. "Saving my money for college."

"I see."

They drove in silence as the rain beat against the car windows, and the wipers swished back and forth, like a metronome. Palm trees thrashed in the wind, and rainwater gushed from sidewalks and splashed onto the street, spilling into the gutters.

Stevie observed Galan's hands on the steering wheel, his long, agile fingers, and she wondered if he were a pianist. More likely a magician. How else could you explain how he'd flipped the gun from the mugger's hand?

She liked his nose, an aquiline nose, she guessed you'd call it, his lips sensual and set in a firm line, giving him the appearance of determination. Something about him appealed to her, a quality she couldn't quite put her finger on. The man was really attractive, but she liked a guy to have enough of a tan to show he exercised outdoors. This man must spend most of his days in an office, unless he really was a magician. If so, he was welcome to perform his magic on her. Sweet, wonderful, dangerous magic.

A glance out the window told her the rain had stopped as quickly as it had begun, and Galan turned off the windshield wipers.

"Turn right at the next light," she said, reaching for her purse, setting it in her lap.

They drove onto a wide street with magnificent oaks, grand houses, and planter islands brimming with impatiens on both sides of the street. As silence pervaded the car, the full force of her attack came back to hound her. The rain-slick street reflected the glow of street lights, a faint illumination that offered scant comfort. This pleasant and shady avenue now appeared treacherous, as if a thief hid behind each tree, and danger lurked on every corner.

"Here we are," Stevie said several minutes later. "Home."

There were so many things she wanted to say to him, but the words got stuck between her brain and her lips. A slew of emotions rattled her as she unbuckled her seat belt. Happy--relieved!--to arrive safely at her apartment, she knew tonight was the last she'd see of her rescuer. She gripped her purse handle as cold reality sank in. Never see him again. Why should that bother her so?

He stopped in front of a fine Georgian mansion with wide pillars, where huge ceramic planters brimful with red poinsettias added a dash of color to a white front porch, and a Volvo and a Lincoln Navigator tenanted a curving driveway. Grateful for the bright floodlights that offered a clear view of the spacious yard and the brick walkway to her apartment, she reached for the door handle.

"No, wait. Permit me to open the door for you."

"Thanks, but I'm halfway out already." Stevie stepped onto the rain-slick sidewalk and smiled at him as he came around to her, unsure of the protocol in such a situation. She'd never accepted a ride from a stranger before. "Thanks again," she said, holding her hand out to him, "both for coming to my rescue and for the ride home. I can't tell you how much I appreciate it. I ... I might have been killed, if you hadn't come along."

His hand was surprisingly cool, yet she found his clasp comforting, like an ice-cold coke on a sultry hot day.

"It was nice of you to drive me home," she repeated to cover her confusion.

"My pleasure, Stevie." He withdrew a small notebook and pen from his shirt pocket and scribbled a number on it, then tore out the page and handed it to her. "My phone number. If you ever need help for any reason, please call me." Black, enigmatic eyes stared into hers, and she couldn't have looked away if a Brinks truck had spilled its loot onto the street.

She tucked the paper in her pants pocket. "Thanks, I'll remember," she said, fishing in her purse for her keys. "I thought chivalry was dead, but I see it's alive and well in Galan Kent."

"Anything for a lady. Now, may I walk you to your apartment?"

"You don't need to," she said, unaccountably downcast at the thought of his leaving.

"Please, I'd feel better if I saw you to your door." He placed his hand lightly under her elbow. "Now lead the way." He walked with a certain masculine grace, but the only sound she heard on the pavement was her own footsteps....

From inside her apartment, she watched his long strides as he returned to his car. A real gentleman, she thought, but not quite as open as she liked a man to be, almost as if he had something to hide. Secrets. He wouldn't even tell her where he worked. Well, she'd had enough of sneaky people, and she could manage fine without knowing another, thank you very much. There was something different about his speech, too, something she couldn't quite put her finger on, sort of old-fashioned. But surely his quaint speech was part of his attraction?

Galan Kent had given her a lot to think about--his dark eyes and deep voice, his old world charm that brought to mind some of those vintage movies from the 'forties. Too bad she'd never see him again.

* * * *

Behind an oak tree across the street, Moloch watched as Galan escorted the mortal woman to her door. It's a good thing I came to Miami tonight, Moloch thought, angling his head past a bougainvillea bush to obtain a better view. His original purpose had been to discuss a troublesome vampire with Galan, but now he was beginning to wonder if Galan himself might cause trouble. Look at how he was consorting with a mortal woman! What was Galan's purpose--to lure the woman, transform her into one of the undead? Yes, that was acceptable. Anything else was not.

Suppose Galan developed an attraction for her? She was pretty--for a human. Moloch folded his arms across his chest, his mind scheming. One thing he knew--he would not permit any attachment between a mortal and a vampire, especially Galan, the one he'd chosen as his successor in the Society of the Undead.

Among all the vampires in the world, Galan had always been the most responsible, the most dependable ... until now. What had happened to change him? Or had he changed? Moloch wondered, realizing he couldn't judge Galan by his actions this one night.

But what was his purpose in taking the woman home? Moloch nodded with determination. He would keep a vigilant eye on Galan, and yes, the woman as well.

If he had to, he would destroy her, and take pleasure in doing so. She was such a lovely thing, and that would make draining her blood all the more erotic.

* * * *

Galan headed back toward Miami, with only mild self-reproach for deceiving the young lady with his fake Police Auxiliary card. As for planting recognition in the policeman's mind--he'd erase the memory when he visited the police station later tonight. No harm done. What a stroke of luck to be in downtown Miami so early, when he usually stalked the city in the middle of the night.

If the young lady only knew he'd stolen the Mercedes from a Philadelphia mobster, along with $20,000--what would she think of him then? Well, it wasn't the first time he'd stolen money from a criminal, and it certainly wouldn't be the last. He didn't need the money, of course--he'd amassed a fortune over the centuries--but it didn't hurt to remind these criminals of their vulnerability.

Stopped at a red light, he recalled Stevie's lovely looks. Long blonde hair framed a pretty and certainly fascinating face, one he knew would haunt his dreams for days to come. She was tall, only a few inches shorter than he. And her hair! He hadn't seen such colored locks in many years, a shade that reminded him of Linette. He sighed. Better not dwell on Linette--the recollections were too painful--but concentrate instead on the lady he'd rescued. He liked her attractive nose with a slight tilt at the tip, and he wouldn't wager on it, but he felt sure her eyes were blue. Like Linette's.

Stevie, a lovely woman. Full, lush breasts, a slim waist, and long legs aroused desire and resurrected a hundred memories that refused to stay buried.

He wanted to see her again--he would see her again--but for now, a more immediate wish demanded his attention.

He needed to feed.

\* \* \* \*

On a deserted street in downtown Miami, Galan held a criminal in his superhuman grip.

"Hey, let me go! Who the hell d'you think you are?" A short, squat man with beady eyes, the malefactor twisted and struggled, helpless against Galan's solid strength.

Galan shook him. "You damned son of a bitch, I saw you, not ten minutes ago, when you ravished a defenseless woman." If only he'd arrived a few minutes sooner, he could have saved her, a regret that deepened his fury.

After he hypnotized the victim a few minutes ago so she'd forget her horrible experience, Galan had sought her assailant and found him two blocks from the crime scene, here in this dark alley.

The criminal squirmed in Galan's grasp. "I never hurt nobody."

Galan slapped him across the face. "Don't lie to me, you bastard!"

He tightened his grip, his nails digging into the man's shoulder. "You'll pay for your sin, oh, yes, you'll pay. Consider yourself fortunate I won't kill you ... this time." He shook him harder.

"Don't ever commit such a ghastly crime again, or I promise you, next time you won't escape with your life."

The man trembled, and frightened eyes stared into Galan's. "Wh--what are you going to do to me?"

"This." Galan sank his teeth into the man's neck.

* * * *

Before the first faint lavender glow lit the east, Galan returned to his home, an old two-story stucco set on one-half acre, tucked among a spreading oak, assorted palm trees, and bushy foliage which hid it from view.

With only a thought, he opened his front door, then stepped into a silent, dark living room. Living room. He chuckled, finding bizarre humor in the oxymoron. Like the rest of the house, this room held elegant, comfortable furniture, plentiful adornment to ensure his part-time housekeeper wouldn't become suspicious.

Galan snickered. Moloch didn't know he only fed on criminals but didn't kill them. What would the fiend think of him then? He laughed, not caring what Moloch thought.

As daylight began to creep into the corners, Galan rushed upstairs to his wide bedroom closet and drew the deadbolt. Satisfied with all the events this night but especially with images of the mortal woman haunting him, he climbed into his silk-lined coffin and pulled the lid shut.

* * * *

The early morning sky remained dark and cloudy as Stevie exited the bus and made her way to the bookstore, a couple blocks to the south. As she walked the empty streets, she thought of her attack last week, which brought to mind her rescuer, Galan Kent. What an unusual first name, an unusual man besides, a guy who'd been in her mind a lot since that night. She sighed, wishing she would see him again.

A cold wind blasted her face, making her shiver. She quickened her steps and pushed her jacket collar up around her neck. She had a lot of books to enter into the computer before the place opened, but first, she had to check on Joe, one of the many homeless who slept on the streets and in the doorways of downtown Miami, one of many unfortunates she tried to help.

"Why do you spend so much time with the homeless?" a close friend had once asked.

Stevie had hesitated. "My father is a property attorney up north, and--this isn't something I like to admit--but he accepted a big bribe from a wealthy developer--"

"A bribe?"

"To persuade the zoning board to let the developer build a high rise. The land was supposed to be used for low income housing."

Her friend gave her a puzzled look. "So what's that got to do with you?"

"I know it's just a drop in the bucket, but it's my way of making up for what my father did." She choked on her words. "It's one of the reasons why I decided to study social work in college, instead of going into law like the rest of the family. I wish I could feel the same way toward my dad as I did when I was younger, but it's too late now...."

Too late now, she repeated as she hustled along the street, sidestepping an empty beer can. A glance at her watch told her the police would soon come to rouse Joe from his sleep and chase him on his way--wherever his way might be.

She arrived at Joe's "home"--and stopped. Sprawled on the sidewalk, he lay with his arms flung out at his side, his skin absolutely white. No pool of blood on the sidewalk, no blood anywhere! A look of terror darkened his face. Cold, nameless dread sent chills along her arms and down her legs, a wave of nausea making her swallow convulsively.

"Joe!" she whispered. No answer. "Joe, wake up!"

Gingerly, she felt his wrist but found no pulse. God, how had he died? Why was his skin so pale? Her knees buckled and threatened to give out. Her heart pounded. She leaned her head against the side of the building, her hands clenched so hard the nails dug into her palms.

Seconds passed before she jerked away from the building and kicked a stray bottle, heading for the bookstore to call the police.


## Chapter Two

Arriving home from work in the evening, Stevie tossed her purse onto the sofa and slipped off her shoes. Countless worries taunted her as she walked to the window and stared out. A full moon was rising, wind ruffling the branches of the trees, tossing the leaves to the ground.

A week had passed since she'd found Joe's body, a time when terrifying dreams had filled her nights with images of dead bodies and pools of deep red blood. She closed her eyes, seeing herself race down dark alleys, a skeletal demon in pursuit. A chill ran down her back and arms.

She rubbed her arms. Stop thinking about it.

After she changed into a T-shirt and sweatpants in her bedroom, she checked her bromeliads, orchids, and African violets posing on a room divider, then did a few stretching exercises. House key tucked in her pants pocket, she went outside for her run, bright streetlights illuminating the area on this cool winter night....

Almost home now, when she could shower--who was that man on the sidewalk, only a few yards ahead who blocked her way? He looked ancient, with long, bushy hair, dressed in a flowing black robe down to his ankles--a bathrobe? Even in the dark, she could see him clearly, a shiny pendant dangling from his neck. She caught his stench, like a dead animal. He had a face like a cadaver, wolf-like eyes blazing with evil.

She glanced behind her, then veered out onto the street, careful to keep her distance from him. As she raced on, she dared a look back, but he was gone. How had he disappeared so quickly? She shuddered, afraid to think about him as she neared her apartment.

Perspiration slicked her face and body as she unlocked her door and stepped into the living room. A porcelain table lamp lit the room with a dim glow. The sweetly-fragrant scent of the brassavola nodosa--the lady of the night--greeted her, lifting her spirits. Now for a shower--

The phone rang.

Stevie shoved sweat-soaked locks from her forehead as she headed for the phone, more tired than usual after a run. And relieved to arrive home safely, that old guy still fresh in her mind. She picked up the receiver. "Hello."

"Stephanie--"

Oh, oh, her stepmother.

"Your father and I want to know if you're coming home for Thanksgiving." No greetings, no preliminaries.

"Sorry, Ellen, we're too busy at work. I'd intended to write a letter, let you know."

"Your father and brothers will miss you, as I will," Ellen quickly added. "You've worked at the book store for a long time. I never heard of a place where workers didn't get at least a week off after a year's employment."

Stevie tapped her fingers on her thigh. "It's not a matter of earning a vacation--I have--but as store manager, I can't take off at such a busy time."

"We'll let that go for now, although I'm afraid your father will be disappointed ... as I am, of course. But I also wanted to tell you that Greg and his wife just bought a new house in Scarsdale, a very spacious house, I might add."

"Hey, great," Stevie replied, happy for her older brother. "I'll want to see the house whenever I get back to New York."

"Right. When you get back. By the way, both your brothers are doing well in your father's law practice, making good money. Bob hopes to eventually add your name to the company."

"Sorry, I don't think that'll happen." Stevie shifted her position, resting her hip against the end table. "You know I have other plans. I've made my feelings plain on that."

"Do you have any idea how your attitude hurts your father?"

Attitude? "Ellen, I can't study law just to please Dad. What kind of lawyer would I be if I entered the profession only to make someone happy?"

"Well, I suppose I'll have to tell him you have other plans."

"Yeah, I guess you will."

After a few minutes of desultory conversation, Stevie hung up, sorry they couldn't have ended the conversation on a more agreeable note. All she wanted now was to take a shower and go to bed, forget Ellen's snippy phone call and the weird man on the street.

Later, when she climbed into bed after a warm shower, a hodgepodge of pictures tumbled through her head: the mugger with the gun, Galan coming to her rescue and the ride home with him, Joe's body on the sidewalk, his skin chalk-white. And what had the police concluded from his death? No more than she already knew, and she sensed an evasiveness about their answer, one that only heightened her worry.

But most of all, the terrifying man tonight. Too much had happened within the past couple of weeks, she thought as she punched her pillow and flopped onto her side. Too much.

Troublesome images taunted her as she fell into a deep, dream-filled sleep....

The young woman plunged through the homewood, weaving her way among the oaks and beeches, their skeletal branches stretching upward to a clear blue sky, like supplicants reaching to heaven. She drew her brown woolen cape closer as a cold wind whistled through the trees and molded her dress to her body. Her long skirt caught on the bramble bushes, and she tugged the material loose, so eager to meet her lover she'd scarcely thought of anything else all day.

She left the woods behind and emerged onto a meadow dotted with violets, where pussy willows bordered a clear, meandering stream that flowed southward, and the pleasant aroma of gorse blew her way.

Her lover waited by the chestnut tree at the water's edge. She ran to meet him. "Galan!"

He met her half-way and enfolded her in his arms, kissing her forehead, the tip of her nose, his lips finally covering hers with a passion that left her breathless.

Shading her eyes, she glanced up at the sun as it arced toward the western horizon. "I fear I can't tarry long. You know I want to stay with you, more than anything."

He drew her close to him again. "If we were married...."

"After Michaelmas, we shall wed," she murmured against his hard chest, his heartbeat strong and steady close to her ear.

"Why must we wait until we marry before we pleasure each other?" he said in his tantalizingly low voice that tempted her to surrender.

She drew away, twisting the folds of her woolen skirt between her hands. "We must not sin...." She shook her head, unable to say anymore.

"What troubles you, dearling?"

"Last night, I saw something fearful in the sky." Tears misted her eyes. "A monstrous light with a tail trailing behind it. Oh, what could it be? Surely an evil sign!"

"I saw it, too," he said with a grim nod. She could tell he tried to act bravely for her sake. "Cometa, the monks call it ... hairy star."

"But what does it mean?" she asked, on the verge of tears.

"I do not know, but it has naught to do with us."

"It is God's warning." She wrung her hands while tears streamed down her face. "Galan, I fear ... I fear it means the end of the world."

"Don't say that!" he cried in a harsher voice than she'd ever heard him use. Quickly, he crossed himself. He cradled her head against his chest, then kissed the top of her head. "My love is yours for all time, Linette. Nothing and no one can come between us."

"But if William of Normandy invades England?"

He shook his head. "He wouldn't dare!"

She choked on her words. "I fear something terrible will happen ... something terrible...."

"Terrible!" Stevie jerked awake, her heart thudding against her chest, her long cotton nightgown damp with cold perspiration. Braced on her elbows, she stared around the darkened room, waiting for her heartbeat to subside. Never--ever!--had she had such a vivid dream, as if she'd actually lived through those events.

What did the dream mean? Galan, of course, she recalled from two weeks ago, a man who'd teased her mind constantly since then. Galan, with his dark, mysterious eyes and a voice she'd remember for the rest of her life, a voice rich and sensual

...enticing, too, as if he could persuade her to do anything he wanted, go anywhere he desired.

Galan. Why had that name appeared in her dream? But more important, another question taunted her like an echo that wouldn't fade. Who was Linette?

* * * *

Galan typed the last word, then turned the computer off with a reminder to proofread the chapter when he returned from downtown. He leaned back in his swivel chair, his hands locked behind his head, the sleeves of his white cotton shirt rolled up to his elbows, his long legs stretched out in front of him.

How he wished he were mortal again, to walk in daylight and bask in the warmth of the sun, to know the love of a mortal woman who would give him children and share his life and home, a woman he could care for throughout eternity. But even if his wish were humanly possible, Moloch would never permit it. Moloch, damn the fiend! By all that was holy, how he hated this living death!

But if he could escape his fate? He heaved a deep sigh. There was no escape. He was doomed to number among the undead for all eternity. The undead.

A constant wish tortured him, even though he realized its futility. All through the centuries, he'd longed for a woman who reminded him of Linette, his love from so long ago. He'd never met such a woman ... until now.

"Linette." The whispered name echoed in the silence of the room, yet even as he spoke her name, another face captured his mind. Stevie, with her blonde hair he ached to caress, her gentle voice, the touch of her hand that made him want to take her in his arms, make love to her as a man was meant to love a woman. He had to see her again.

If it were true, as the mortals believed, that you met your soulmate in one life after another, why had he never met Linette again? Why? Why?

A glance at the desk clock revealed it was after two, and surely, Stevie would be sound asleep: a good time to visit. In their naiveté, the mortals believed that a vampire couldn't enter one's house unless invited. Stupid mortals.

In a blink, he found himself in Stevie's bedroom, where she lay on her side facing him, the slow rise and fall of her chest an indication she slept soundly. Her scent tantalized him, a blend of spices and lilac, a poignant reminder of the home he once knew in England, distant centuries in the past. A wash of moonlight spilled through her open window, but he needed no moonlight to study her features.

"Stevie," he whispered in the dark, "why can't I get you out of my mind?" He reached forward to touch her hair, then let his hand drop to his side. "Why do you haunt my dreams?"

Lustrous blonde hair fanned out in splendid disarray down her back and onto her pillow, her slender fingers resting on the bedspread. His gaze followed the swell of her breast, her slender waist, the curve of her hip. He yearned to take her in his arms, devour her with his passion. The sweep of her long eyelashes enthralled him, a lovely embellishment that added to her charm, more exquisite than diamonds. The rapid movement of her eyes under their lids told him she was dreaming.

"May only pleasant dreams accompany your sleep," he whispered.

Her beautiful pale throat offered a temptation almost painful in its intensity, a lure he feared he couldn't refuse.

Yet he knew he must.

His gaze was drawn to the pulse at the base of her throat where its beat, beat, beat, pounded in his ears, louder than a thousand drumbeats, beckoning like a siren song. With his long fingers, he reached toward her throat, aching to touch the soft flesh, to feel the delicate warmth, and--

No! He jerked his hand away, his body throbbing with desire. Resolved to fight this craving that chased every rational thought from his mind, he took several steps back, too well aware he must leave ... and never return.

By St. Aidan! How long could he resist her?

## Chapter Three

On a balmy Sunday afternoon in late November, Stevie figured now would be a good time to catch up on several odd jobs around her apartment. She especially needed to water her orchids outside, all of them hanging from the wooden fence or the limbs of a grapefruit tree behind the "big house." After slipping on her loafers, she headed outside, grabbing her water can that waited by the door.

The leaves of the grapefruit tree fluttered in a pleasant breeze that gave no hint of the coming winter. In her Carpe Diem T-shirt and blue jeans, she was quite comfortable.

Her landlady approached along the walkway, giving her a friendly wave.

"Stevie, I've been thinking--if you're not going home for Thanksgiving, why not have dinner with us? You know we'd enjoy having you." She raised her eyebrows. "Unless you have other plans."

"No other plans." Stevie retrieved her watering can, moving to a phalaenopsis, its plastic pot dangling from a thin branch of the grapefruit tree. "But I wouldn't want to impose on you."

"How can one more person be any trouble? It'll just be us." She squeezed Stevie's hand. "Besides, I always wanted another daughter." Her finger grazed a mottled green leaf of a paphiopedilum. "You have a lovely orchid collection here."

"Thanks, I love orchids! Have for years, ever since a high school boyfriend gave me a cattelya corsage for the prom." She tapped the phal pot. "See this one? When it blooms, it'll have light green flowers, almost the color of your blouse. So pretty! It's called Misty Green. I'm going to enter it in the Miami Orchid Show."

"Sounds great. I can't wait to see it bloom." She bent over to brush a leaf from her slacks. "We'll have dinner at one, but come whenever you like."

Stevie flipped an ant from the leaf of another phal, a hybrid of gorgeous white flowers with pink spots. "What can I bring?"

"Just yourself. I've already bought everything, and dinner is all planned."

"If you're sure..." She thought a moment. "Mrs. Shipley--"

"Hey, why so formal? Just call me Melissa."

"Okay, Melissa." She paused, feeling like an idiot. "Have you seen a strange man around here, an old guy with long, bushy hair? I've seen him a couple times when I'm out on my nightly run. Do we have someone new on this block?"

Melissa frowned. "Someone new? Not that I'm aware of. And you know me," she added with a smile. "I always get all the neighborhood gossip. What did he do?"

Stevie shook her head. "Nothing, really. Funny thing, he just stands on the sidewalk and stares at me, like I had two heads or something. Then he sort of--now, this is going to sound real weird--but he just disappears." Goosebumps broke out over her body.

"Disappears?"

"Yeah, like--" She snapped her fingers--"a puff of smoke." Boy, did that sound stupid. "Must be a logical explanation. After all, it is at night when I run. So he probably just walks off before

I'm aware of it." Yeah, sure. "Anyway, I think I'll stop my nightly run for a while. I thought this area was safe--"

"So did I." Melissa chewed her bottom lip. "I'll ask around, see if anyone else has seen him." The phone rang from inside the house. "Oops, better go. Talk to you later."

Melissa hurried away, leaving Stevie no closer to an explanation than before. With a shrug, she resumed her task. Really, it wasn't like her to let a few incidents rile her, but that man sure was creepy.

Another man aroused thoughts better left forgotten. Galan Kent. Now there's a man for you, she thought, her heart beating faster. He was a real gentleman, so different from all the other men she'd known--maybe too different, as if something set him apart from other men, a quality she couldn't put her finger on. Besides, he seemed so secretive, definitely not honest and open, the way she liked people. Yet she couldn't deny his fascination, like a monster magnet tugging at her.

Anyway, she didn't need any more undependable people or complications in her life. If she'd wanted that, she would've stayed with Jason, the rat. For over a year he'd sworn he loved her, but then he'd gotten another girl pregnant. It'll be a long time before I trust someone again, she thought as she finished watering her orchids. If ever.

\* \* \* \*

A cool wind blew in through Stevie's open living room window, but she liked the chill as she prepared to exercise. A wave of fatigue washed over her, prompting her to wonder if she'd be able to finish her workout. She'd always been in good health, so what had made her so tired? She dismissed her worry, finding solace in her usual remedy: if she didn't think about it, the problem would go away.

She strolled out to the tiny kitchen where she kept her CDs and her player in the cramped space on the counter. After she inserted a CD, she padded back to the living room, heading for her ab machine in the corner. She adjusted her tights, then knelt by the machine and began her exercises to the rousing strains of The Beautiful Galatea. She'd finished fifty reps when a knock at the door interrupted her.

She pushed herself to her feet and strode toward the front door, rolling her shoulders to get the kinks out.

As she peered through the peep hole, her heart lurched. Galan! She never thought she'd see him again. "Come on in," she said, opening the door, determined to keep her voice even.

"Good evening." His gaze met hers, and he entered her living room with a bouquet in his right hand. He moved with animal grace, radiating raw energy. He was all potent masculinity, self-confidence oozing from every pore. She could swear excitement hummed in the air and vibrated off the walls. In his long-sleeved black polo shirt and black jeans, he appeared quite debonair, as handsome as she remembered.

His eyes caught her attention, those dark, mesmerizing eyes. Then her gaze shifted to his tousled black hair. As though following her look, he ran a careless hand through the windblown mass of curls.

With a slight bow, he handed her the flowers. "These flowers were so lovely, they reminded me of you. And oh, yes, I would have called, but I didn't know your number."

How could she ever forget that voice--rich and velvety, like chocolate ice cream, but as warm as summer in Miami.

"How nice!" She inhaled the sweet-spicy scent of pink carnations, fingering the delicate petals of the yellow roses, delighting in the exquisite aroma of the white freesia.

"Thanks for the compliment and the flowers. I'll write down my phone number for you after I put these in water and turn my CD player down."

"Don't lower the volume. Die Schone Galatee." He smiled. "Von Suppe has always been one of my favorites."

"Mine, too. I especially like his overtures." She held up a hand. "Be right back." She grabbed a tall avocado vase and made her way to the kitchen. Within a few minutes, she returned to set the vase on the coffee table and took a moment to admire the effect. Flowers! When was the last time a man had given her flowers? She couldn't remember.

Brushing her hair from her forehead, she glanced his way. "Sit on the sofa, why don't you. Would you like some tea, coffee, wine?"

"Nothing, thank you." His smile was dazzling, like bright sunshine after a thunderstorm. Her heart slammed against her rib cage and jumped up to her throat.

"Rather a coincidence to hear classical music here," he said after she gave him her telephone number and joined him on the leather sofa, "because I have tickets to a Viennese string quartet at the Gusman Theater next Friday night. Would you care to join me?"

Would she care? Does it snow in Alaska? She smoothed her hand across the leather sofa. "I'd like that." A slight pause. "By the way, my last name is Novak."

"Yes." He said it as if he already knew. Had she told him her name? She must have.

"You have an unusual first name," she said, frantically searching for something to say. "Don't think I've heard it before."

"An old name, goes back hundreds of years." He stretched his legs out. "That reminds me, I've made a study of names. Take Stephanie, for instance--"

She laughed. "You take Stephanie. I like Stevie better."

"Ah, but Stephanie is a lovely name. Now let me tell you its derivation and what it means...."

Those wonderfully expressive hands fascinated her as he spoke, each gesture meaningful and succinct. His voice had a penetrating quality, and even though he talked in low tones, something told her his voice would carry a great distance.

And his eyes. What did she see in those dark eyes? Secrets he'd never reveal. Secrets she wished she knew.

They fell silent while The Beautiful Galatea reached its climactic conclusion. She slanted a look at him, shocked to see the intense expression on his face. She'd give anything to know his thoughts. Would he always remain such a mystery?

\* \* \* \*

As silent as a shadow, Galan left the deserted warehouse directly north of downtown Miami where a graveyard of neglected buildings polluted the landscape, and garbage cluttered the sidewalk. An occasional car sped past on the Boulevard, its headlights cutting a swath through the early morning darkness.

Enough feeding for now....

Within seconds, he arrived in his backyard, among the magnificent oaks and Australian pines. A glance upward revealed a quarter moon floating among the Pleiades, an array of brilliant stars lighting the night sky. The hibiscus bushes swayed in the breeze, a cool breeze, he supposed, but temperatures meant nothing to him.

Unable to banish morose memories, Galan recalled the events of almost one-thousand years ago, and all that had happened since then. Far better if he had died on the battlefield....

\* \* \* \*

*Hastings, 1066*

With no moonlight to guide them, Galan and Moloch clambered down Telham Hill, stepping warily among jutting stones and tree roots, while a cold Channel wind whipped tree branches, blowing dust into their eyes. The cries of the wounded echoed in Galan's ears, fusing into memories that would haunt him for the rest of his life. Moloch seemed not to notice.

"Where are we going?" Galan asked as he brushed a speck of dirt from his eye, his parched throat crying for a drink. "Moloch,

I'm grateful you saved my life, but I want to return to my family." And to Linette, his troubled heart reminded him. Oh, God, to hold her in his arms, kiss her sweet lips ... "Please let me know how I can repay you, and if possible, I shall."

How had Moloch saved his life? The question taunted him, tortured him, but he feared to know the answer. Briefly, he considered escape from this demon--for he could think of no other name for him--but just as quickly, he realized the effort would prove useless.

Stepping over a gnarled tree root, Moloch gripped a chestnut branch for support. "We'll discuss payment later. And soon, you may return to your family."

"Why did you choose to save my life?" Galan pointed back toward the battlefield. "Why didn't you save another man's life, or all their lives?"

Moloch stopped to stare at him, his skeletal hands gesturing in the darkness, his wrinkled face a picture of sinister emotions. "Must I have a reason? I save whom I want to save. I have neither the time nor the patience to rescue so many." He chuckled, a dry, raspy sound. "'Many are called, but few are chosen.' Doesn't your Bible say that?" he asked as his long, bushy hair blew across his face, his voluminous black robe billowing about him.

"I ... I believe I've heard the priest read those words."

"Let us hurry," Moloch said when they reached the bottom of the hill. "We have much to do this night."

Galan gave him a sharp look, increasingly worried but afraid to speak. Besides, Moloch had saved his life. The least he could do now was to follow him. Later, he would have to get away ... if he had the chance.

They plodded through a marshy valley, the cold water seeping through his woolen leggings, making him shiver. Like giant monsters, tree branches thrashed in the howling wind.

As they followed a dirt path that edged a vast forest, so many questions plagued him, frightful suspicions making his mind churn with anxiety.

After a mile or so, they arrived at a church in ruins, its stone walls jagged and uneven, the black sky its roof. Why had they come to a church? A chill raced along Galan's arms and legs. An oaken door hung from broken hinges, banging back and forth in the wind. Neither speaking, they entered the nave where the cold stone floor under his wet leggings made him shiver uncontrollably.

With eyes now accustomed to the dark, Galan observed the cobwebs that festooned the wooden cross on the altar, the shattered baptismal font, the wrecked wooden pews. His gaze took in several multi-branched candelabra, each one filled with tall candles. All these things paled beside his intense thirst, a thirst so strong it threatened to consume him.

"Why ... why are we here?" he asked, every word an effort. "I beg of you, let us go where we can find a drink. Mayhap someone lives nearby...."

"One thing at a time," Moloch answered in his caustic voice. "This is my home, and--"

"You live here? You would defile a holy place--"

"--abandoned, as you can see," Moloch said, pointing to the dark sky that stretched above them. "Destroyed by the Vikings." He chuckled, a hissing sound that reminded Galan of a snake. "What better place for my ... uh ... residence?" A demonic gleam lit his eyes.

Moloch moved away, a spectral figure in the blackness of night.

The hairs at the back of Galan's neck prickled. An icy tremor of fear passed through him. Despite his thirst, his wariness increased, deepening into a strong desire to escape this Moloch. Run! a warning in his head sounded. He remained immobile, as if caught in a spell.

"Now let us have light," Moloch said, "and then I'll give you a glass of wine, the finest wine you've ever tasted."

Galan had never tasted wine, only ale, but no matter. His parched mouth begged for satisfaction.

Moloch moved from one candelabrum to the next, lighting each wick with a touch of his fingertip, and soon, the nave blazed with light. How does he perform these miracles? Galan wondered, unable to remove his gaze from Moloch. He surely must be a warlock. The flickering candlelight cast wavy shadows on the stone walls, distorting Moloch's body, his shadow a grotesque monster on a far wall. A fiend.

The church brighter now, Galan noted the dust that layered the floor and floated in the air, the scattered leaves that rustled along the stone floor, like the whispers of the dead.

"After I quench my thirst," he said while Moloch lit the last candle, "and after you've told me how I can repay you, I must return to my family, my loved ones." Especially Linette. He hungered for her, ached to hold her in his arms, kiss her sweet lips.

Why had Moloch brought him here? Why? Why? The question plagued him, a continual torment that made his head throb, his heart pound, his knees shake.

Moloch swung around to stare at him, a diabolical gleam glazing his eyes. "Yes, of course," he replied, as if the matter were of little consequence. "Now, for the wine." He stepped up to the marble altar to retrieve a crystal decanter of wine and a glass goblet.

His face set in concentration, Moloch poured the wine, then handed the glass to Galan. "Drink to your life!"

The crystal goblet pulsated with a rare radiance, glowing golden by the candlelight. Galan shook with fright. He wanted to run, but a power beyond his control stopped him.

"Are you not drinking any?" he asked, his throat on fire with thirst.

Moloch waved a languid hand. "I had a glass shortly before I found you. Too much wine does something to my brain," he said, tapping his bony forefinger against his head. "But please, partake of your drink."

Galan forced himself to take a slow sip. It had been more than a day since he'd eaten, and if he weren't careful, the wine would make him ill. Although desperate for more, he waited a moment to let the tart taste linger on his tongue.

With an appreciative smile, he raised the glass to his mouth again. After the second sip, everything within the nave blurred, the room spinning around him.

"No!" He slumped to the floor, and the glass slipped from his hand to shatter into a hundred pieces. The last thing he remembered was Moloch standing beside him, laughing. "Now you shall join the undead!"

Hours later, when he awakened from his drugged stupor and discovered his body's ghastly transformation, he'd lain on the cold stone floor for the longest time, each passing second an agony. He stared at his hands, absolutely pale, as white as the snow in January. That much he could tell, even in the dark. And cold, dear God, so cold! Tears streamed down his cheeks. He clenched his hands at his sides, his nails scraping the stone floor.

Moloch's final words echoed in his brain ... the undead ... the undead.

By all the saints, what has happened to me? Blessed Virgin, how have I sinned that I should suffer so? He'd never see him mother and father again, nor his brothers and sisters. And never again know Linette's love. He rocked back and forth, pressing his hand to his head, sobbing uncontrollably. Through a haze of despair, he prayed for the strength to endure his body's unspeakable change.

God, please, oh, please....

An odd, salty taste fouled his mouth. When he touched his lips, his fingers came away stained red with blood. How had that outrage happened? In the dimmest recesses of his mind, he remembered Moloch saying, "Drink, now drink my blood," and holding a wrist to his mouth.

Without warning, the demon came to stand beside him, his lips drawn back in a feral grin. "So you're awake now."

Too shocked to stand, Galan raised himself on his elbows, anguish in every word. "What have you done to me?"

Moloch cackled. "Now you are as I am. A vampire!" He walked away, leaving Galan to his misery. Before he stepped out of the church, he called over his shoulder, "I shall return. I must feed now." With one last burst of laughter, he left.

The undead. A deep, burning hunger gnawed at Galan's insides, a craving like nothing he'd ever endured. He sobbed brokenly for his family, for Linette, for all he'd known and would never know again. Please, God, he prayed, let this be only a nightmare.

The years and centuries stretched ahead of him, an abyss without love or hope, when he'd remain forever separated from his family and friends, from Linette, all those so dear to him. Blessed Virgin, how would he live? But he wasn't alive now, he was dead ... and not dead.

His craving had finally driven him from the church, that, and Moloch's harsh tutelage, but it had taken him years to become accustomed to drinking human blood.

Throughout the centuries, he had to answer to Moloch, the fiend who always lurked in the background. Moloch, his mentor. His tormentor. Always careful to conceal his desire for mortality from Moloch, he wished, more than anything, he could elude that demon....

But there is no escape, Galan agonized, returned to the present, where he stood beside an oak tree in his backyard. He pressed his hand against the rough tree bark, all his thoughts on Stevie. Strange how one person could make such a difference in his life. Of course, she reminded him of Linette, but Stevie had an inner grace, a personality all her own. Something told him he'd feel an attraction for her, even had he never loved Linette.

He frowned, his mind raging with impossible dreams. If he were mortal again, if Stevie could learn to care for--

"In the name of Lucifer, what the hell's the matter with you?" Next to a hibiscus bush several feet away, a too-frequent intruder sneered. "You look as if the last mortal had disappeared from the earth."

Alarm sliced through Galan like a saber through cotton. Moloch! Stay calm.

"Surprised to see me?" Moloch strolled toward him, his tangled hair blowing across his face, the long-sleeved black robe billowing in the night breeze, booted feet making a path through the grass.

Galan folded his arms across his chest. "I should be used to it by now."

"Agreed." Moloch joined him by the oak tree, the aged vampire's face as vicious as ever. "Why have you been acting so differently lately, as if you don't appreciate all I've done for you? Look what I've given you," Moloch said, spreading his cadaverous arms wide, "power, immortality." He shook his head. "Such ingratitude."

"Have I complained?" Galan asked, his conscience warning him to protect Stevie.

"Lately, you've changed," Moloch said. "What's happened? That woman you drove home--"

Galan caught his breath. "How do you know about her?"

"I know everything. Don't think for one minute you can keep a secret from me. Why do you even bother with this mortal wench?" Moloch asked, his eyes narrowing to slits.

A muscle twitched in Galan's jaw. By all the saints, he wanted to destroy this demon, drive a stake through his evil heart, burn him until he was nothing but ashes. "She's my concern, not yours."

"Never forget--I'll not permit any bonding between a vampire and a mortal."

Raw fear churned inside Galan. What might Moloch do to Stevie? Kill her? Transform her into a vampire? He shuddered but spoke in cool tones. "I repeat, let her be." Not giving a damn about himself, he knew he must tread carefully for Stevie's sake.

An expression of wicked pleasure warped the demon's face. "Don't you ever dictate to me. For your own sake, forget about this mortal woman. That kind will always be denied you. I'll see to that."

Moloch placed his bony hand on Galan's shoulder, and it took all of Galan's willpower not to shove the hand aside.

"You will not mingle with mortals. You will remain only with your own kind. Plenty of the undead in this world. How long before this woman figures out what you are?"

"Why should she discover it at all? I've given her no grounds for suspicion. And if she should suspect me, then I'll do as you suggest." By St. Aidan, how could he bear never to see Stevie again?

"If she even questions what you are, her doubts would cause difficulties for us. What if she goes to the police with her suspicions?"

"The police?" Galan laughed. "For certain, they'd be vastly amused."

"Don't be so sure of that. Remember the vampire hunts of the last several centuries, and how so many of our people suffered? Have you forgotten Budapest in 1760? You escaped that persecution only because of the vanishing powers you'd developed over the centuries. Newly-created vampires lack that ability."

Galan scoffed. "So you think there'll be public burning again? Vampires roasted alive, like two-hundred years ago?"

"It could happen, boy. If your lady friend--"

"She's not 'my' lady friend." Unfortunately.

Moloch sighed. "Never forget--I could destroy the mortal woman without a thought. Neither you nor any of the undead could stop me. But since you're one of my favorites, I'll let you transform her into one of us."

Galan felt his heart ease. Perhaps there was a way to fool Moloch and pursue Stevie at the same time. What a splendid idea, Moloch!

He nodded. "Ah, I can see it already. A partner for eternity. Only let me toy with her for awhile, tease her a little, then the metamorphosis will be so much more exhilarating." Rubbing his hands together, Galan hoped he gave a credible performance.

Moloch wagged a gnarled finger in front of his face. "Fine, have your way with her. If she begins to guess what you are, shun her like holy water. Or better still, turn her into one of the undead as soon as she suspects. You understand?"

"Perfectly." Galan understood something else, a painful reality he yearned to deny. Because of Moloch, he would remain a vampire until the end of time.

Unless he could rid himself of the fiend.

Chapter Four

Darkness crept over Schloss Oberau, a remote thirteenth-century castle Moloch had acquired centuries ago, nestled near the foothills of the Alps. He stretched his skeletal limbs and awakened, then stepped over the side of the casket, bare feet hitting the stone floor of the great hall.

With its crumbling stone walls outside, the castle looked a hulk of its former self, presenting the appearance of a derelict, deserted habitation, an image sufficient to keep away any curious visitors. And that was fine with Moloch.

Inside, the castle revealed a different story. Splendid tapestries decorated the stone walls, and finely-crafted oaken furniture added an enchanting charm to the vast room. Purple velvet draperies fluttered at the windows, catching the light of the Waterford chandelier that glittered from the majestic ceiling. Too bad he couldn't enjoy these amenities more, Moloch thought as he ran his fingers through his bushy hair. He slept in his coffin during the day, and at night--ah, the night!--he prowled the world.

A stiff wind gusted through the wide open windows, billowing his robe about him, and his unkempt hair whipped across his face. A black cat snoozed against a far wall, flat on his back, his paws upright.

Moloch stopped by the long trestle table, thinking of all the protégés who demanded his supervision, most particularly Galan. What should he do about that nightwalker? The young man was giving him problems, yet he realized that Galan's very stubbornness and contrariness were desirable traits for a leader.

Galan's not telling the truth, he fumed, and that mortal woman could spell trouble yet. Moloch's jaw clenched with determination. He'd get the truth from him, no question about it.

Occasionally a vampire longed to regain mortality, an inexplicable truth Moloch had learned centuries ago. This desire didn't happen often, not once among a million vampires, but even once was enough to make him seethe with fury.

Not to his surprise, this wish always involved a member of the opposite sex, a mortal.

Could a vampire regain his mortality? A persistent rumor lingered at the back of his mind, now and then erupting to taunt him to distraction. He'd heard tales of an elixir that could reverse the process of vampirism and make one of the undead mortal again. Did such an elixir really exist? Were there any former vampires now living mortal lives? He'd never known of any, but he'd sell his soul to find out ... if he had a soul.

Why would one of the undead want to become human again? Why would he want to relinquish his strength, his powers, his ability to transport himself from one place to another without benefit of plane, boat, or car? To relinquish all that, just for a weak, insipid mortal?

Galan won't get away with it, Moloch vowed, staring out the window at the snow-capped Alps in the distance as he tapped his fingers on the stone window ledge. After all the time and machinations he'd invested in Galan, the ingrate had better stop this foolishness and content himself with his vampirism.

An idea came to Moloch. The best way to get at Galan was through the mortal woman ... the shifty, deceitful female, definitely an obstacle to his plans.

He sat down on a high-backed chair with its intricate carvings and pulled on his short leather boots, then rose and fastened a thick leather belt studded with gemstones, a recent find from his last trip to Barcelona. Behind him stood a magnificent glass-fronted oaken cabinet, an adornment he'd acquired over two-hundred years ago, a genuine Chippendale.

Moloch reached inside the cabinet and fingered his latest treasure, a Faberge gilt-painted cup from the Victoria and Albert Museum, another addition to the objets d'art.

He grinned in sly anticipation. One of these nights, he intended to visit the Tower of London and add the crown jewels to his collection.

After one last affectionate look at his accumulation, he strode toward the outer ward, where the cat dozed in sleepy contentment, unaware he blocked Moloch's path.

Moloch aimed a vicious kick at the cat. "Get out of my way!"

Cringing with fear, the feline hissed and slunk away into the deepest recesses of the castle.

And that's how Galan should kick the mortal woman out of his life. Kick her until she screamed for mercy, kick her to death!

* * * *

Shivers skimmed along Stevie's arms and legs as she stepped off the bus in downtown Miami. Brr. Sweater weather. Early for work today, she strode toward the New World Tower, a sleek, modern office building with a brown marble facade and wide gleaming glass doors. She wanted to check on Nick, one of her "adopted" homeless, who always slept near the building's entrance until she woke him each weekday morning before the police could chase him away.

Sound asleep, Nick lay curled on his side, his head on his knapsack. Stevie knelt beside him and shook his shoulder, aware from past experience that often these desolate people slept like the dead. A spurt of alarm stopped her for a moment, the sight of the dead homeless man still horribly fresh in her mind. It took several minutes of patient shaking, but finally Nick roused, wiping the sleep from his eyes. He stared at her in sleepy recognition.

"Nick, I brought you something for breakfast--two big poppy seed muffins," she said, handing him a plastic bag that held the treats. "Oh, and another thing." She reached into her purse to give him a couple of dollars. "Remember that refreshment stand on Flagler Street I showed you? Why don't you get orange juice and coffee."

"Thanks, ma'am. Sounds like a good idea."

"Happy to do it, Nick." She had considered job possibilities for him, too, some she would mention later after she had more facts.

She looked toward the east, where the rising sun peeked up over Biscayne Bay and sent the water sparkling like crystal. She rose to her feet, smoothing the wrinkles in her cotton slacks. "Don't forget about your juice and coffee. 'Bye for now."

"'Bye, ma'am, and thanks for everything."

With a smile and a wave, Stevie left him then, on her way to the bookstore.

* * * *

Should have known things never go as planned, Stevie thought as she hustled to the bus stop in the late afternoon, when dark clouds hid the sun, and a fierce wind whipped across the streets. Since she had her date with Galan this evening, she'd decided to leave the bookstore fifteen minutes early, but several picky customers had detained her, making her fifteen minutes late, darn it!

The bus arrived ten minutes late and was already crowded, but at least she got the last empty seat. As usual, cars, buses, and trucks crawled along Biscayne Boulevard, slower than a snail on Valium. Stevie closed her eyes and tried to relax while countless conversations buzzed around her, most of them in Spanish and a few in Creole, but none in English.

She dashed home from the bus stop and started to throw off her clothes once she stepped inside her apartment.

Foregoing her supper, she took a quick shower. She dressed carefully for her date, selecting her only good dress, a light blue short-sleeved silk. She slipped the whisper-soft material over her head, loving its slinky, luxurious feel. She stepped into her black three-inch slingbacks, completing her ensemble with a pearl necklace and gold earrings, legacies from her mother. With a touch of rose lipstick on her mouth and a dab of powder on her nose, she hoped Galan would like the effect.

And speaking of liking--she wondered if Galan would like to go to the beach with her, maybe her next Sunday off, if it was a warm, sunny day. She sure would enjoy a day at the beach, and Galan could definitely use a tan. Possibly she'd ask him sometime soon, she decided, checking in the mirror to make sure her slip didn't show.

Galan arrived on time, elegant in a black suit, white shirt, and burgundy tie, the dim light adding color to his face. He looked as if he'd just stepped off the runway of a Milan fashion show. Her heart revved like a Dodge engine at a NASCAR race. His eyes were dark and mysterious, like the night ... full of secrets. Catching a scent of sandalwood, she sighed. Sexy!

His dark eyes assessed her. "You look lovely," he said with a warm smile, his deep, sensual voice washing over her. "That shade of blue is your color. Matches your eyes."

"Thanks, you look nice yourself." She reached for her white linen jacket. "Shall we go?"

"Indeed." He helped her into the jacket, his hands resting on her shoulders a bit longer than necessary. Tempted to lean back against him, she gathered her wits and told herself he was only a date. Besides, she didn't want to get close to him ... or any man. Each minute with him made it more difficult to resist his considerable charm. She wondered how she'd last throughout the evening, concealing her feelings from him.

They arrived at Gusman Theater downtown with time to spare and the best seats, ten rows from the stage. There wasn't an empty place in the theater, and most of the audience was middle-aged and well-dressed, sophisticated people who talked quietly among themselves. What a difference from the rock concerts she used to attend, Stevie mused as she settled herself.

While the quartet played Mozart's whimsical Eine Kleine Nachtmusik, she occasionally slanted a look Galan's way, feeling a rush of warmth as she observed his straight nose, the firm set of his jaw. She studied his hands in his lap, those expressive fingers, like the violinist in the quartet. What would it be like to have his hands on her, touching her, caressing her? Despite the air conditioning, the prospect sent her temperature soaring about twenty degrees.

Once, their gazes met and held, and he smiled at her, an expression that added another twenty degrees to her overheated body. When he turned away, her gaze strayed downward to his thighs and the trim fit of his black trousers, as if they'd been tailored especially for him. He reminded her of a tiger she'd seen on a National Geographic program, poised to pounce on its prey. She'd bet no one ever got the best of him, either. Master of the universe. She smiled to herself. There went her crazy imagination again.

At the end of the performance, they filed out of the theater with the other patrons, a neat, orderly exit, no pushing or shoving, reminding her again of the contrast with a rock concert.

Outside on Flagler Street, Galan peered down at her. "Please wait here whilst I get the car from the parking lot. Only be a few minutes."

"Hey, I'll walk with you."

"Very well, then." Tucking her hand through his arm, they strolled in companionable silence toward Galan's green Mercedes, less than a block away. A cool wind lifted her long hair from her shoulders and fluttered her dress around her knees, prompting her to button her jacket. Her stomach growled, a reminder she'd missed her supper....

"Do you attend these concerts often?" she asked on the way home, searching for a way to fill the silent void between them.

He smiled her way. "Not as often as I'd like to ... with you."

Would their friendship end with this night? Or would they have more times together? His words sounded promising.

They stopped at a red light, and her stomach growled again, her face warming with embarrassment.

He smiled his toothpaste bright smile. "Stevie, it would please me very much to offer you dinner. There's a fine restaurant a short distance away." Another smile in her direction. "Does that suit you?"

"Sounds great."

Once there, a protest formed on her lips. "This restaurant looks awfully--" She started to say "expensive" but caught herself, not wanting to question his ability to pay "--nice."

"So I've heard. I've never eaten here, but this gives me an opportunity to spend more time with you," he said as the valet came around to open her door.

Although they had no reservations, the maitre 'd quickly led them to a small table in a corner of the dimly-lit dining room with turquoise walls and glistening crystal chandeliers. Every linen-topped table was full, she noticed, with lots of well-dressed older people, but a few young people, too.

She studied the meat, fish, and poultry selections on the menu, hoping they wouldn't have a long wait for the entree. She was dying of hunger! Fingering a pink carnation in a crystal vase, she saw that Galan had already set his menu aside.

"What will you have?" he asked after she placed her menu on the table.

"Chablis for now. The chicken a la Kiev sounds good."

Galan ordered her Chablis and red wine for himself, and when the drinks came, he gave the waiter her dinner order.

She looked at him in surprise. "You're not eating?"

He raised his glass. "Only the wine. I'm not hungry now. But please, don't let that keep you from enjoyment of your meal."

The pale overhead light softened his features, moderating its harsh lines and muting the pearlescent quality of his skin. It was an arresting face, but one that never betrayed his thoughts.

There was so much about him she wanted to know. Unsure where to start, she reached for her glass, her gaze on him. "I remember you told me you don't work downtown," she said.

He sipped his wine, then set the goblet down. "I work at home. I'm a writer."

"A writer! Science fiction, mystery, or--"

"Non-fiction. History. I'm writing an account of the Battle of Hastings."

"Ten sixty-six," she interjected. "History was my favorite subject in high school."

He nodded. "I feel that I know so much about the battle, it seems as if I actually fought in it."

"I've often felt it was a shame the Normans won," she said, "when right was on the side of the English."

"King Harold should have prevailed! We--uh, the English held the high ground." He studied his wine glass. "But the English lost the battle to the deceitful Normans, and thus, lost England."

He sure sounds as if he fought the battle, she thought as she selected a roll from the bread basket and buttered it. "You almost finished? With your book, I mean."

"I've several more chapters to go, but it's coming along quite well. There's a publisher in New York who's already expressed an interest."

"Wow! That's great! I'll want an autographed copy when it's published," she said with a smile.

"It would be my pleasure. I shall make certain you get a copy."

She bit into her roll, puzzled as ever by Galan's speech. She couldn't put her finger on it, but certain words and phrases he used sounded stilted. And the more she heard him speak, the more she caught a trace of an English accent.

"Did you ever live in England?" She sipped her Chablis, keeping her eyes on him.

"A long time ago. Enough about me. Tell me, will you go home for the holidays?"

"Can't take time off from my job."

"Then your loss is my gain. I wondered if you'd enjoy seeing The Nutcracker."

"I'd love it! I've never been to a ballet." She thought for a moment. "Can you get tickets this late?"

"I've already bought two tickets."

"Oh." She didn't know what else to say. Was he so sure of himself?

He seemed to be able to read her mind. "If you hadn't been able to go, I intended to go by myself."

She finished her roll and wiped her hands on her napkin. "You wouldn't want to waste a ticket."

He gave her a steady look. "Indeed, it is my good fortune."

Her salad arrived, rendering her momentarily silent while she dipped her fork into the most luscious combination she'd ever tasted, a vegetable melange with a light dressing, topped with watercress. Boy, did that taste good!

He rested his arms on the table, fingers entwined, silver cufflinks gleaming. His eyes seemed to probe her, as if he could see into her soul, discern every secret. "Tell me about yourself. I know you work at the bookstore, but have you any special interests?"

"I help the homeless and--"

"The homeless--why?"

"Because I want to. Well, I help them as much as possible, and I try to get them jobs." She sighed. "Not always successful there. Whenever I get a chance, I spend a little time talking with them, even after I work late in the evening."

He frowned. "Miami's a dangerous place at night, as you should well know."

She knew he was thinking of her mugging the night they'd first met. "I'm more careful now."

"'Careful' doesn't count for much. Miami is full of criminals. I see so many...." He paused, as if he'd said too much.

"So many--what?"

"Crimes!" he said with a dark look. "Criminals everywhere!"

"How do you see all these so-called crimes?"

"I see them," he replied in a voice that brooked no contradiction.

"Maybe you don't realize it, but in this country, a man is innocent until proven guilty."

He shook his head. "I see all the proof I need."

"Well, I don't want to argue about that now...." She thought quickly. "My father...."

"Yes?"

She twisted her napkin in her lap. "He's a lawyer, and he once made a deal--took a bribe, in other words--that kept many poor people from having adequate housing. Helping the homeless is my way of making up for it."

"You are not responsible for your father's sins."

She shrugged. "I do what I can." She sipped her Chablis, looking up as the waiter brought her entree.

"Let's talk about something else," he said. "Do you like poetry?"

"I don't like--" She made a fluttery movement with her hands "--poetry that doesn't rhyme."

He smiled. "Well, I think you'll like this one."

> "It was many and many a year ago
> In a kingdom by the sea--

"Edgar Allen Poe!"
Smiling, he nodded.

> "That a maiden there lived whom you may know
> By the name of Annabel Lee...."

She concentrated on every word, fascinated by his deep, rich voice, as smooth as a butterscotch sundae. His voice, like his eyes, had a mesmerizing quality. Hearing him heightened all her senses, as if she'd never really lived until now. If only his voice had that effect on her, what might a kiss do?

> For the moon never beams without bringing me dreams
> Of the beautiful Annabel Lee
> And the stars never rise but I feel the bright eyes
> Of the beautiful Annabel Lee
> And so, all the night-tide, I lie down by the side
> Of my darling, my darling, my life and my bride
> In the sepulcher there by the sea
> In her tomb by the sounding sea

"That was very impressive!" She returned to her dinner, unaware until this moment that she'd forgotten her meal, forgotten everything except his voice and the poem. It seemed as if they had the restaurant to themselves, just Galan and she.

"Perhaps I should go on the stage," he said with a self-deprecating smile.

"You'd be a hit!"

Galan studied her while she ate, every gesture, every facial expression. He liked the way her eyes lit up when she talked, no matter her mood. She tucked a strand of hair behind her ear, a simple gesture but exquisitely enchanting. Even by the dim light, her skin glowed with life, and the sweep of her eyelashes, the gleam of her blonde hair by candlelight captivated him. Inhaling her lilac scent, so many memories rushed through his mind, of meandering streams and grassy meadows, of the white chalk cliffs of Dover.

In spite of himself, he observed the pulse at the base of her throat, the pumping of her blood that tempted him almost beyond endurance. He wanted to reach across the table and touch her warm, delicate skin, but if he did, he'd be lost, helpless to deny the hunger that clawed at him. No, he could never hurt Stevie, who meant so much to him. Willingly, he would give his life-- such as it was--before he'd let any harm come to her.

As he drained his glass of wine, he struggled to constrain his appetite. He'd have his own dinner later, after he drove her home. Hunger tortured him, a deep, urgent desire for food. Yet he longed for some nebulous attribute that went beyond mere sustenance, a goal forever out of reach. He gazed at her while she ate, seeing all he'd never have, everything denied him, from now until eternity.

After Galan paid the waiter, they left the dining room, descending a few steps to the entrance, where a crowd of patrons waited to be seated. There, glass cabinets lined the walls, each filled with porcelain dishes and figurines, a pleasant attraction she'd missed when they first arrived.

"Oh, look at the pretty porcelain!" Stevie headed for one of the cabinets, catching her reflection in the glass.

He came to stand beside her. "Quite an interesting collection."

She saw him next to her but she didn't see his reflection in the glass. What? She looked at the glass again. Strange.

With a muttered exclamation, he lurched back, away from the cabinet.

She turned in his direction. "You okay?"

"Yes, of course. Why shouldn't I be?"

"I don't know...." Her voice trailed off, and she, too, stepped away from the cabinet, wondering why she hadn't seen his reflection. A trick of the light, she supposed.

What else could it be?

## Chapter Five

The last faint stars disappeared from a slate blue sky as Stevie stepped off the bus in downtown Miami, the Miami Herald clutched in her hand, her leather purse slung over her shoulder, and a lot of worries plaguing her mind. What made her so tired? she agonized, trudging along Biscayne Boulevard, thinking how worn out she'd felt for weeks. Adjusting her purse strap, she sighed. She supposed she'd have to see a doctor, but she sure didn't want to, especially since she had no medical insurance.

Later this evening, she had karate class, but she didn't feel up to that, either. Should she cut the class? Better not; she was becoming pretty good at defending herself, and here in Miami, you never could tell when that skill might come in handy.

Huge Christmas wreaths bedecked light poles, and silver garland added an extra holiday touch, brightening the streets and lightening her mood.

She glanced at the newspaper in her hand. The headline screamed at her. UNEXPLAINED DEATHS--VAMPIRE MURDERS? She skimmed the article, her throat suddenly dry. "A number of mysterious deaths...."

A sick feeling churned in her stomach, slowing her steps. The dead man from several weeks ago jarred her memory, his skin milk white, as if all the blood had been drained from his body. Now, more, similar deaths.

Of course, she didn't believe in vampires.

* * * *

Alarm jolted Galan as streaks of lavender and rose tinged the eastern horizon, a precursor of the deadly dawn, when all of the undead must take refuge in darkness. If he didn't hurry home.... He shuddered. After a visual check convinced him the street remained deserted, he felt the slow pulse of his victim and rose from his feeding, leaving the man in a weakened, hypnotic state.

Sounds and aromas bombarded his senses. He smelled the salt water of Biscayne Bay, a pleasant smell he'd become used to. The sweet fragrance of fruit the vendors sold several blocks distant floated up his nostrils, but too quickly, a car's exhaust nullified the delectable scent.

Mindful of the urgent need to transport himself, he caught sight of a form down the street, about a quarter of a mile away. With lightning speed, he covered the distance, only to discover a dead body, its skin alabaster white, sightless eyes staring up to heaven. Galan raked his fingers through his hair. When had this happened, and how could he have missed it?

Several moments later, he turned away from the corpse, at a loss to know which of the many vampires had killed the man. Moloch? Damn the bastard! But how could he think when his thought processes became lost in the cacophony echoing inside his brain? He heard two security guards talking on the fifth floor of the New World Tower, heard a leaf fall from a ficus tree at the end of the block. He heard--footsteps!

"Stevie!"

"Galan, what are you doing so earl--?" Her gaze slid to the lifeless body. "But that's Nick! He looks like a ghost!" Not another vampire murder! She swallowed convulsively, turning her head to the side, her skin turning hot, then cold.

Gently, Galan took her by the arm, easing her away from the horror. "I came upon him myself only a few minutes ago, and--"

"But just look at his skin!" Her newspaper fell to the sidewalk, forgotten. Her eyes brimmed with tears, and she choked on her words. "What's happened to him?"

"Nothing we can do for him now," he said in soothing tones, "but I intend to call the police from my cell phone." He drew her into his arms to comfort her, temptingly aware of her body warmth, of her breasts pressed against him, the firm pressure of her hips through her cotton slacks. A stiff wind blew a lock of hair across his face, an unimaginably sweet allurement.

A pink glow lit the sky, and his brain flashed another warming. By all the saints, Stevie must not catch his trepidation.

With light fingers, he brushed a strand of hair from her face. "You knew him, didn't you?"

Silently, she nodded in his arms. Galan loosened his hold and stepped away. "I wish I could stay with you, but I must leave."

"But where...?"

The sky became brighter, the sun's beams touching the streets and buildings with an amber glow.

"Important business," he murmured. Go home, go home!

"Business? Now?"

"I'll phone you tonight," he called over his shoulder as he dashed around the corner.

"Hey, wait!" After a few moments of indecision, Stevie rushed after him. She didn't see him anywhere! How could he disappear so quickly? A crazy thought froze her blood. Galan's disappearance--like that old man she'd seen in the evening.

Her attention shifted back to Nick. She wondered what--or who--was causing these deaths. And how come Galan just happened to be standing next to Nick? Did he have something to do with--? She shook her head. Uh, uh, that was too crazy to even consider. But why in the world had he left her so quickly, as if he suspected the police would be after him? He couldn't take a few minutes to say 'good-bye'?

The hell with you, Galan Kent!

* * * *

Galan roused from a deep sleep and headed downstairs as night crept over the land. His steps slow and halting, he stopped by his glass-topped coffee table and picked up the telephone, then dialed Stevie's number. Four rings later, he heard it pick up.

"Hi, this is Stevie. Sorry I'm not here to take your call, but if you leave your name and number, I'll get back to you as soon as possible. Thanks!"

Curse these human inventions; imagine talking to a machine.

"Stevie, this is Galan. I wanted you to know I called the police about the dead man." He paused, aware she was disturbed with him for leaving her so precipitously this morning. "I hope to see you in a few days." How could he bear the wait?

Sighing, he hung up the phone.

Long moments of charged emotions passed, then he left his living room and went back upstairs. There, he sat at his desk for countless minutes, too distracted about Stevie to write.

How warm and endearing she'd felt in his arms this morning, an ephemeral treasure he could never call his own. He clenched his hands on the desk as anguish tore him apart. God help him! Someday, Stevie would meet a mortal man to love, a man who could give her the happiness she deserved. Then she'd marry him, this man who would hold her close at night and savor the exquisite passion that surely must lie within her.

He drummed his fingers on the desk, waiting for the words to come, aware of the need to finish his chapter. Folding his arms across his chest, he stared off into space, as if he would find inspiration from within the room.

An eerie premonition sent every coherent thought flying from his mind, and he sensed her presence before he saw her.

"Rosalinda."

A slender woman glided out from a dark corner, reeking of musk, her black taffeta gown whispering along the carpeted floor.

She came to stand beside his desk, a tall, regal figure, the décolletage of her gown revealing voluptuous breasts. Curls of ink-black hair rose over a foot atop her head, and he could swear that was a real bird's nest tucked among the dark tresses. Diamonds glittered from her neck and ears, a diamond bracelet dangling from her wrist.

"Galan!" She smoothed her hand along the back of his neck, tangling her fingers in his hair. "I've missed you terribly. You have no idea." She pouted prettily. "Life is so empty without you."

"Moloch."

She frowned. "Who?"

"Moloch sent you, didn't he?" He glanced up at her, resolved to ignore her full breasts, her sensual hips. He mustn't fall into her trap, and the scheme stank of that wily fiend.

With ringed fingers, she patted her coiffure, the gems sparkling in the dark, calling attention to her long, blood red nails. "Moloch? Why do you speak of him? I came of my own volition." She bent low to kiss his neck. "How I've missed you."

"Let us stop playing games, shall we? We parted over two-hundred years ago. Why this sudden revival of interest in me?"

She pouted again, but now a trace of anger blazed in her green eyes. Peevishly, she plucked at a speck of lint on her sleeve. "Is this any way to treat a lady? You were always such a gentleman. What's happened to change you?" She hurried on. "We were friends once, nay, lovers! Let us resume that friendship, revive the feeling we once shared."

Galan shoved a book aside on his desk. "It's over, Rosalinda. The feeling is dead." But was it really? Memories of her bedroom charms taunted him, and it took all of his willpower to refuse her now. But refuse her he would, because it was only Stevie he wanted, for now and all time. "It's over."

"How can you say that, Galan? How can you hurt me so?" Rosalinda pressed a hand to her bosom. She bent over and traced her fingers along his thigh. "Remember what wonderful times we had together?" She rained light kisses across his neck. "And how happy I made you in bed?"

Passion stirred inside him, and he was tempted to the point of no return. But he must not--would not--give in. "I never realized what a good actress you are." Leaning back in his swivel chair, he threw her a look of wry humor and eased her hand from his thigh. "With the world of the undead to choose from, you surely can find another lover, one who is worthy of your charms. One who can please you more than I," he said as he bowed his head in mock humility.

"You'll be sorry for this." Venom blazed in her eyes. "Just you wait. You'll regret--oh, how you'll regret--you ever spoke to me thusly." With a swish of her gown and the scent of musk lingering like spoiled fruit, she disappeared.

Galan slammed his hand on the desk. Damn it! What was he thinking? By rejecting Rosalinda, he might have put Stevie in danger.

Glowing red numerals on his desk clock revealed the time, 3:12 a.m.

In a heartbeat, he found himself in Stevie's room, where she lay on her stomach, her long hair a golden mantle down her back. She whimpered in her sleep, and he longed to take her in his arms and comfort her, tell her she had nothing to fear. That wouldn't be the truth, though. She had plenty to fear, if she only knew it.

A window stood partially open, lacy white curtains fluttering in a breeze. Smells drifted in through the open window, dried grass and flowers, exhaust from a car zooming along the street.

Galan studied Stevie's outline under the thin blanket--the gentle concavity of her back, the swell of her buttocks, the silhouette of her long, shapely legs. She had such a lovely body, one that would forever bewitch him, but one that would never belong to him.

But heaven help anyone--mortal or undead--who dared to harm her, because he'd guard her with his life. By God, he'd risk anything to ensure her safety.

Lost in a whirlwind of emotions, he stood in a corner of her room, prepared to make a quick departure if she awoke. Night sounds became magnified within the small space: a dog barked down the street, a frog croaked outside the window, a train whistled and rumbled in the distance. In the backyard next door, a snake slithered through the grass, its tongue flicking in and out. A fox and its mate gamboled in a yard, two houses down.

Night after night, he kept vigil by her bed, forsaking nourishment to ensure no evil befell her, but by the fourth night, hunger clawed at him with an eagle's talons. The lure of her seductive body drove him wild. The carotid artery in her neck pulsed like a thousand crashing cymbals, the sweetest sound on earth. It would be easy, so easy....

By all that was holy! He couldn't fight his hunger any longer. He had to feed!

But what might happen to Stevie when he wasn't by her side?

\* \* \* \*

"Galan."

Several nights had passed since Stevie had last seen him. Galan stood at Stevie's open door, a bunch of yellow roses in his hand, a contrite expression on his face.

He handed her the flowers. "I fear there's nothing I can say or do to make amends for leaving you downtown, except to tell you I'm very sorry."

Indicating an easy chair, Stevie took the roses, inhaling their sweet-spicy aroma. "Thanks for the flowers. Sit down while I put these in water." She retrieved the avocado vase and filled it with water at the kitchen sink, then returned to the living room. Not knowing all the circumstances, she decided to give him the benefit of the doubt for leaving her so hastily earlier in the week.

Nevertheless, worries haunted her. Nick, dead on the street, would remain a vivid nightmare for the rest of her life.

Legs stretched out, he rested in the chair, his presence a powerful force in the room. Why is it, she wondered as she set the vase on the coffee table, that this man always has such complete control of himself? She sank down on the sofa opposite him, at a loss to understand him.

"You'll still attend The Nutcracker with me?" he asked with a dark and brooding look.

She hesitated. "Right, I'm looking forward to it."

Silent moments passed while they exchanged glances, his eyes holding her prisoner. She'd heard the phrase before, had always considered it trite. Now she knew better. It seemed as though he could see into her soul, read her innermost thoughts, undress her with just a look. She shifted her position on the sofa and glanced away, wondering if he would always remain a mystery, wondering, too, why she should care.

"It's getting late," she said after a stretch of aimless conversation, afraid she sounded rude but growing uncomfortable under his gaze. "Got a lot to do tonight." Not true on either count, but she needed time to herself now.

"Very well." He gave her an endearing smile, the first he'd favored her with this evening. "I shall call you later this week."

* * * *

At her tiny kitchen table, Stevie finished her breakfast of oatmeal and an English muffin topped with strawberry jam, then rinsed her dishes in the sink. In her pink knit nightshirt and white terry cloth robe, she headed for the front door to get the Miami Herald. Outside, a cool, wintry wind swept across the yard, prompting her to draw the robe closer about her.

Bending over, she glanced toward the jacaranda tree and-- She stopped as icy bumps rippled along her arms. The old man with long, bushy hair stood by the grapefruit tree, only a few yards away. He stared at her with murder in his eyes. Who was he, and why was he looking at her like that? She rushed back inside, slamming the door behind her.

Call the police! A deep breath and a few quick steps led her to the phone. With trembling fingers, she dialed 911. After she hung up, she dashed to her bedroom and grabbed the first clothes she found, then headed for the bathroom to dress. She finished in time to hear a knock on the door.

"Ma'am," the Miami Shores policeman said, "I've checked your yard, and I didn't see any strange man like you described. If you see him again, please don't hesitate to call us. After I leave you, I'll check the whole area again. Next door, too. Could be a visitor there."

"Maybe." But she knew better.

* * * *

The Nutcracker was more thrilling than Stevie had imagined, Galan's presence adding an exciting dimension to her enjoyment of the performance.

After The Dance of the Toy Soldiers, Galan glanced her way. "How did you like that?"

"Beautiful." And it was--the music, the costumes, the elements of fantasy, everything that comprised this lovely ballet.

She forgot her money worries, her uneasy relationship with her family, until all she could think about was the ballet.

And Galan.

Especially Galan.

Never mind that he was full of mystery. He was a man like no other she'd ever met, one who could captivate her with only a look.

During intermission, he bought her a wooden nutcracker, and with his prize-winning smile, he handed her the memento. "Something to remember me by."

"Thank you." She turned it over in her hands, delighting in the painted face and uniform of the soldier. "That was so nice of you." Something to remember me by. A wave of sadness washed over her, and she was at a loss to understand why. If he walked out of her life now, would it matter so much? Her heart answered for her. Yes, it would!

Once, her arm brushed his, and every sense came tingling to life, as if sight, sound, and smell had lain dormant until now, only waiting for one special person to resurrect them. Apparently, the contact aroused him, too. His gaze met hers, his look dazzling, hypnotizing her, as if she had no will of her own. He smiled at her, and with only his look, she knew she'd never really lived until she'd met him.

The performance ended with several minutes of loud applause and a bouquet for the lead ballerina. Soon they filed out of the Theater of the Performing Arts, and within minutes, reached an immense parking lot. A chilly wind swept the other patrons to their cars, and Stevie shivered in her white woolen jacket.

As they walked to Galan's car, her fatigue crept back, a debilitating weakness that slowed her steps and sent a jolt of alarm crashing through her. Funny how she'd forgotten about her tiredness during the ballet. Too bad she couldn't forget about it all the time, she thought, tightening her collar around her neck.

Galan tucked her arm through his. Clad in only a black suit, he looked as if the cold didn't faze him, yet the temperature must be in the low fifties. "Are you cold?" he asked with a worried look.

"A little," she said, her teeth chattering. "Miami weather is so changeable, don't you think? Only a few days ago, the temperature was in the eighties, and now it's as cold as the iceberg that sank the Titanic."

"I'll have you home soon," he murmured in his low voice, "or would you like a drink first? I know of a quiet bar in the Beacon Hotel, although I suppose you'd like some place that's livelier," he said with a faint smile.

"Galan, if it's okay with you, I'd just as soon go straight home." She hesitated, then plunged ahead. "Don't know why, but I've felt kinda tired lately."

"Tired?" His face and voice registered alarm. "What do you mean--tired? Do you have any other symptoms?"

She waved her hand. "No big deal. Just working too hard, I guess, and I have had a lot on my mind. Haven't felt feverish or had a sore throat, any other cold symptoms. Probably be fine if I don't think about it. Maybe I'll start taking iron supplements." Yeah, now that she thought about it, that might be a good idea.

He stopped on the street, frowning as he ran his finger down the side of her neck. The wind whipped his hair across his forehead, his eyes dark and penetrating, as if he could read her thoughts.

She grabbed his finger. "Hey, what are you doing? Think you have a medical degree or something?"

"Only checking to see if you have an inflammation." Sinfully rich, his voice teased her senses, making her forget her troubles.

Despite the cold, his touch sent a rush of warmth through her body. She spoke quickly. "Like I said, I've been working hard lately, saving my money for college. So maybe my tiredness is just a bunch of things put together." Even to her, the excuses sounded lame. Her activities shouldn't wear her out like this, and she'd always been healthy, rarely needing to see a doctor. Now, when she should have enjoyed every minute with Galan, she only wanted to go home to bed.

They reached his car, and Galan squeezed her hand. "Take care of yourself. I wouldn't want anything to happen to you."

"That goes for me, too, but I'll be okay after the holidays." This night had been special, full of magic. She still couldn't figure Galan out, but he seemed interested in her. Never can tell where this relationship might lead, she thought as he opened the car door for her. But wait a minute. Did she want this relationship to lead anywhere?

She shrugged. Unwilling to dwell on her friendship with Galan, she brought her mind back to her health. She had nothing to worry about.

She hoped not.

## Chapter Six

Shortly after arriving home from work, Stevie changed into jeans and a T-shirt, comfortable attire for the spring-like weather, although January hadn't arrived yet.

With an armful of dirty clothes, she headed for the cubbyhole off the kitchen and loaded jeans, shirts, and blouses into the washing machine. Her mind drifted as she leaned against the machine and poured soap into a cup. Was it only two days since Galan had taken her to see The Nutcracker? Vivid recollections of the ballet flitted through her mind--the dances, the costumes, the scenery, the exquisite music, images she'd remember for the rest of her life.

But especially, she thought about Galan with his solicitous manner and courtly ways, definitely a gentleman, a man whose gallantry made her feel more like a woman. Would she have enjoyed The Nutcracker as much with another man? Not a chance.

Humming The Little Drummer Boy, she closed the washer door when the phone's ringing drew her back to the living room.

"Hello."

"I'd like to come see you," Galan said in his low, sensual voice. "Do you mind if I visit this evening?"

Mind? Never! "Come on over," she replied, plugging in the multi-colored lights on her miniature Christmas tree. She tucked the phone under her chin and adjusted the angel with a white flowing nylon gown and silver wings on top of the tree, straightening it so it wouldn't tip over. "How've you been?"

"I have been well, and thinking of you...."

Her heart raced as she hung up the receiver. What did she mean to him? Don't read anything into his visit, her head reminded her heart, and don't try to figure him out. After all the times she'd been with him, she still felt as if she hardly knew him, this puzzling man.

Minutes later, Galan arrived at the front door, his smile making her heart do somersaults. As he stepped into the living room in his confident manner, he raked his fingers through his windblown hair, giving her an ice-melting smile that sent all her resolutions flying out the window.

He handed her a gorgeous pink phalaenopsis nestled in a wooden basket, tied with a pink and white bow. "Present for you. I know how you like orchids."

"Thank you, it's beautiful." Mindful of the other flowers he'd given her, she asked, "Where do you work, in a florist's shop?" She smiled up at him as she set the orchid on the coffee table.

He grinned. "Let us say I like to buy you flowers."

She shoved a strand of hair behind her ear. "How about tea or coffee, or maybe wine?"

"Nothing, thank you." He sank into the brown leather chair, his arms loose at his side, legs crossed at the knees. He leaned forward, his gaze focused on her throat. "I've been ... concerned about you. How have you been feeling--still weak?"

Stevie sat on the sofa, drawing her legs behind her. "Not weak, exactly, just a little tired. The holidays," she said in a rush of words, "lots to do--Christmas shopping, mailing packages, not to mention we've been extra busy at the bookstore."

"Is there no way you can take a vacation?"

She shook her head. "Too busy this time of year." She took a deep breath. "After the holidays, I'll be good as new." Right.

"Let us hope overwork and not illness is the reason for your malaise." He tapped his long fingers on the arm of the chair. "Would you like to see a film with me this Saturday?" he asked in his rich-as-chocolate voice. "You may choose which one."

"Cool! There's a new Brad Pitt movie I'm dying to see." An idea raced through her mind. "Since the weather has been so nice lately, why don't we go on a picnic this Sunday? I know a place--"

"During the day?"

"Well, I guess so," she said, struggling to keep the sarcasm from her voice. "When else would you have a picnic?"

"An evening picnic would be pleasant. We could have champagne...."

"Have to work every evening at the bookstore, since one of the other workers is on maternity leave. How about Sunday afternoon?"

"I can't." He gave her a quick smile, as if to take the sting from his words. "There is still much to do on my manuscript. Please try to understand."

"But really, you should get out in the sun more. Your skin is so pale. Don't you know you need--?"

A noise erupted from his throat that sounded suspiciously like a growl. "I'm very busy during the day," he said evenly. "My, uh, deadline, you see."

She looked at him, wondering what thoughts were concealed behind his dark, unfathomable eyes. He couldn't spare a few hours on a Sunday afternoon? A riddle wrapped in a mystery inside an enigma; she'd heard that expression somewhere, a rendition that pretty well summed up Galan.

"Try to understand," he repeated, a hint of a smile on his face. He shifted in his chair and uncrossed his legs, a movement that revealed the hard muscularity of his thighs, the trim fit of his pants.

"Okay, I'll try," she replied without conviction.

Silence stretched between them, long moments which gave her a chance to study his features. With only the dim glow of a lamp, his face didn't appear so pale now, yet the dull light did little to soften his chiseled features.

"Stevie...." He shook his head but said no more.

Her look met his, then his gaze slid down to her throat. He clenched and unclenched his hands, as if struggling against an unseen force. His gaze flew to hers again, and a tremendous lassitude came over her, rendering her helpless. My God, what was happening to her?

Yet this feeling aroused her like nothing she'd ever known. Had he cast a spell on her? Didn't she have a mind of her own anymore? She wanted him now, this minute, as she'd never wanted anyone. She wanted to taste his kisses, feel his arms around her. If only he would--

"No." The single word fell from his lips, scattering her wishes to the winds. A fresh rush of heat flooded her face, prompting her to turn away from him, afraid he'd sense her confusion. Could he really read her mind?

"Best I leave now, although I realize this has been a short visit. I wanted only to ask you about the film, but I fear you must arise early tomorrow." In one easy movement, he rose from his chair, as always a dominating presence whose face revealed perfect control.

Still enclosed in a cocoon of passion, Stevie stood too, wanting to go wherever he led her, do whatever he desired. She gave herself a mental kick. What had happened to all her resolutions to keep him at a distance? She sighed. Out the window. She tucked her T-shirt inside her jeans and smiled up at him, hoping to present an image of serenity, as if her whole body wasn't brimming with sensual excitement.

Galan came to stand beside her, giving her the full impact of his heart-stopping charm as he brushed a lock of hair from her face.

"Sweeting," he whispered.

Sweeting? She'd heard that endearment before, but where? She thought hard, but caught in the lure of his old-world charm, she couldn't summon the answer.

He bent low to touch his lips to hers. "I'll call you later in the week." After one last smile, he turned and left, opening and closing the door behind him.

She ran her hands across her breasts, down to her belly and past her hips as waves of soul-wrenching need flooded her. She sank into the chair he'd so recently vacated, inhaling his faint sandalwood scent and wishing he didn't rattle her so. And wishing she could drive him from her mind.

\* \* \* \*

For days after his visit to Stevie, Galan cursed himself for not taking her in his arms and kissing her as he'd dreamed of for so long. In his bedroom, he brooded over her, his need a continual torment with no hope of satisfaction.

Moloch. By all the saints, he despised the fiend, hated him for the hideous transformation the wily vampire had performed on him. Hatred burned inside him, hotter than a flaming torch, more persistent than a raging inferno.

It struck him anew that from now until the end of the world, he was doomed to live only by night and never live a normal life, never know the true love of a woman, a woman like Stevie. Who was he deceiving? He desired Stevie, everything about her.

He slammed his fist against the bedroom wall, heedless of the flash of pain in his knuckles. There would be a day of reckoning when Moloch would pay for his sins.

\* \* \* \*

At Schloss Omerau in mid-December, Moloch convened a meeting of all the vampire representatives scattered throughout the world. Arms folded across his chest, he stood in the great hall and counted over one-hundred delegates, each representing his own bailiwick. Tall, short, fat--the delegates ran the gamut. Some wore silks, others denim, but none were dressed warmly, since the cold meant nothing to them, unlike the puny mortals, who suffered from every imaginable weakness. A stiff wind whistled through the open windows, tugging at Moloch's bushy hair and fluttering gowns, tunics, and robes, like laundry left hanging in a storm.

Shoving loose strands of hair from his face, he looked on in silent satisfaction while the great hall hummed with hundreds of voices from Arabic to Urdu, most of which languages he understood. The vast majority of delegates were men, but an occasional woman stood out in the crowd, like a vixen among foxes.

Finished with his silent perusal, Moloch pulled out a chair and sat at a wooden trestle table, while others stood or sat on the worn benches lining the four walls.

The master vampire spoke in his raspy voice, and the din stopped, like turning off a water faucet.

"I must tell you the reason for this meeting," he said, his gaze focused on the nightstalkers. He paused for emphasis. "One of the undead has fallen under the spell of a mortal."

Shocked glances and gasps erupted throughout the hall.

Moloch spoke with cold fury. "I will not allow any attachment between a human and one of the undead."

Octavius, a renegade vampire, slunk into the hall and stopped at the outer edge of the assembly, far from Moloch. Clad in a snow-white toga, with graceful folds falling to his ankles and leather sandals on his feet, he liked to project an image of distinction and dignity, an impression often at odds with his true feelings. He hoped his perpetual sly grin gave him the appearance of one who considers life--or rather, death--one grandiose joke.

The other vampires viewed him with disdain, throwing anxious looks at Moloch, but the leader appeared oblivious to the sideshow.

A red-haired nightstalker sneered. "What are you doing here? You're not a representative."

"Get out of here," a second vampire snapped.

The maverick's grin widened. "That's what I always like, a warm welcome."

"Keep your mouth shut, or we'll make you leave."

Octavius held up a hand. "I want only to listen."

Moloch paused dramatically. "It is Galan who has fallen in love with a mortal. He should have transformed the bitch into one of us long ago, or enjoyed the taking of her blood while she begged for her life."

More shocked murmuring.

Tall and blonde, with a military bearing, Helmut raised his hand and was acknowledged. He sported a Waffen SS uniform, complete with high black boots polished to a shine, his cap with the silver death's head set at a jaunty angle. "With all due respect, sir, why don't we turn this mortal woman into a vampire?"

Moloch shook his head. "Don't want to antagonize Galan. I have great plans for him. I've been at the helm for almost two-thousand years, and eventually someone must take my place as leader of the Society of the Undead. Not yet, mind you, but within a few centuries." And would any of these nightstalkers want to take his place? Not likely, self-centered bastards that they were.

"Kill the mortal woman!" Screams and hisses and curses rent the air, everyone talking at once, the voices bouncing from stone wall to stone wall. "Drink her blood! Suck her dry! Burn her 'til she's only ashes."

"Quiet!" Moloch waited until the room became silent again.

"Ich glaube nicht!" muttered Helmut.

The head vampire gave him a harsh look. "You doubt my word?"

"Nein, mein Fuhrer. It just seems so ... so preposterous one of us would want to become mortal again."

Moloch scowled. "And despicable. Of course, we can't permit Galan to continue to see the vapid wench. We must drive him away from her," he said, pounding his fist on the table.

"But, sire." A young man clad in an Elizabethan costume of a deep red doublet, stiff white ruff, and black silk hose stepped forward. "If Galan is so unreliable, why would you consider him for leadership?"

"Because I want him for the position," Moloch said. "Until Galan met this mortal woman, he was the very representation of what a leader should be--trustworthy and dependable, able to make decisions and act on them." Unlike the rest of you, he thought, painfully aware these delegates were the best he could scrounge up. "Because of these admirable traits, I consider him the best candidate." Resolve deepened his voice. "What we must do is lure Galan away from this wench."

Rosalinda stepped forward, her look bold and confident, as if her actions determined the fate of nations. Adorned in a deep green velvet gown that swept the floor as she moved, she wore her long hair loose to her waist. Gold glittered from her neck, ears, and wrists, sparkling in the nighttime darkness.

She spoke in a firm voice. "I did my best. Galan and I were lovers once, and I tried to resurrect our affectionate relationship. I did everything I could, as you ordered, but he spurned me."

"You didn't try hard enough, my girl." Moloch's sharp gaze raked her from the crown of her head to the six-inch black spike heels on her feet. "With all your, um, feminine charm, you surely should have drawn Galan away from this mortal. So try again, and no excuses. I'll not accept failure a second time." He held up a hand. "But no harm is to come to Galan or the woman." He waited a thoughtful moment. "Not for now, at least." "Yes, sir." She bowed her head, her long hair tumbling in front of her face. Gathering her dignity about her like a cashmere shawl, she eased to the back of the room, already planning her next move.

* * * *

As Galan prepared to go downtown for his feeding, a figure appeared in the room.

"Octavius! What brings you to my humble abode?" A mocking grin on his face, Galan rose from the bed to embrace his friend. "Haven't seen you for a long time--what is it?--over a hundred years, I'm sure." In his white toga and leather sandals, his visitor looked the picture of a distinguished Roman senator, but Galan knew his garb was an affectation, for Octavius had served as a Greek slave in the Roman Empire. He even doubted Octavius was his real name.

Octavius returned the grin. "Only thought I'd look up an old friend. You know what a sociable creature I am."

"You never were a good liar," Galan replied with a rush of affection. "Now tell me your real reason for being here, not that I don't appreciate having you. But it might be helpful to know why."

Octavius sat on the bed and swung his legs around, resting his back against the headboard. He adjusted the folds of his toga with concentrated precision. "Very well, let's get down to business. Moloch is concerned about you ... no, maybe 'alarmed' is a better word."

Filled with countless anxieties, Galan sank onto a cushioned chair, facing his friend. "Tell me something I don't already know." He remained silent while the full meaning of Octavius' message sank in. "And he related his concerns to you."

"If only it were that simple," Octavius said with a worried look. "He called a meeting of the vampire delegates, and--"

"By St. Aidan, no! It is no one else's business." Galan frowned as another thought came to him. "But you're not a representative, are you?" Neither was he, Galan silently admitted. At one time, yes, but now he wanted only to keep his distance from the fiend.

Octavius winked. "I invited myself. I believe the modern term is 'crashing the party.'"

"Why should he call a meeting just because of my--" Galan paused, more worried by the minute,"--my relationship with a mortal? That was the purpose of the meeting, I suppose?"

Octavius studied his fingernails, each one painted a different vivid color. He wiggled his matching toes. "Partly. He's considering you as his successor."

Galan snorted. "Why in Hades would he consider me? I have no interest in the position."

"My friend, you refuse to recognize your sterling qualities."

"I've managed to put up a good pretense for all these years--centuries! And I'll continue to do so, especially now that I must protect the mortal woman." Galan crossed his legs and leaned back in his chair. "At one time, I would have assumed leadership of the Society, hoping to guide it along more, uh, compassionate lines. But now I see there is no changing Moloch."

Galan frowned in puzzlement. "Why are you telling me these things about Moloch and the meeting?"

"You helped me once," Octavius said. "Remember the jealous nightstalker who threatened me because I took his woman from him? And how you threatened him by vowing to tell Moloch of some nasty remarks he made about our esteemed leader?"

"Ah, yes, Morcar. And the girl, I believe, was Lilith."

"Right on both counts. So this is the least I can do to repay you." He changed his position on the bed, a sober frown on his face. "No, I'm not being entirely honest. How did Moloch ever get to be leader of the Society of the Undead? No one asked me how I felt about him. And something else--I don't like his methods, his constant supervision, as if we were all children he must discipline." He folded his arms across his chest. "Now, there, I've said my piece, and I wouldn't be surprised if you agree with me."

"Most definitely." Galan's mind churned with new worries. "Rosalinda's been here once. I'm concerned about what she might do--not to me, but to the woman I care for."

"You leave Rosalinda to me," Octavius said, smoothing his fingers over his slicked golden hair. "I've taken rather a fancy to her, and I am not without a certain amount of charm. I'll make myself so irresistible, she can't refuse me." He exuded absolute confidence, polishing his nails on his toga.

"Which still leaves Moloch," Galan said, close to panic. "And Stevie," he added, sotto voce. What could he do about her? He couldn't walk out of her life. He needed to see her again and again, but more important, he had to protect her.

Octavius snapped his fingers. "I have an idea! I shall create a diversion--don't worry, I'll think of something--that will keep Moloch occupied, so he'll forget about you and your beloved." He frowned. "At least, for the time being."

"Yes, for the time being. Those are the operative words." Galan ran his fingers through his unruly hair as his troubles tormented him, with no resolution in sight.

A moment of silence stretched between them. Octavius opened and closed his mouth, fidgeting on the bed.

"What is it, my friend?"

"Is it true you wish for mortality?" Octavius blurted.

Galan's head jerked up. "Moloch told you that, didn't he?" He held up a hand. "No need to answer. Until recently, I've been able to hide my feelings from the fiend. But now ... now, since I met the mortal woman, things have changed. My life-- such as it is--has changed." He cracked his knuckles. "Anyway, why wish for an unattainable goal?"

Octavius gave him a long look from under his lashes. "I've heard rumors of an elixir that can make a vampire mortal again and--"

"What?" Galan jerked in his chair, his mind reeling with the meaning of this revelation. If it were true, oh, God, if such an elixir really existed....

"Only a rumor, you understand." Octavius gave him an apologetic smile. "Possibly I shouldn't have brought up the subject now--"

"But I'm glad you did." Galan stood and paced the floor, running his fingers through his hair. "It gives me hope."

"False hope, I'm afraid, my friend. I'll try to find out more about it ... somehow. If Moloch should hear about this elixir, or that I've been asking about it ... well, you see the difficulties."

"By St. Aidan, yes! Don't put yourself in danger for my sake. But if you do hear anything...."

"I'll let you know, believe me."

"And I shall try to find out more, too." Galan returned to his seat, resolved to calm his emotions, not wanting to get his hopes up, only to have them dashed. And many problems still remained. He leaned forward, resting one ankle on the opposite knee, forcing himself to speak with confidence. "My friend, I can't tell you how much your help means to me, but sooner or later, Moloch will return to deal with me."

And he'd have to deal with Moloch. Which one of them would win?

## Chapter Seven

"Hi, Dad, how are things in New York?" Steve lounged on the sofa, her left leg slung over the back, phone cradled against her ear. In jeans and a T-shirt, she was quite comfortable on this balmy evening in late December. She tossed a romance paperback onto the coffee table and held the phone closer to her ear.

"Everything's okay here. Just wanted to see how you are. We missed you at Thanksgiving and Christmas. Too bad you had to work." Was there a trace of sarcasm in his voice, or did she only imagine it? "You going to work at that bookstore for the rest of your life?"

"Hardly. I intend to start at Barry University for the fall semester."

"Studying what?"

She took a deep breath. "Sociology. You know I want to go into social work."

"Social work! There's no money in that."

"Give it up, Dad. There's more to life than making a lot of money."

"Like what, for instance?"

"Job satisfaction, for one thing."

"I'm perfectly satisfied with my profession, and I make good money besides. The two are not mutually exclusive."

"But I like to help people." She slipped her leg from the back of the sofa and sat up, leaning forward. "And maybe I can even make a difference in someone's life."

"Lawyers help people every day, Stephanie. I wouldn't mind if you studied one of the other professions, like medicine or accounting. But social work...!"

"I'm not going to change my mind, and please don't try to change it for me. This is what I want to do."

"Where are you going to obtain funds for tuition? From what you make at the bookstore?"

"I've applied for a student loan, but I haven't heard back yet."

"If you studied law or any of the other professions, you know I'd gladly pay your tuition, no strings attached. Don't forget I already paid for two years at Columbia--"

"I haven't forgotten."

"--and then you quit because you couldn't decide what you wanted to do with your life. I don't see any point in advancing more money--"

"I'm not asking you to."

"--when you intend to go into some useless line of work."

"It's not useless!" She gripped the receiver, her heart pounding. "Dad, I'm a different girl now than I was a few years ago. I intend to get a degree in social work."

"Then don't ask me for money, no matter why you need it."

"Don't worry, I won't. I'm paying all my living expenses, as you know, and the student loan should pay for my education. I can get by on my own, and there's really no more to say." Stevie hung up.

She flexed her tense fingers, wishing they could have finished their conversation on a more agreeable note. No matter what her dad said, she knew she could do anything she set her mind to. Only a matter of determination.

Within seconds, the phone rang again. Was her father calling back to apologize or to argue further? After three rings, she picked up the receiver. "Hello."

"Don't think you can escape," a raspy voice said. "I'll get you sooner or later."

"Who is this?"

Silence.

"What a jerk!" She slammed down the phone and headed for the kitchen. Halfway there, a crazy idea halted her steps. Was he the same man she'd seen a couple of times in the neighborhood, the last time right outside her apartment? Shivers raced over her body. Who was he? And what did he have against her?

* * * *

With only minutes to spare before daylight, Galan flung his front door open and slammed it behind him. No sign of Rosalinda, and he'd checked all her usual haunts from Sao Paulo to Frankfurt to Tokyo. He thought of all the nights he'd kept guard by Stevie's bed, but what about the times hunger had driven him away?

What if the vampiress had taken advantage of his absence to feed on Stevie? That would explain Stevie's fatigue. God, no! Simple enough for Rosalinda to discover Stevie's address, because she had only to follow him to her apartment, clandestinely, of course. Nothing was impossible for the undead.

And what about Octavius and his promise to entice Rosalinda away from him? Where in Hades was he?

More than anything else, he wondered about the elixir, a possibility that drove every other thought from his mind ... except Stevie ... and keeping her from danger.

Which brought him back to Rosalinda ... if the vampiress reappeared in his life, he'd stifle his resentment and greet her like the lover she'd been, so long ago. He'd do anything to keep her away from Stevie. Heaven has no rage like love to hatred turned, nor hell a fury like a woman scorned. He should know that by now, as surely as he knew Rosalinda's every mood, damn the bitch!

Drowsiness dragged him down as the early morning darkness lifted, and the rising sun sent bright shafts of light through the closed window blinds. With no time to lose, he raced upstairs, heading for his wide closet. Inside his coffin, he shut the lid and closed his eyes, soon falling into a deep sleep. Hours later, as the sun sank below the horizon and semi-darkness shadowed the room, Galan roused from his slumber. Slowly, he raised the coffin lid and sniffed. Was that musk he smelled? Aha! Rosalinda! After all his searching, she'd come to him.

But where was Octavius? It would be just like that knave to forget his promise and leave him to deal with the vampiress.

Pasting a smile on his face, he tucked his shirt in his trousers and opened the closet door.

"Galan!" Attired in a deep green satin gown, her long black hair rippling down her back, Rosalinda rose from the bed with one easy, fluid movement, like a snake. Blood red lipstick presented a vivid contrast to her pale skin. Lavender eye shadow and ebony mascara embellished her eyes. Diamonds glittered on her neck and wrist, a ten carat diamond flashing on her right ring finger. She was a walking advertisement for a jewelry store.

She threw her arms around him. "My Galan, as handsome as ever."

"Rosalinda! How nice to see you again!" Like hell.

She smiled coquettishly. "Well, this is a pleasant surprise. When last I visited you, you weren't very happy to see me," she said with a questioning look.

He drew her down onto the bed next to him. "My mistake. I've been thinking about you--and missing you so--it occurred to me, why don't we take up where we left off two-hundred years ago?" He slipped his arm around her waist. "We had splendid times together, didn't we?"

"The best I've ever known." She leaned her head on his shoulder, the musk aroma making his eyes water. "Let us resume our relationship, darling. We can go anywhere we want. The world is ours!"

Galan hugged her waist, hating himself for this pretense while he wondered how long he must continue. "Where shall we go? Paris? Rome?"

"London!"

He nodded. "London it is."

"We'd better leave now," Rosalinda said as she smoothed the folds of her gown, "if we want to take in everything there is to see and do. Don't forget about the time difference."

"I haven't forgotten." He stood up to take her hand. "Shall we leave, then?"

She slipped her arm through his, an eager smile on her face. "There's so much I want to fetch from Harrod's."

"Anything you want." Facing her, he held her lightly by the shoulders. "Before we leave, there's something I must know, and I demand an honest answer."

"Of course, Galan." She stared up at him, green eyes wide with innocence. "When have I ever lied to you?"

More times than I can count. "I have a mortal friend, a woman...."

"Another woman!" Jealousy burned in her eyes, her lips curling with contempt.

"Only a casual friend," he said, as always determined to protect Stevie. And surely Rosalinda knew about her, since Octavius had related the meeting at Moloch's castle. "She's spoken of fatigue lately, an alarming malady in such a young lady. Have you--?"

"I swear by all that is evil, I've not gone near her." She threw him a look of hurt indignation.

He peered into her eyes, searching for any sign of falsity ... and found none. For now, he'd take her word. But if she dared touch a hair on Stevie's head, he'd drive a stake through her wicked heart and burn her, so she'd never threaten anyone again.

"Forget this silly mortal," Rosalinda said with a coaxing smile. "She could never make you happy as I have. Kiss me, Galan," she whispered, leaning closer, eyes shut.

Galan touched his lips to hers, a light brushing of mouth to mouth. He recalled the passion they once shared, temptation beckoning him. But no one could take Stevie's place, especially not Rosalinda, the witch.

She pulled him ever closer, kissing him fiercely, running her fingers through his hair. An exultant smile on her alabaster face, she drew back with a slow sigh. She ran her hand past her hips and thrust out her breasts. "You're mine, aren't you, darling?"

"For always." Stevie, Stevie, his heart cried. If only she were you.

The vampiress reached for a large alligator tote bag on the bed, her long hair falling forward, concealing her face. "Let us go, then." Bag clutched in her hand, she straightened and brushed the long flow of hair over her shoulders.

They closed their eyes in fierce concentration, and a rush of air tugged at them. Images swept past, the Atlantic Ocean glittering in the moonlight below. Within a minute, they arrived in London at the spot Rosalinda desired, in Knightsbridge, near Brompton Road. Mostly rowdies and hooligans roamed the streets of the city at this early hour of the morning, but Galan didn't spare a worry about them, well aware they posed no threat to him or his companion.

Tiny, dry snowflakes spiraled down from a coal black sky, caught in the dull glow of streetlights. A strong wind blasted through the avenues, whipping Rosalinda's hair across her face and molding her dress to her body. Under the streetlight, her skin shone as white as the snow that dusted the sidewalks, her thin lips a slash of scarlet across her face.

Lit up like a centenarian's birthday cake, Harrod's dominated the block, with its many elegant windows showing all manner of goods, from costume jewelry to evening gowns. I suppose Rosalinda will want to visit every counter, Galan fretted.

Face pressed against a window, she studied a shoe display. "Oh! Look at those shoes. I can take my pick of them before we leave," she called to Galan, who'd strolled past her, glancing at the other department store windows. "So--"

A punk with spiked green hair and gold pierced earrings zipped around the corner and grabbed for her purse. "Give me yer--"

Galan rushed to her rescue but found, as always, Rosalinda could take care of herself. She hissed and spat at the bloke, a steady stream of thick, deep red blood spurting from her mouth.

The would-be thief jerked back, frantically brushing his hand across his face. "Blimey!" He turned and raced down the street, nearly slipping on the ice, as if the entire London police force were after him.

Rosalinda smiled sweetly. "Shall we go in now, darling?"

Impervious to security devices, they entered the magnificent emporium, a store so huge you couldn't see from one end to the opposite. As if she were a new heiress with an embarrassment of riches, Rosalinda flitted from counter to counter, Galan in tow. Both of them easily eluded security guards inside the store, their vanishing ability as potent as ever.

They stopped at a perfume display, where a variety of elegant bottles graced the counter, like debutantes at a cotillion. Rosalinda tried every scent that caught her fancy while Galan leaned against the glass, a study in nonchalance, hating himself for this charade. The vampiress sprayed a heavy mist on her neck and wrists, a mixture of musk, patchouli, and myrrh.

A cloud of perfume surrounded her face. "How do you like this scent?"

Like it? The stench overpowered him, like a whiff of poison gas. "It's lovely. Your type of perfume."

"Very well, I'll take it." She dropped the bottle into her bag as her gaze covered nearby aisles. "Now let's see about the jewelry, then I'll get a few pairs of shoes from the display window before we leave."

Passing the men's jewelry display, Galan spied a pair of eighteen carat gold cufflinks, an adornment he'd always wanted. He grabbed the pair and pocketed it, leaving fifty pound notes on the counter to cover the cost. He followed Rosalinda to the fine jewelry department, where locked glass cabinets posed no impediment.

By the time they left Harrod's, Rosalinda had snitched a ruby pendant, a sapphire bracelet, and the creme de la creme, the most exquisite emerald and diamond necklace, priced at maybe half a million in American dollars. Not to mention the perfume and three pairs of shoes.

"A most profitable visit," she declared as they drifted through the heavy doors, once more eluding security guards. "Now on to Sloane Street."

Galan's nostrils flared, his hands itching to shake her senseless. Would he ever get rid of the bitch?

Stevie, what are you doing now? He missed her more than he'd ever thought possible, imagining what she must be doing at this time--probably coming home from work.

And where in Hades was Octavius? Had he changed his mind? With centuries to fine tune their skills, ancient nightstalkers could easily home in on another's location. He done it many times himself. Continually glancing in all directions, he had only a faint hope the renegade bloodsucker would arrive soon ... if he ever did.

No doubt Rosalinda would latch onto Octavius without thinking twice, and then he'd be rid of her. He hoped.

"Why are you always looking over your shoulder?" Rosalinda asked as they passed Chez Enfant. She snorted. "Don't tell me you're worried someone will attack you."

"Not likely. But perhaps I'll see an acquaintance," he blandly replied, vowing to be more circumspect. "Think of all the nightstalkers here in London."

"Wait 'til later." She stopped to admire a variety of hats in a shop window. "I'll wager we'll see more nightstalkers than we can count in Picadilly Circus. We can feed then, too," she said with a sly smile, "together. Remember what fun that was?"

Fun? Like everything else, Rosalinda fed to excess, going from one victim to the next, prolonging the agony of the sufferers, gorging herself until her skin turned a fiery red. The very thought sickened him.

"Ooh, Galan!" she cried, her voice rising as she pointed to a hat in the window. "Love that chapeau."

"It's yours, then...."

A half-hour later, they left the shop with Galan carrying two hat boxes under his arms, the handle of a third dangling from his forefinger. If he hadn't stopped her, Rosalinda would have emptied the damned store. By all the saints, how he wanted to leave her and get the hell back to Miami.

Where was Octavius! Hunger gnawed at Galan's belly, an agonizing reminder he couldn't postpone feeding much longer-- but by himself.

A few blocks later, they prowled the streets of Picadilly Circus, this section a jumble of neon lights, tacky stores, and garish signs. Drunken revelers made a ruckus, garnering a disdainful glance from Rosalinda.

"Stupid mortals," she hissed. "I'll get them soon enough." Bloody saliva dripped from her mouth, her long nails sharper than talons, like an eagle poised to pounce on a rabbit.

Fierce hunger tortured Galan, as if red hot knives gouged his stomach. He had to get away. Couldn't wait any longer. He had to--

A flash of white appeared around the corner, a young man with blonde hair, his long robe falling to his ankles, leather sandals on his feet.

"Octavius!" The laggard joined them at a street corner where a porno shop flanked a store that sold nothing but condoms. Where the hell have you been?

"Galan." Octavius greeted him with a curt nod, then turned all his charm on the vampiress. "And Rosalinda!" he cried, his gaze devouring her. "A vision of loveliness." Bending low, he raised her hand to kiss the back, his look deep with desire. "What a coincidence to see two of my best friends here in London, of all places! Mind if I join you?"

Rosalinda hesitated. "Galan and I are having such a good time, and we were just going to feed together."

Galan shot her a glance. We were?

Octavius smiled winsomely. "Oh, but Rosalinda, some of our nightstalker friends in Paris are giving a party this very minute. Think how you enjoy those revels! Everyone we know will be there, even Lilith, I'll wager. You have a score to settle with her, if I remember correctly. So why not come with me?" He glanced in Galan's direction and winked. "You, too, Galan."

Rosalinda clapped her hands. "I love parties! And when I see Lilith, I swear I'll scratch her eyes out." She threw an appealing glance at Galan. "Let's go to Paris."

Galan made a gallant bow. "Two's company, three's a crowd. It breaks my heart to leave you, dear Rosalinda, but I mustn't keep you from a good time." He pressed his hand to his heart as he caught Octavius' sly grin out of the corner of his eye. After another bow, he handed the hat boxes to Octavius. "I bid you both adieu."

His face set in studied control, Galan left them, anxious to return to Stevie, although it was still too early to see her in secret. He'd visit her later, when she'd be sound asleep and he could resume his surveillance. Octavius had come to his rescue this time, but Galan's intuition told him his luck wouldn't hold much longer. Sooner or later, Rosalinda would be back, a greater threat to Stevie than ever.

Moloch, too.

He had to defeat them both.

\* \* \* \*

In the hazy darkness before dawn, Galan lay in his coffin. While he slept, images flooded his mind, finally coalescing into a dream so real, it was as if he'd actually lived through the experience. Yet even while sleep embraced him, he knew it was only a dream....

A warm summer breeze drifted across the meadow as Galan leaned against a massive chestnut tree to wait for Linette.

He looked off into the distance where the grassland met the green-garbed oaks and beeches in the thick woods. With an ever quickening heartbeat, he saw his loved one's slender figure as she hurried toward him. Passion engulfed him, his desire at a breaking point.

"Linette!" He stopped to stare at her. "Linette?"

Clad in jeans and a pink T-shirt, she rushed into his arms. "Galan!"

He shook his head to clear it. "Stevie?"

She laughed, the breeze lifting her long blonde hair from her shoulders and molding her T-shirt to her breasts. "Galan, don't you recognize me?"

"Ah, yes, my Stevie!" He gathered her in his arms and kissed her long and hard. "I've waited a lifetime for you. Many lifetimes."

They found a spot within the shade of the wide oaks, where not even the sun could witness their lovemaking. She kicked off her moccasins and unzipped her jeans, then stepped out of them. With tantalizing slowness, she tugged the T-shirt over her head and unhooked her lacy bra, letting the garments fall to the ground.

She slipped her silky panties off and tossed them with the rest of her clothes. She stood before him naked, the loveliest sight he'd ever beheld, an image that rendered him speechless. His gaze took in her high, proud breasts, the flat belly, the entrancing curve of her hips.

His fingers fumbling, he drew off his tunic and untied his woolen braies, tossing them to the ground. His undergarment shoved aside, he laid his tunic on the leafy forest floor for her to lie on.

"Come, darling." Galan eased her onto the warm ground and lay down beside her, amidst the shady foliage. He drew her into his embrace, all his restrained love and longing finding release in each shared kiss, each caress, every whispered endearment.

"I love you," she murmured as she returned kiss for kiss, touch for touch.

"Dearest, I want you so much."

"Then make me yours," she said, "for all time, through all our lives together."

Love and passion drove him on, and he couldn't have stopped if day had become night, if the world had ceased spinning, if the sun had burned to ashes.

He nuzzled her neck. "You're mine, forever."

"Yes!"

Words no longer had any meaning as their rapture spiraled to an undreamed of pitch, ending all too soon in their cries of ecstasy.

"Linette," he murmured after he kissed her softly on the lips. "My Linette."

Indignation flashed in her eyes. "I'm not Linette! I'm Stevie!"

Stevie! Galan jerked awake. Pushing locks of hair from his forehead, he thought about Stevie, her blonde hair and blue eyes, every dear gesture, and how much she reminded him of Linette.

Of course!

## Chapter Eight

But why now? Lifting the coffin lid, Galan considered all the years--almost a thousand!--that he'd roamed the earth. Why had he met this dear woman only now and not in a previous century? He drew the deadbolt back and stepped out of the closet, the answer bursting upon him. Perhaps the time wasn't right. He paused while he closed the door. The time wasn't right? What in Hades did that mean?

Every muscle tense, he gripped the doorknob. How much longer could he pretend to be a mortal? How much longer before Stevie would discover what he really was? The thought sickened him. Oh, he'd been brave enough when he'd assured Moloch that Stevie would never guess his true essence, but he didn't think he could keep his unspeakable secret from her much longer. Sooner or later, she'd discover what a monster he was. He slumped against the door. God, he prayed, please don't let it be sooner.

Seize the moment. With renewed energy, he moved about the room, slipping on a steel gray silk shirt and inserting the gold cufflinks from Harrods. He exchanged his black jeans for charcoal gray woolen trousers and stepped into black Ferragamo loafers. He'd make the most of every evening, every minute with her, for he never knew when their time together might end.

* * * *

At Galan's side, Stevie left the movie theater and walked onto the parking lot. Under a sliver of a moon and a few bright stars brave enough to compete with city lights, they headed for Galan's Mercedes.

"What a balmy night," Stevie said as she gazed up at the clear sky. A night made for love, and here she was with Galan. If only-- A stiff wind molded her light blue sweater to her breasts and plastered her long rayon skirt to her legs, the filmy material tangling between her knees, hindering her movements. As she bent over to loosen her skirt, she caught his eyes on her, his look undeniably sensual. A rush of heat made her forget the cold, forget everything but this man's presence. If someone asked her what movie she'd just seen, she could no more have told them than she could have sprouted wings and flown.

His familiar scent whirled around her, that aroma of sandalwood that seemed as much a part of him as his dark hair or ebony eyes.

He opened the car door for her, then walked around to his side and slid in beside her. "I meant to ask you about your Christmas," he said, starting the engine, "but holidays often slip past me, I fear." He glanced her way. "Did you have a pleasant day?"

She set her purse on the seat between them. How could Christmas, of all days, slip past him? "The people I rent from invited me to spend the day with them. But since Christmas is for families, I didn't want to spoil their time together, especially when they don't see their kids that often. So I spent the day by myself. What about you?" She studied the unreadable lines and angles of his face.

"I spent it by myself, also."

While he drove through the heavy traffic, she made small talk, unaware of her words, every thought on him. She admired his hands on the steering wheel, those long, expressive fingers. It seemed such a shame. They could have spent Christmas together.

She glanced at him out of the corner of her eye, observing his mouth, wondering what it would be like to have his lips on hers, those expressive hands on her body. She grew warmer, and an ache blossomed inside her, a fierce need to be in his arms, to have his body close to hers. She shifted her position, certain he could sense her desire.

They arrived at the Shipley mansion a short while later, where Galan parked in the curving driveway, a few yards from a newly-planted crepe myrtle tree. Christmas lights brightened the yard, revealing a mass of red poinsettias on the wide front porch. As she waited for him to open her door, she nervously twisted a long strand of hair around her index finger. She wanted him to kiss her, but would he? The pleasant ache mushroomed into full-blown desire as he held the door open for her, his gaze meeting hers. What did his look mean? Her imagination ran wild, every thought on those dark eyes, his intense expression, his firm yet gentle hands.

In meaningful silence, they walked hand in hand to the apartment, past the jacaranda tree whose branches whipped in a stiff wind. Her hanging orchid pots swung back and forth from the branches of the grapefruit tree, like monkeys on a jungle gym. A vast canopy of night sky stretched above them, studded with countless constellations.

All these things she took in with only a look. Galan's nearness, his strong fingers wrapped around hers, sent a rush of heat from her head to her toes and to every body part in between. She sensed a certain barbarism in him, waiting to escape but barely kept in check. The thought brought a smile to her face. His fingers caressed hers, her desire skyrocketing. Kiss me, Galan, she wanted to say as they reached her door. Let me know what it's like to have your arms around me, kissing me until I can't think of anything, anyone but you.

The moonlight shone on his face, accentuating his paleness and casting silver lights on his hair. His eyes were darker than a thousand midnights, his gaze as deep and bottomless as the Atlantic Ocean.

"Sweeting," he murmured as he stopped to face her.

"Why do you call me that?" More than anything, she wanted his kisses, but his language confused her. "That's the second time you've used that word."

He brushed a stray lock of hair from her face, his touch gentle. "It's an old term, goes back hundreds of years. Yet it's how I think of you--sweet and lovely, everything a man could want in a woman. And I want you--"

Without another word, he swept her into his embrace, binding her to him, as if for all time. He pressed his mouth to hers in a kiss that took her by surprise, a kiss like nothing she'd ever known. She wrapped her arms around his neck, returning his kisses, aching to keep him by her side. If he wanted to make love to her now, on her front doorstep, or carry her into her bedroom, she could never refuse him.

His kiss deepening, her body became weightless, as if she floated in space. Good lord, his kisses! She was drowning in sensuous pleasure, caught in a floodtide of warm passion, floundering, like a ship lost in a hurricane. If only she could stay in his arms forever, become part of him and never leave his side. Time no longer had any meaning as he pressed her ever closer, their bodies melding as one. Time present blended with time past and time future.

He whispered her name again and again, sending a fresh rush of heat through her body and leaving her so weak she feared her legs couldn't hold her. A trail of kisses from her mouth to her jawline sent her emotions spinning out of control.

Then he stopped, his lips pressed to a spot on her neck. He licked the spot, his teeth nibbling at her skin. A low growl erupted from deep in his throat, a savage sound that sent a jolt of alarm racing through her.

She felt his shoulders tense beneath her fingers.

"Galan ... what is it?"

"No," he moaned. "Oh, no!"

Slowly, he drew back and stared down at her, a look of agony twisting his handsome face. How could he stop now, just let her go?

"I must leave now," he whispered.

"Leave, already?" Desolation twisted inside her.

"Stevie, I'm so sorry." After one last embrace, he was gone down the walkway before she could ask him what troubled him. So quickly, she'd hardly had time to comprehend his words.

Chest heaving, Stevie grasped the doorknob as she watched him climb into his car and drive off. She stared at the Mercedes until the taillights disappeared around the corner. Her body throbbed as silent moments slid past. A cat screeched from the backyard next door, interrupting her troubled musings. What was the matter with him? She unlocked the door, then stepped into the dimly-lit living room, where the sofa, chair and tables dwelt in shadow. She'd never known a guy like him, never in her life.

She slumped into a chair and unbuttoned her coat, then slipped off her slingbacks. Why bother dating him? No sense in going with a man so full of secrets you never knew what he thought or felt. A man whose actions often bordered on the bizarre. A man who always left her aching for more.

* * * *

Mindful of his promise to Galan, Octavius headed for Schloss Omerau. How could he distract Moloch, make the fiend leave Galan alone? He scratched his chin, a plan forming in his mind. The more he thought about it, the better it sounded. But could he stand before Moloch without stammering or shaking? The demon had always terrified him.

Arriving at the castle in the early evening, he found Moloch at the long trestle table in the great hall, a flagon of wine and a crystal goblet half-full of burgundy in front of him. Moloch's skeletal fingers clutched the glass, as if it were the elixir of youth, his ticket to eternal happiness.

A gust of wind through the open windows sent the purple velvet draperies whipping out from the wall, the glass of the crystal chandelier tinkling, like a thousand miniature chimes. In contrast to the splendor of the room, a black feline reposed in a far corner as it daintily licked its paws, the remains of a rat at its feet.

Clad in a long black robe and short leather boots, Moloch threw Octavius a sullen look. Octavius swallowed hard, his stomach knotting. With his perpetual frown and downturned lips, the master looked like a starving dog deprived of its last bone.

"What do you want this time?" Moloch said in a deceptively mild voice.

Octavius bit his bottom lip. This time?

Moloch slammed his hand down on the long wooden table, knocking the goblet over. The wine spilled across the table and onto the stone floor, where it formed a crimson puddle.

"What's the matter? Lost your tongue? Tell me what you want!"

Don't let him upset you. He's only a vampire, like you. "I don't want anything. But Morcar--"

"Morcar! That troublemaker!"

"My feelings exactly. It seems he's spreading rumors about you again--"

"Again?"

Octavius nodded. "As he did a couple of centuries ago. Back then, Galan stopped him with a threat, very convincingly, I assure you. Now, Morcar's saying you've been at this position too long, that you're too stuck in your ways. 'Your fossilized' thinking, I believe is the term he used." A muscle twitched in his jaw. Had he gone too far? "Morcar believes he could do a better job as leader. So--"

Moloch half rose from his chair, his long, slender fingers clenched on the table edge. His mouth hissed steam. "Where did he say this?" Black, piercing eyes stared at Octavius.

The maverick's legs shook under his toga, and he took a deep breath. "At a recent party in Paris. Hundreds of nightstalkers attended, more than I could count. He made no secret of his opinions, going from one vampire to another, spreading his vicious lies." Would the fiend believe him? Octavius forced himself to breathe evenly. After all, it was the truth.

Moloch stood so quickly, his chair fell back on the stone floor, echoing like a clap of thunder in the room. He nodded with determination, his dark eyes flashing venom. "You leave him to me." He snapped his fingers. "You're dismissed."

\* \* \* \*

On a cold, frosty morning a few days after the New Year, Stevie dragged out of bed, feeling tired and listless, wishing she had a thermometer. I don't feel like going to work today, she thought as she slid her feet into her fluffy slippers and headed for the kitchen.

A short while later, after grabbing her beige slacks from the closet, she sank back down on bed. Forcing her legs into the slacks, she thought about Galan. She'd never figure him out, this guy with his moody personality, his secrets.

Her fingers trembled as she zipped her pants, then she headed for the chest of drawers to get her blue cotton sweater. Outside her window, she heard the rumble and whistle of the Florida East Coast Railway train in the distance. She pressed her hand to her throbbing head, hoping she'd make it through the day.

She tugged at the drawer, her fingers so stiff she could barely grasp the knobs. Damn, damn, damn! She tugged hard, sending a Lladro angel toppling. After checking the angel for knicks, she set it aside and tried again. One deep breath and a hard tug opened the drawer. She'd suffered from fatigue for months, and now this! For the past several weeks, she'd lost her appetite, and now her clothes hung on her like garments on a broomstick scarecrow. A rush of alarm chilled her. She'd have to see a doctor.

## Chapter Nine

In the narrow aisle of the Bookworm's Delight, Stevie tried to shelve a volume between two other books while she clutched a pile of new arrivals.

"Damn!" The book fell to the floor with a hard thud, barely missing her foot, followed by other volumes. She stifled a cry as she leaned over to retrieve the books, bending cautiously as a sharp pain shot from her knees down her leg.

"Oops, looks as if you have a problem here." A tall, good-looking man with light brown hair and a pleasant smile crouched beside her to help pick up the books. "There!" he said, setting them within a bare spot on the shelf. In brown wool pants, a white shirt and a beige sweater--cashmere, if she wasn't mistaken--he presented a picture of studied casualness, reminding her of photos she'd seen of English country gentlemen. He probably carried a pipe in his pocket. His face was familiar, too.

He grinned. "Now I know what they mean when they say 'heavy reading.'" His hand supporting her elbow, he helped her rise to her feet. "You okay, now?"

Stevie leaned against the bookcase. "Yeah, guess I just tried to do too much all at once," she said with a smile. "Thanks for your help."

"You're welcome." He paused. "By the way, I'm Mark Farrell. Come here whenever I get a chance. But I won't take up any more of your time." He nodded, backing away. "See you later, then." After another nod and a smile, he left the store.

What a nice guy, Stevie thought as she watched him walk out. A gentleman, too, and you don't see much of that kind anymore. A gentleman, like Galan. She sighed, wondering why she hadn't heard from him.

One of the employees hurried over from across the room, a worried frown on her face. "What's the matter, Stevie? I've noticed lately you're not your usual cheerful self." Julie gave her a close look. "Not pregnant, are you?"

"Pregnant?" Stevie wished she could laugh but feared it would hurt too much. "Hardly." Tired and feverish, she rested against the bookcase. A week had passed since she'd noticed the stiffness in her hands, and look at her now. A lot worse! "Been a little tired lately. Don't know why. Getting old, I guess," she said with a wan smile.

"Old?" Julie laughed. "No one gets old anymore. We all stop aging at twenty-five. But seriously, if you have

problems ... do you want to talk about it?"

"I just don't feel good." Stevie shifted her weight to ease her sore joints. Might as well have it out in the open. "I kept thinking I'd get better, but sometimes I have to drag myself out of bed in the morning. Guess I'll have to see a doctor." She brushed her fingers across her forehead. "Don't want to, though."

While customers milled about the aisles, taking books down from the shelves and turning the pages, Stevie touched Julie's arm. "Here, let's move out of the way." They headed for a far corner.

"There's a lot of flu going around," Julie remarked, "and if you have something contagious, you know the rest of us won't mind helping out until you feel better."

Stevie changed her position again, her knees aching like crazy. "Probably a good idea to take time off from work. You can take my place until I come back. Maybe a week or so. Hope it's no more than that. I'll tell the others."

She'd ask the brothers at Camillus House, the Catholic shelter for the homeless, if she could use the free clinic. Since she often served meals to the men and women there, they wouldn't charge for a checkup, would they? And if they did? Well, then, she'd have to dip into her savings.

In spite of her pain, a rush of emotion made her catch her breath as she thought about Galan. She wanted to be in his arms, feel his mouth on hers, his body close to hers. How was it possible to miss someone so much, that you thought about him every minute, day and night? But she didn't want him to see her like this. She'd wait 'til she got better. And she would get better, wouldn't she?

\* \* \* \*

Like an explosion, the alarm clock jolted Stevie out of a restless sleep. Flat on her back, she ached in every joint.

Come on, girl, get up! With a moan, she forced herself out of bed, and after dressing, headed downtown to Camillus House. If they let her in the back door, she could avoid a long wait.

After a half-hour's ride on the bus and a short walk to the shelter, she got into the doctor's office right away, thank God for small blessings. In the small, plain office, she related her symptoms.

The doctor fiddled with his fountain pen. "Could be rheumatoid arthritis, but we'll--"

"Rheumatoid arthritis?"

He made a few notes in a file folder. "We'll need to take X-rays and do a blood test. Then it'll be three days or so before we get the results...."

A short time later, Stevie left the clinic, not knowing any more than before. Three days to wait. Like three years.

Aching in every joint, she tried to walk normally, telling herself that many young people had much more serious ailments. So quit feeling sorry for yourself, she thought, walking along the dirty, trash-laden streets. Easier said than done.

\* \* \* \*

I must see Stevie again. By St. Aidan, he missed her so, every minute away from her a constant torment, worse than the most desperate hunger. Unable to reach her by phone, Galan didn't want to arrive at her home unannounced, as he had on his first visit. Worry about her kept him awake during the day and haunted his dreams when sleep finally came.

He surmised Rosalinda spent her time with Octavius now, but the unruly vampiress was as unpredictable as a roulette wheel, damn the bitch. What if she weren't with Octavius now? What if she posed a danger to Stevie, as he'd feared before? He must never let his guard down.

Even if Rosalinda left Stevie alone, Moloch had an army of vampires and revenants to destroy her. Revenants! Monsters, neither living nor dead, not even undead, but creatures caught somewhere in limbo between life and death.

One quick glance at his desk clock told him Stevie would be sound asleep. His intuition warned him--he'd better go to her, now!

Within seconds, he found himself in her bedroom, and--Rosalinda! Red-hot rage exploded inside him. God! He wanted to destroy the bitch. A neutral expression fixed on his face, he forced himself to stay calm, knowing he could think more clearly if not blinded by anger. But it wasn't easy.

Unaware of Galan, Rosalinda approached Stevie's bed. Bloody saliva dripped from her mouth, her hands poised to strike, long, sharp nails curved like tiger's claws. Clad in a red and black striped silk dress, she wore her hair in an upsweep, a jewel-encrusted dagger tucked among the coiling tresses of the crown.

Fearful of waking Stevie, Galan whispered, "Rosalinda."

She swung around, shock plain on her face, but guilt, too. "What are you doing here?"

"That's my question for you."

She shot him a defiant look. "I can go wherever I want, whenever I want. Nothing and no one can stop me."

By God, how he hated her. To think they'd once been lovers! He struggled to smile. "I thought you spent your time with Octavius now."

She smirked. "He's so boring. Not nearly as exciting as you. Besides, he's having a little altercation with Morcar. Morcar's been spreading lies about Moloch, in case you didn't know."

"Yes, I did know."

Turning onto her side, Stevie mumbled in her sleep. He laid a gentle hand on her forehead, returning her to slumberous oblivion. With the greatest effort, he drew his hand away, wanting to touch her hair, caress the silky locks, run his fingers down her cheeks.

Galan nodded toward Stevie. "I want you to leave her alone."

Rosalinda glared at him, hands on her hips, her eyes flashing. "Who the hell do you think you are, to tell me what to do! I go when and where I please. The world is my playground, the mortals my playthings, to tease and dispose of as I want."

"Then I'm begging you. Stay away from her."

She laughed, a brittle, mocking sound. "She really means that much to you? How can you possibly care for this mortal who lacks my charm, my powers? She is bound by the laws of nature, of physics, if you will. But I ... and you, can do anything we want." She made a wide gesture. "Nothing is impossible. Why, only think how we can travel through time. And look how we can visit any place we desire without benefit of transportation, like the mortals need. You would forsake all that to stay with this ... this miserable excuse of womanhood?"

A murderous urge erupted in him, but she was one of Moloch's favorites, and he didn't dare antagonize the master fiend. Damn them both to hell!

He reached for Rosalinda's hand, struggling to suppress his fury. "Leave her alone. Come away with me instead. The world is our playground, our powers without limit." God, how he hated this deceit, but he had no choice. "Let's go away together. Where would you like to go?"

She smiled with triumph. "Brussels!"

"Brussels, then. One of my favorite cities. Why, only think of all our friends we'll meet in the Grote Markt."

When would he see Stevie again? His stomach twisted in knots. Would he ever see her again?

"You must promise me something," she said with a sly look.

"What's that?"

She flicked a disdainful glance at Stevie. "That you'll never go near her after this night. Otherwise, I'll kill her."

* * * *

Heavy rain and falling temperatures told Stevie a strong cold front was moving down the peninsula into south Florida. Oh, boy, just what she needed. Cold weather. Rain drummed on the roof and gushed onto the ground below, forming a puddle outside her bedroom window, and trees thrashed in the wind, their branches swaying.

More fatigued than ever, Stevie trudged to her bedroom closet to get a thick cotton blanket from the top shelf. Can't believe I once liked cold weather, she mused as she raised up on her tiptoes to reach the blanket, wincing with the pain. Now winter weather made her joints so much worse, stiffened her knees and swelled her hands and fingers. She'd taken a week of sick leave from the bookstore, hoping against hope she'd feel better by Monday.

And if she was still in pain? She'd go back to work, no matter what.

Blanket clutched to her chest, she plodded to the living room to watch TV, anything to get her mind off her worries, help her forget the pain. Anyway, it was still too early to go to bed, and the last thing in the world she needed was to lie in bed, tossing and turning for hours.

Getting settled with her blanket tucked around her chin, she flipped the remote control from one channel to another, finally stopping at the educational channel to watch a special program on vampires....

VAMPIRE MURDERS. The Herald headline ricocheted in her brain. Silly, how could anyone believe in such creatures?

Despite her doubt, she watched the first half of the program in fascination, while the narrator related tales of vampires throughout the centuries. The undead, he called them, with a brief history of Count Dracula. So there really was a Count Dracula? He wasn't just a figment of Bram Stoker's imagination? Well, what do you know.

"And here's a vampire for you," the narrator said after a public service announcement, "an actual woman who lived in the sixteenth century. She tortured and murdered hundreds of young women." The TV screen showed an actress who'd played the part in an old movie. "Does she look like a vampire to you?" he asked. "Just goes to show you never can tell what one of the undead looks like." He laughed, an eerie, mocking laugh. "Beware of strangers when you're out walking after dark."

So what's a vampire supposed to look like? Stevie wondered as she bent to scratch her foot. She sat back up and straightened the blanket around her shoulders.

"Here's something most people don't know," the narrator continued. "Not until the nineteenth century were vampires shown with fangs." First I ever heard that, Stevie mused. An old movie actor from Nosferatu appeared on the screen, fangs as prominent as the devil's horns.

"Now listen to this," he said. "According to vampire lore, they have no reflections and so avoid mirrors or any glassy surfaces."

Stevie pressed her hand to her head, thinking hard. Something about a glass cabinet...The thought remained out of reach, as elusive as a winning lottery ticket. All those aspirin she'd taken a while ago had dulled her brain, but she'd think of it if she just gave it time.

"Some people still believe in vampires, and many claim to number among the undead. Why, they even form vampire societies." So what do they do at their meetings? Stevie wondered.

Drink each other's blood?

The program ended with a long, ghostly laugh. "Better watch out, all you mortals out there."

Not so stiff now--maybe those aspirins had helped--she wrapped the blanket around her and trudged to her bedroom, thinking about Galan every step--his dark eyes, his smile, everything about him. He called her every evening and left a message on her answering machine, but she didn't want him to see her now, not like this. Strange, he hadn't called tonight. She swallowed a lump in her throat, trying not to think of him, wanting to put him out of her mind.

What would he think if he saw her now, when she could walk only in shuffling steps? Uh, uh, she'd wait until she got better. If she ever did.

* * * *

One evening the following week, a dense fog--unusual for Miami--veiled the city, blurring houses and trees. Concealed behind the jacaranda tree, Galan waited to see Stevie as she arrived home from work. Water from last night's rain dripped from the trees and glistened on the pavement. Cars driving by made a whooshing sound on the rain-slick streets, their dim headlights cutting a pale swath of light through the mist.

Moisture from the branches dripped onto his head and down his face, but he ignored it. Dead leaves littered the lawn and driveway, like an assembly of lost souls. A squirrel across the street climbed up an oak tree, the scratching of its claws multiplied a hundred-fold in Galan's ears.

Rosalinda, the slut! had remained in Brussels with Morcar and Octavius, the latter two having resolved their differences. When he'd left them, all three were indulging in an enthusiastic, vigorous sex romp at a deserted apartment on the outskirts of the city.

"Galan," Rosalinda had implored, "don't you want to join us?" She'd laughed, a low, throaty laugh. "The more the merrier."

He made a mocking bow. "Forgive me, dearest, but I must plead hunger," he said, hoping he was giving a credible performance. "I bid you farewell, but please, I beg of you, don't let my absence spoil your fun...."

With another impatient glance down the street, he tapped his fingers against his side. Fearful of arousing Rosalinda's suspicions, he knew he must return to Brussels.

How much longer must he live this life--this death! Would he ever discover the secret of the elixir? Fast losing hope, he searched his mind for a means of learning more, for Octavius remained ignorant of its source.

Minutes slid past as he stood under the tree, and--there she was, a spectral figure in the haze. But this wasn't the Stevie he knew, not the woman who'd told him she ran five miles every night without tiring, not his dear one with the warm smile and the easy laugh. As still as a frozen corpse, he watched as she approached the apartment, her steps slow and halting, a troubled expression on her face.

In God's name, what ailment afflicted her? Go to her, his heart urged. Take her in your arms and comfort her. And stay with her, for all time.

Agony sliced through him, as painful as the Norman arrow at Hastings. He clenched his hands, his mouth working. If only he could remain here with Stevie, discover what caused her suffering. But no, he had to part from her, never to see her again.

Never see Stevie again.

## Chapter Ten

"Where the hell were you?" In a wrinkled cotton chemise, her matted hair hanging to her waist, Rosalinda looked and sounded like a shrewish fishwife from Billingsgate. Careful to mask his feelings, Galan viewed her with revulsion. Leaning against a mahogany tallboy, he observed her in the bedroom of their spacious Brussels apartment as night lingered over the city, and streetlights cast a dull glow through the crimson velvet draperies at the wide front window. The huge rumpled bed gave evidence of Rosalinda's frolic with Morcar and Octavius, but where those two were, Galan didn't know and cared less.

"I waited and waited for you," she said.

"I told you," Galan answered patiently, "I had to feed."

She shoved her forefinger at his chest. "Liar! You went to her, didn't you? To the mortal woman."

"Madam, please do not call me a liar. I haven't touched her for a long time." Galan went on the offensive. "And if anyone has a right to ask questions, it is I. If I remember correctly--and believe me, I do--when I left here you were taking turns with Octavius and Morcar."

She lifted her chin. "What I do with my body is my own business."

"Then what do you want me for?" He held up a hand. "No, don't tell me. It's only for spite, to make sure I'll stay away from the mortal woman." Immediately regretting his words, he affected an anguished look and placed his hands on either side of her waist. "Dear Rosalinda, surely you know I'd rather be with you than anyone. How could one of our kind prefer a human woman to you?"

A tear trickled down her cheek. "You really mean it? That you'd rather spend your time with me? Remember, I asked you to join us."

"Three men and one woman?"

"Why not?" Rosalinda slid closer and wrapped her arms around his waist. "I'm always ready for something new. Make love to me," she whispered. "It's you I want, no one else."

Weary of pretense, he eased out of her embrace. "I can't make love. I fear I've lost my powers."

"Another lie! It's because of that ugly mortal. No matter what you say, you want only her." She brushed her hand across her eyes and sniffed. "You have no use for me anymore."

"Not true," he protested, proud of his acting ability, almost as good as Rosalinda's. "I simply haven't fed as I used to. Many things have kept me far too busy. Not everyone gorges on mortals as you do," he said, no longer able to keep the sarcasm from his voice.

"It's the only way to keep your powers. Do you want to be weak like a mortal? Wouldn't you rather have the strength of twenty men?"

"If it's strong men you want, you should have stayed with Octavius," he replied, well aware that he, Galan, could best any vampire in physical prowess.

"But Octavius isn't nearly as exciting as you." Her blood red lips twisted into a pout. "I'm getting so tired of this century, and I can't stand it when you go near another woman." She cradled his face in her hands. "Darling, let's go back to the eighteenth century. Remember how much fun we had then? And oh! do you remember that French chateau where Morcar killed all the mortals?" She giggled. "Then none of their stupid kind would live there because they thought the place was haunted. Let's go back there," she said with a coaxing smile. "Morcar's been eluding Moloch, in case you haven't heard and--"

"Of course I've heard. Rosalinda, I do manage to keep abreast of the news."

"Well, maybe we can persuade Morcar to give a ball and invite all our nightstalker friends." Her face hardened. "Not only friends, but enemies, too. I didn't see Lilith when I accompanied Octavius to that party in Paris, and I've got a few matters to settle with her."

Galan knew he must handle Rosalinda with care. But when would he see Stevie again? When, when? "Sounds like a fascinating idea ... France, I mean." He thought for a moment. "Clothes," he mused aloud. "We must dress appropriately."

She clapped her hands. "Oh, there are scads of armoires in the chateau, full of gowns, coats, and breeches. Shoes, too. Plenty of clothes for both of us."

\* \* \* \*

*Rambouillet, France 1777*

A vampire string quartet occupied the dais of the magnificent salle de bal at the chateau, where glittering crystal chandeliers glowing with spermaceti candles illuminated the rose marble floor and pale green damask draperies. The strains of the stately minuet competed with voices and raucous laughter. Must be at least two-hundred party-goers here, Galan estimated with a glance around the room. Everyone was dressed in splendid colorful silks, satins, and laces. Scents of musk and patchouli hung over the room like a fog over London.

Attired in a peacock blue velvet coat and cream-colored breeches, a yellow silk embroidered waistcoat and diamond-buckled shoes with two-inch square heels, Galan clasped Rosalinda's hand as they moved to the measured beat of the dance. A powdered wig with tight curls and a black velvet ribbon completed the look of the archetypal aristocrat, the very image he desired.

He held Rosalinda at arm's length, grateful the wide pannier of her pink satin gown prevented proximity as they stepped to the dance's stately tempo. Her heavily-rouged cheeks, ruby red lips and a heart-shaped black patch by her mouth gave her the appearance of a courtesan. And that's pretty close to the truth, Galan thought, slanting a look her way.

Diamonds as brilliant as the crystal chandeliers sparkled from her neck, ears, and wrists. Her coifed and powdered hair extended more than two feet above her head, a porcelain sailing ship anchoring the crest.

What a contrast to Stevie and her simple, unaffected look. Playing his part to the hilt, Galan tried to discard his depressing memories, concentrating instead on pleasing the painted bitch.

Rosalinda was all smiles and coy glances, like a virgin on her first date. A spurt of alarm skimmed over him as he saw her gaze light on Lilith across the room, her mouth tightening. Why couldn't those two sluts resolve their differences as Octavious and Morcar had? Knowing Rosalinda's moods, he feared trouble loomed ahead. Grave trouble.

In the course of the dance, they separated, Galan taking Lilith's hand.

"Galan!" the crafty vampiress exclaimed, "this is the first chance I've had to talk to you all evening. I swear you've been ignoring me." She preened, raising the hem of her gold silk gown and wide pannier to reveal long, shapely legs up to her thighs. "See what you're missing?"

"Ignoring you? Certainly not." Galan caught Rosalinda's malicious look as she paired with another dancer, and a jolt of alarm raced through him again. "I could never disregard such a lovely lady."

"You are such a gallant," Lilith gushed, dropping the hem of her gown. She turned away, throwing him a teasing glance over her shoulder.

Continually changing partners, Galan kept Rosalinda within his peripheral vision, watchful of her venomous expression. By God, she looked like a witch. Best for him to stay away from Lilith. No use tempting fate.

At the end of the dance he headed away from the rest of the crowd. Heels clicking, he strode along the marble floor, his frock coat swinging behind as he kept to the edge of the room, careful to avoid several groups of vampires forming a quadrille. Perhaps if left alone, he could think his thoughts of Stevie without fear of interruption, and remember all the things that made her so precious to him.

Rosalinda waylaid him before he reached his destination. Damn her! Did she have to hang on to him every minute? She grabbed his arm as he passed a nude statue of a Greek slave woman, set on a mahogany stand beside a marble pilaster. With a neutral expression fixed on his face, he suppressed his murderous rage and managed a faint smile.

Rosalinda fluttered her ivory fan, jewels flashing on every finger. "What did she say to you?" she snarled.

He looked at her in bland innocence. "Who?"

"You know who--Lilith!"

"Oh, she merely said it's been a long time since she's seen me," he improvised. "The last time we met, I believe, was in Venice in 1457 at the doge's palace." He bent his arm and adjusted the froth of lace at his wrist.

"I'll kill her!"

"Why this antagonism against Lilith? What has she ever done to you?"

She snapped her fan shut and rapped it against his arm. "The wench is a man stealer. She'd better stay away from you, if she knows what's good for her. You're mine, you know."

"Have I ever said otherwise?" By St. Aidan, how much longer could he keep this up?

"What does anyone see in that old hag?" She smiled slyly, tugging at her bodice, revealing nipples painted as red as her lips. "Now tell me something--does she have my beauty, my charms?"

He shook his head. "Rosalinda, you're in a class by yourself."

"Then remember that," she said with a second tap of her fan. One more sly glance and she slithered away, her silk gown rustling along the marble floor, the scent of musk lingering in the air.

Minutes later, while Rosalinda joined in a country dance with Morcar, Galan leaned against the marble pilaster, one leg crossed in front of the other. Rosalinda and Morcar, now there's a good pair. He raised his gold-framed quizzing glass to study Rosalinda, alert to every nuance in her expression.

A strong fragrance of patchouli drew his attention, Lilith at his side.

"Galan, darling!" She linked her arm through his, smiling with bold confidence. Wary of Rosalinda, he tried to ease out of her grip, but she held fast, like an eagle clutching its prey.

She threw him a provocative glance from under her long lashes, pressing closer against him. "Let's sneak away to my room, where we can be by ourselves. No other man here or anywhere can compare to you. Just the thought of you makes me hot all over," she said with a mocking laugh. "I want you to make love to me. Now!" she hissed.

"I fear I can't," he said in a kind voice while Rosalinda threw dagger looks at them from across the room. "You're a lovely, desirable lady, but my heart belongs to Rosalinda. Surely another nightstalker here would appreciate your

charms ... Morcar, for instance."

"Morcar!" she said with a dismissive wave of her fan. "I'm tired of him."

"Well, I--" He paused as he noted Rosalinda's approach, her steps quick and purposeful as she elbowed her way through the dancers. Her eyes blazed hatred, her mouth a firm slit of furious determination.

"You bitch!" Rosalinda slapped Lilith hard across the cheek, the blow echoing like a thunderclap in the room. Bloody saliva dripped onto her breasts and trailed down her gown, her fingernails curved like claws. "You stay away from my man!"

"Your man!" Lilith looked her up and down, lips curled with contempt. "What a laugh!"

Silence enclosed the ballroom. The musicians stopped playing and left the dais. All the nightstalkers gathered around the two vampiresses, like spectators at a boxing match.

Lilith sneered. "What does he see in you? An ugly has-been who can't keep any man. They all leave you sooner or later, don't they?"

"Why, you--" Rosalinda aimed another slap, but Lilith blocked it with a quick movement. Talk and laughter issued from the other vampires as they formed a circle around the two antagonists and made bets.

Arms folded across his chest, Galan watched the contretemps in fascination. Really, he should stop them, but he wondered how far they'd go.

"You ugly toad!" Lilith grabbed Rosalinda's coiffure and sent the ship toppling to the floor, where it shattered into a hundred pieces. Shards flew in all directions, and pins scattered to the floor, sounding like shot bullets in the charged atmosphere. Puffs of flour clouded the air, as thick as battlesmoke.

Galan jerked each vampiress by the arm, his arms straining to hold them apart. "Ladies, please, this is most unseemly. You're spoiling the party."

Exchanging glares, they thrashed in his arms, but he held them tight. The scents of musk and patchouli clashed in front of him, making his eyes water.

"No more!" Galan didn't give a damn if they wanted to kill each other, but he wished they'd take their disagreement elsewhere.

Hands curled into fists, the two women glowered at each other, hissing and spitting, hurling insults, like rounds from a cannon.

"Slut!"

"Painted whore!"

"Strumpet!"

"Harlot!"

Galan gave Rosalinda an appealing glance. "Please." After several long moments, she visibly relaxed. Uneasily, Galan released her, inch by cautious inch.

Rosalinda stalked away, but not before she hurled one last vicious look at Lilith. "I'll get you later, you hussy!"

"I'll see you in hell first," Lilith screeched.

The others drew back, muttering among themselves. Deprived of amusement, they dispersed as the first hint of daylight seeped through the heavy damask draperies....

Hours later, after a long, deep sleep, Galan emerged from his coffin to find Octavius in his room, perched on the edge of the canopied bed. Galan set the coffin lid down and eyed his friend with a questioning look.

Octavius sprang from the bed, excitement tingeing his face. "Have you heard the news?"

"What news?" Galan asked as he smoothed the wrinkles from his coat. "I've been asleep until now."

"Lilith killed Rosalinda. The usual way ... drove a stake through her heart."

With studied control, Galan sank onto the bed, striving to conceal his elation. One thought and one woman dominated his mind.

Stevie!

*  *  *  *

Another meeting brought the vampire delegates to Schloss Omerau. They're all here, Moloch mused. All except Rosalinda. Damn Lilith to hell!

Moloch rose from the long table and looked out over the noisy assembly. A ferocious wind blasting through the open windows lifted strands of gray hair from his shoulders and whipped the folds of his black robe. He clasped his long, skeletal fingers in front of him as his eyes assessed the group.

"Enough talk!"

Quiet descended over the group, every eye focused on the master.

"You've all heard the news by now. Rosalinda is dead." A fierce scowl twisted his face. "Lilith killed her, but we shall deal with the traitorous bitch some other time. Never doubt she will pay for her wicked deed. Our main concern now is Galan and that mortal woman."

A mass of voices hissed in unison. "Kill her! Kill the mortal!"

"Tear her from limb to limb!" a vampire screeched. "Torture her until she screams for mercy, then let her die."

Helmut worked his way through the crowd. "But sir, what about Galan? He deserves punishment for consorting with a mortal." His gaze covered the congress of delegates, as if seeking confirmation. "We all know the only reason he stayed with Rosalinda was to protect his lover. He should be made to pay for his transgressions."

"We shall see," Moloch replied to murmurs of agreement. "I still have hopes for Galan. After this mortal woman is destroyed, perhaps he will see the light." He raised his arms in a dramatic gesture. "Let this be a lesson to all the undead, and to all the humans who would dare entrap them. Get rid of the mortal female!"

Screams echoed from wall to wall, bouncing off the ceiling. "Yes, kill her! Suck all the blood from her useless body until she's only a shell." Voices rose, swelling to a roar. Fists thrust high in the air as angry emotions crackled within the castle walls.

After the voices died down, Helmut spoke again. A look of cruelty creased his face, his eyes blazing with sadistic excitement. "Sir, I would have the honor of killing the mortal woman. It would give me great pleasure to end her life."

Another vampire raised his hand. "No, I want to kill her!"

Shrieks and screeches reverberated throughout the hall.    "Let me do it!"

"I'll kill the bitch!"

"This is what I live for. I'll suck her dry!"

A low rumbling hung over the hall, and Moloch clapped his hands for attention. "Quiet!" His dark gaze covered the quarreling delegates. He leaned forward and spoke in clear tones. "Let me tell you how I plan to kill the mortal wench."


Chapter Eleven


I must see Stevie again. Back in Miami, Galan stepped from his coffin as twilight cloaked the city, and the first evening shadows darkened his bedroom. Fully awake, he left his room and headed downstairs, past the living room and Florida room, then outside.

A quarter moon floated in the night sky, west of the Pleaides. The dark night enveloped him, a part of him, as he would always be part of the night.

Love and despair clashed inside him, a painful amalgam that weakened him at a time when he needed all his powers. His anguish became palpable, pulsing, pulsing, pulsing, like a million beating hearts. He stared up at the deep lavender sky, where Jupiter joined Venus in their nightly sojourn across the heavens, as he wanted to join Stevie, for all time. A poignant ache tightened his throat, encapsulating the sadness of his whole benighted life.

Memories of Stevie raged through his mind, every smile, every facial expression, that made her so dear to him, the only woman he could love. He remembered the long flow of her golden hair. How he wanted to touch each lock, to let each silky strand slide through his fingers like sand. Visions of her lovely body taunted him to madness--her breasts, her hips, her slender waist, her long, slim legs with their shapely calves and ankles--every inch of her that he yearned to touch, caress, to drive them both insane with joy. His recollections deepened his desolation, like a thousand remembered kisses from a long-departed loved one.

As if she were with him now, he heard her easy laugh, saw those blue eyes flash with pleasure or defiance, depending on her mood. She had so many moods, each catalogued in his brain, and as precious as rare gems. Rubies, emeralds, sapphires.

But what if he told her what he truly was? A vampire. Would she believe him? He laughed without humor. If he revealed his true essence, she'd run from him as he would flee from a crucifix or holy water. If only he could find out more about the elixir to make him mortal again ... Far better had he never heard of this potion, than to have this continual heartbreaking disappointment. But he'd never give up searching for it, even if he had to cover every part of the earth.

By St. Aidan, if he were with Stevie now, he'd hold her close and beg her to tell him what painful affliction she suffered from. And if he could--oh, God! if only he could--he'd make her well again.

He glanced at his Rolex, counting the minutes until she arrived home from work. He'd call her then and make arrangements to see her. How could he bear the wait?

No, he didn't dare! He'd only endanger her if he went near her. Why hadn't he thought this out? Ah, but he knew why. As usual with Stevie, he let his heart rule his head. Rosalinda no longer posed a threat, but only look at the army of slaves and revenants Moloch had to command. How could he forget?

Galan gritted his teeth. May Moloch rot in hell.

\* \* \* \*

Deep in sleep, Stevie was having a wonderful dream. Each sensory image flashed through her brain, as though she lived through this experience. She and Galan were dancing in the most gorgeous hotel ballroom she'd ever imagined. Potted palms lined the walls, and crystal chandeliers twinkled overhead, the entire scene a rich fantasy of the senses.

"It's been a long time since I danced like this," she said, peering up at him.

"A slow dance?" His voice penetrated her very essence, a song in her veins.

"Not since the high school prom. But with you, I could make a habit of it."

He kissed the top of her head. "And I could make a habit of you, for always. You're a drug inside me," he said, "stronger than cocaine, more potent than laudanum."

"So you're hooked on me?" she asked with a smile.

"For life."

She sighed against his hard shoulder. "Um, the feeling is mutual."

Round tables accommodating hundreds of patrons occupied the space beyond the dance floor. Vaguely aware of her surroundings, Stevie glanced at the starched linen tablecloths, the crystal and china.

She heard the mumbled voices of men and women, smelled the rich aromas of food and wine. But sights and sounds blurred beside Galan. Other dancers shared the floor, but all she saw, all she felt, all she knew, was Galan. All she wanted.

She breathed in the faint scent of sandalwood as he drew her ever closer, their bodies moving as one.

In her slinky midnight blue gown of shimmering satin with its low neckline, Stevie caught Galan's dark gaze and roguish smile, his look plainly sensual. With his set jaw and firm lips, he reminded her of a medieval warrior, eager to slay dragons in his lady's defense. Fanciful? Maybe, but this was how she'd always think of him.

Dressed in a suit of the finest black wool, a white shirt, and burgundy tie, he looked every inch a man of fashion. No other man could ever compare with him.

She knew the time was the present, yet the group on the bandstand reminded her of the Big Bands from the '40s. Clarinets mingled with trumpets and tubas, drums, and a piano as the band entertained the customers with a love son she'd never heard. Galan knew the words. Why should that surprise her? He eased her closer and softly sang the lyrics in her ear.

She leaned into his embrace, never wanting him out of sight. A rush of desire raced from her fingertips to the pit of her stomach, where it lingered as a pleasant but urgent ache.

After the song ended, he held her closer and whispered in her ear, "Let's go upstairs."

Anticipation warmed her cheeks. "Thought you'd never ask."

Her hand in his, Galan led her past the other dancers and they mounted the carpeted stairs, neither saying a word. Heat sizzled between them, so tangible she could reach out and catch the feeling in her hand, store it to savor another time. By the time they neared the top, she simmered with passion, ready to explode.

At their approach, the door to their bedroom swung open, but by some trick, she found herself in an English meadow, her brown peasant dress discarded on the ground. The forest surrounded them, dark tunnels and sweeping arches of oaks. The warm spring air caressed her bare skin.

She and Galan lay under a spreading oak, the faint rays of sunlight filtering through the branches. The spring breeze whispered through the canopy and rustled the violets that blanketed the meadow. What a contrast to the passion that raged inside her.

Why, this must be the Middle Ages, she thought, fingering the rough material of her plain dress. How could that be?

With murmured endearments, he feathered kisses from her jaw to her breast as his hand roamed her body. He eased her legs apart, where his fingers found the core of her passion. Gently, he stroked her as he raised up to watch the emotions playing across her face.

An unbearable ache grew within her, surprising her with its intensity. "Take me now!" she cried. "I've wanted you for so long."

"No one else, for all time," he murmured as he entered her.

And then, there was no need for words, only a desperate need to give and receive pleasure.

Which they did, in full. Whispers and moans and gasps of ecstasy were the only sounds to fill the air, their lovemaking all that mattered.

"Galan!" she cried as a shattering force shook her whole body, hers and Galan's together.

"You're mine, Linette!"

\* \* \* \*

In his bedroom, Galan paused while he slipped his keys into his pants pocket. Pictures flashed through his mind, a cavalcade of visions that teased his senses. He stopped, clutching the edge of his chest of drawers. By all the saints, what was happening here? He saw himself with Stevie, leaving a dance floor, climbing carpeted stairs, hand-in-hand approaching a hotel bedroom.

But wait--where were they now? Not in a bedroom but in a meadow, its tall oaks and chestnuts reminding him of England, his former home.

Eyes closed, he watched as Stevie undressed, and he lay back on his bed and moaned. The flow of her golden hair down her back, her bare breasts and rose-tipped nipples, all her lovely charms carried him on a rich floodtide of emotion that flowed on and on.

"Stevie!" He grasped his blue bedspread, his fingers digging into the cotton, the images too real to ignore.

By St. Aidan, how long could he live without her?

* * * *

The last traces of passion ebbed inside her as Stevie awoke in her dark bedroom, sighing in sleepy pleasure from the sensuous dream. The pain of arthritis forgotten for the moment, she stretched, every image of her dream still vivid. Linette, she puzzled, remembering another dream. Who was she? Why did that name crop up in her dreams, like a long-forgotten memory? She delved into her brain but came up blank.

Her gaze covered all the familiar objects in the tiny room--the mirror above her chest of drawers, the end table with its mosaic crystal lamp and collection of porcelain rabbits grouped on a lace doily, a miniature straw hat with pink ribbons and masses of pink roses on a far wall. Another end table hugged a far corner, her computer occupying the entire space.

But something was wrong, terribly wrong.

A putrid odor wrenched her gaze to a far wall, several feet away. She jerked upright and stared at--oh, God, what was it? A monster? Couldn't be, couldn't be. She closed her eyes, then blinked them open again. This was no nightmare! This was real!

A long, dark robe covered the creature's stumpy body. The sleeves hung past his wrists, revealing long, claw-like nails. What was he going to do to her?

Her breath came in gasps. She swallowed convulsively and hugged her arms. Her pain returned, every muscle aching, throbbing. She glanced toward the corner again in one last, desperate hope that this sight, too, was part of her imagination.

Empty yet glowing eyes stared from a dull face with a flattened nose and sagging mouth. As if to taunt her with his presence, he stood immobile, reeking of rotten meat and stale urine. Long, tangled hair scraped his shoulders, strands of saliva dripping from his mouth. Who--what was he? Why was he here? God, please, this can't be happening.

Raw fear turned her stomach to ice. Blood pounded in her ears, her temples, her cheeks. Tears filled her eyes. She forced her sleep-drugged brain to react. Flinging her bedcovers aside, she urged her painful limbs to move, move, move! She clutched her flannel nightgown and headed for the door. Socks on her feet made her slip and she bumped into the door, dazed with the impact. Don't stop. Get out of here!

The monster lurched, panting behind her. Terror clogged her throat; she couldn't even groan. She squeezed her hands so hard the nails dug into her palms. Fright drove the air from her lungs.

Run! Go outside!

She reached the front door and gripped the doorknob--not fast enough! He pulled her back, his long, sharp nails scratching her wrist as he tossed her to the floor. She landed on her left hip, a jolt of pain racing down her leg.

Galan, help me. Please!

He grabbed for her. She rolled away, finding her voice at last. "Oh, God, no!" She scrambled to her feet and rushed to the sofa. Grasping the edge of it, she kept it between them. A stubby, hairy arm reached for her, but she jumped back. Every part of her body shook as they circled the sofa. Tears streamed down her face. She brushed her hand across her eyes to clear her vision.

Eyes now adjusted to the dark, she could see his jaw working furiously, his thick tongue flicking across his drooping mouth. Sharp incisors gnashed together, grinding like scissors, snapping up and down. Saliva streamed from his mouth like blood from a wound.

Her heart thudded hard and fast. Waves of dizziness washed over her. God, no, she couldn't faint, not now.

The police! If she could reach the phone, she could call for help, but she didn't have time.

A weapon, she needed a weapon. Perspiration streamed down her face and soaked her nightgown as she scanned the end table. A metallic glint caught her eye. She grabbed her letter opener just in time. Pushing sweaty locks of hair from her eyes, she thrust it at him.

"Damn you!"

Another thrust. "Damn you!"

The monster deflected each blow, like an enraged grizzly bear beating back a feather. He was toying with her! He could kill her whenever he wanted.

The freak grabbed her and squeezed her throat. His stubby fingers closed around her, tighter, tighter, tighter. His fetid breath fanned across her face like sewer fumes. Nauseated, she turned her head away.

She felt blood drain from her head. Stars burst in front of her eyes. Her ears rang as dizziness washed over her. Wobbly legs threatened to give out.

She would not die without a fight. She raised her tingling arms and pressed her fingers against his eyeballs. She bit down hard on her lower lip and tasted blood.

Screeching with shock and pain, he released her.

She tried to scream for help, but only a groan tore from her throat.

Galan, please help me!

Get outside! Get outside! She raced for the cubbyhole off the kitchen, where a door led to the backyard. She gasped, one quick breath after another. Her flannel nightgown tangled between her legs. She yanked the fabric up and rushed for the door.

Behind her, he grabbed hold of her gown. Razor sharp nails slashed the material and scratched her thigh, but she broke loose. Stabbing, burning pain tortured every joint in her body. A hammer pounded relentlessly in her head.

The monster followed her, his clumsy footsteps shaking the apartment. A painting crashed to the floor.

Almost there! Out of breath, she grasped the doorknob, her hand slippery with sweat.

As the knob turned beneath her trembling fingers, he jerked her back and thrust her against the dryer. Snarling with fury, he raised his hands to her throat.


Chapter Twelve


"How do we know Rosalinda is truly dead?" Now back in the present, Octavius faced Lilith in the spacious bedroom of her luxurious Paris apartment. Outside, bright streetlights illuminated the city, like sparkling crystal scattered across black velvet. Having arrived only a second ago, Octavius aimed to catch the vampiress by surprise.

Which he did. She gasped as she swung away from her mahogany dressing table, frantically waving her hands. Long, auburn tresses flowed past her waist, glowing golden by the light of the ornate crystal lamp on her bedside table. With white, flawless skin and a generous mouth, she had the look of a seductress.

After long moments of charged silence, her sapphire gaze slid over him, cold and calculating. Cat's eyes. Adorned in a black silk gown with a revealing neckline and lace insets in the sleeves and hem, she looked quite the lady of the night ... fit to kill, he thought on a note of wry humor.

She smiled slyly. "Rosalinda? That's my secret. You'll just have to believe me." She returned to her silver jewelry box, rummaging among glittering bracelets, ear rings, and necklaces, all set with precious stones. An emerald necklace sparkled around her slender neck ... Rosalinda's, no doubt.

"We have no proof." For Galan's sake, he must have an answer, and yes, for his sake, too. He'd developed a fondness for the dark-haired vampiress and he missed her in his own inimitable way. He moved closer to Lilith, as if to taunt her with his presence.

She slapped her hand on the table. "You doubt my word?"

"Let's just say I don't accept it as the Gospel truth."

She jerked back, as if he'd driven a stake through her heart. "Don't use that word around me!"

"What--Gospel?"

"Stop it!" she snapped. Her hands fluttered about, twisting rings on her fingers, knocking over perfume bottles.

"Very well." Octavius made a mocking bow. "Your wish is my command." He gave her a cautious glance. "Moloch is angry with you for destroying Rosalinda. Aren't you afraid he'll come after you?"

Her eyes flashed with indignation, her voice rising. "Rosalinda instigated the trouble." Lilith lowered her voice. "I'll tell him I killed her in self-defense."

"You think he'll believe you?"

"It's the truth!"

"So you have no proof that Rosalinda is dead?"

She rolled her eyes. "I already said you'd have to take my word for it."

"What if I don't believe you?"

She shrugged. "No blood from my veins."

Making the best of an unsatisfactory situation, he performed an exaggerated bow. "I shall leave you now, my dear Lilith. Do come visit next time you're in Brussels. We can do the city together." With a wink and a wave, he disappeared.

* * * *

Galan, please help me!

Stevie! Galan stopped midway between his living room sofa and the front door. A strong warning flashed through his brain, tugging at his heart.

In less than a second, he arrived inside her apartment, next to the dryer. By all the saints, no! A revenant threatened her. Fierce, red hot rage exploded inside Galan. He wanted to kill, kill, kill the bastard!

The monster turned from Stevie and looked at him, blinking his soulless eyes with incomprehension.

Stevie's face revealed pure relief, but puzzlement, too. "Galan, how did you--?"

"Not now, later!"

Galan jerked the revenant and banged the monster's head against the opposite wall. "You bastard!" After he killed the beast, the whoreson would disintegrate. God, Stevie must not see this.

"Stevie, please go to your room and close the door."

"Are you crazy! I'll get out of the way, but I will not close the door," she said, turning to rush from the room.

"Don't call the police," he shouted as he struggled to subdue the monster, his hands busy, every muscle straining.

The revenant's jaw dropped open, a look of confusion on his face as he glanced from him to Stevie.

Needing more room to maneuver, Galan grabbed a plastic cup from the washing machine and threw it into the kitchen. He watched in grim satisfaction as the revenant turned in that direction. With one quick movement, Galan shoved him beyond the cubbyhole into the kitchen.

The monster lashed out at him, slicing sharp nails across his face. Galan jerked back in shock. Pain stung his cheeks. His gaze scanned the kitchen for a weapon. And saw none.

A low growl erupted from the beast. It lunged for him again, swinging his arm in a wide arc. Galan stepped aside, the arm missing him by inches.

"You son of a bitch!" Desperation propelled Galan. Next to the oven, he gripped the revenant by the throat, clasping, pinching, pressing, determined to choke him to death. The revenant gagged, his eyeballs bulging, his skin slimy.

The revenant broke free and shoved him aside. Still needing more space, Galan rushed for the living room. Like a puppet, the creature followed him.

Two quick strides took Galan to the sofa. Now to--

The revenant lurched for him, but Galan flung him away. The monster grabbed him in a steely grip. Locked in a macabre dance of death, the two antagonists jerked about the living room, dashing, bashing, crashing into an end table, sending a vase tumbling to the carpeted floor.

Hunger weakened Galan. He couldn't last much longer.

* * * *

Stevie's heart pounded, faster, faster, faster. She stood in her doorway, hands clasped as she watched Galan and the monster. Noises sounded throughout the apartment, gasps and grunts and moans, a struggle of life and death. Scared witless, she bent her head as waves of dizziness washed over her. God, she prayed, please take care of Galan.

But how had that thing gotten into the house? Both front and back doors were locked, a deadbolt secured at each. For that matter, how had Galan gotten in?

And what was it?

Breathing hard, she rushed from her bedroom to the living room. She skirted the two fighters, fear making her sick.

In the kitchen, she grabbed a sharp knife from a drawer, her hand trembling. Sweat greased her palm, and the weapon clattered to the floor. Shot with pain and terror, she bent down to reclaim the weapon. She rushed back to the living room, knife clutched in her trembling hand.

Galan and the beast remained locked in a deadly embrace.

How she wanted to escape this nightmare, but she couldn't leave Galan.

* * * *

Galan shoved the creature against the wall, banging his head again and again. The revenant pushed him away, back, back, back, until he bumped into the sofa. Galan saw Stevie, the knife in her hand. Relief flooded him, but worry, too. What if the bastard turned on her again?

His strength ebbing, he slammed the revenant to the floor. The beast landed on his stomach, legs thrashing. Wordless sounds escaped his throat. Saliva pooled on the rug.

"Give me the knife!" Galan ordered.

"I can do it!" Stevie raised the knife and slashed it into the creature's massive back.

The revenant lay still at last.

Crouched on the soles of his feet, Galan looked up at Stevie. He sighed heavily. "Good work. Now please wait in your room. I'll handle matters here." Another glance revealed her white face. "Perhaps you should lie down."

"Yes!" Hand pressed to her mouth, she rushed to her room and slammed the door behind her.

Oddly bloodless, the revenant lay quiescent, not yet dead. Galan jerked the knife from his back and turned him over, then plunged the knife through his heart.

In slow motion, the revenant disintegrated, his skin sloughing off to reveal his desiccated organs, until those, too, disappeared. His bones crumbled until only ashes fouled the floor, the steel knife as solid as ever. For countless moments, Galan waited for his exhaustion to pass.

After he fetched a pan from the kitchen, he scooped up the ashes and headed for the back door. In the inky blackness of night, he threw the ashes to the winds. There in the backyard, he breathed in the fresh air, reveling in the breeze that caressed his face, its sweetness washing the stench of the revenant from his nose and throat.

Back inside, he strode through the living room, then cautiously opened Stevie's bedroom door. She sat on the bed, clasping and unclasping her hands, her long hair hanging in front of her eyes. At his entrance, she looked up, an unspoken question on her lips. By the blessed Virgin, if only she knew how her anguish tore him apart.

"You ... you killed him?"

"With your help." Galan hurried to her side and sat beside her, wrapping his arm around her waist. "Don't know how to mind, do you, sweeting? Should have stayed in your room," he said as he brushed strands of hair from her cool face.

Turning toward him, she lifted her chin a notch. "If I hadn't gone to the living room when I did...."

"Yes, yes, I know. Without you...." He shrugged, afraid to say anymore.

She looked past him into the living room. "Where's the body? And my God! What was it?"

"Never mind what it was. You don't want to know. And as for the body, don't worry. It's ... let us say it's taken care of."

She drew back, alarm flashing across her face. "You buried him in the backyard!"

"So quickly?" He laughed a little. "Not even I could do that in such a short amount of time."

"Not even you?"

Curse his foolish tongue! "I mean, as a man, I'm stronger than you. But I couldn't dig a deep hole so fast, especially in the near frozen ground."

"Then where is he?" Anguish marred her pretty features.

"Don't worry. He won't bother you again." Galan reached for her, but she edged back.

"He escaped!"

"No. Please ask no more questions. Believe me, he won't cause any more trouble."

"Shouldn't we call the police now?"

"No, I fear a call will only prompt unwanted questions."

"What do you mean?"

"I mean, it will accomplish nothing. Please, Stevie," he implored, easing her close to him. "He is gone. He is no more."

A look of bewilderment crossed her face. "I still don't understand." A moment of silence passed between them, her forehead creased in thought. "Something else I don't

understand--how did you know to come to me--that I needed you? Not that I don't appreciate your presence," she added, twisting her fingers together.

Gently, he ran a forefinger down her cheek. "Don't you know by now how closely we're attuned?"

She nodded, her head against his chest. How he wanted to hold her ever closer, kiss her to drive them both to distraction, help them forget this night's events.

"I don't understand that either," she said, "but I think you have something there." She glanced up at him. "Another thing--how--how did that thing get in? You, too? The doors were all locked."

"That will have to remain a mystery ... for now. Later, I will tell her everything." Yes, even tell her what he was, although he knew he would lose her forever.

"But--"

"No more questions." There remained one more act of love he must accomplish--erase every memory of this night from her mind. Lightly, he raised his fingertips to her forehead, his voice deep and hypnotic. "Go to sleep, Stevie. You will forget about the revenant. And my visit, as well."

Her eyes fluttered closed and her breathing became shallow. With tender hands, he stretched her out on the bed, her head touching the pillow, then he drew her covers over her. Mindful of the scratches on her arm and thigh, he bent over her to brush them with the healing touch of his lips. He gave her one last, loving gaze, as if to imprint every feature in his memory.

Wanting only to stay and hold her throughout the night, he left, first returning the vase to the table, the painting to the wall, the knife to the kitchen. A hundred problems plagued him ... how to protect Stevie from Moloch's wrath, how to discover what ailment afflicted her, how to help her ... if he could.

* * * *

After he returned from feeding the next night, Galan resolved to confront Moloch. Who else but that fiend had sent the revenant to kill Stevie? Familiar with the head vampire's habits, he knew he'd find him at the castle now.

He closed his eyes in concentration, and within seconds, arrived at Schloss Omerau. A light dusting of snow frosted the crumbling towers and turrets of the old castle, like a lace mantilla on an aged crone. Majestic and blanketed with snow, the Alps rose in the distance.

In the blink of an eye, Galan arrived at the great hall, where Moloch sat at the long table, a silver goblet by his side. A furious wind blasted through the open windows, sending the draperies whipping out from the wall. Snowflakes swept inside the room and glistened like ice on the cold floor. The chandelier swung wildly from the ceiling, its crystals tinkling with an incessant clamor.

The head vampire looked up in surprise, then set the goblet on the table with a soft thud. "What brings you here?" He smelled of wet rot and things that creep in the darkness.

Squaring his shoulders, Galan approached the table and spoke without preamble. "I've come to make a bargain with you."

Moloch scowled. "I don't make bargains." He raised the goblet to his mouth, never taking his gaze from Galan, then dabbed a linen napkin across his lips.

"Hear me out." He remained standing, so Moloch would have to look up at him. His voice held a note of steely determination. "I'm telling you to leave her alone."

"You're telling me?" Moloch snapped. "Of whom do you speak?"

"You know who--the mortal woman."

"The mortal woman!" Moloch looked puzzled. "But I sent a revenant--"

"Dead. I killed him." Stifling his smile of satisfaction, Galan delighted in Moloch's furious look.

"You dared to defy me!" Moloch hissed, a cloud of steam exiting his mouth.

"In this case, yes. Only listen to what I have to say." Galan paced about the room, forcing the ancient vampire to follow his movements. He stopped beside the colorful tapestry, pretending to examine it as if it were an exquisite piece of Royal Doulton.

Moloch's gravely voice echoed from behind him. "I don't have all night!"

Galan left the tapestry and faced Moloch again. "I fear she suffers from some illness, and I would help her before--"

"All humans suffer from some illness." Moloch sneered. He tipped the goblet back and drained it, smacking his lips in satisfaction.

"The woman is all that concerns me," Galan said as he stared out the window at the pine trees that dotted the foothills, the snow-laden mountains that towered to the clouds. The wind tore through his hair, lifting the locks from his scalp, tossing them across his face. The frenzied howling of wolves broke his concentration, but only for a moment. "I want to see her again and ascertain her affliction." He turned to give the fiend a sharp look. "With no interference from you."

"You son of a whore! You're giving me orders?"

Galan held up a hand. "Hear me out. I want to help her, if possible. With that accomplished, I'll promise never to see her again." He swallowed hard, conquering the lump wedged in his throat. Never see her again! "I shall remain content with my vampirism, only seeking to serve you." God, how it hurt.

Moloch studied him, stroking his wrinkled chin. "How do I know you'll keep your promise?"

Galan shrugged. "You don't. You'll have to accept my promise, as I'll have to accept yours ... that is, if you agree. And one thing more--whenever you want to retire from your present position, I shall gladly assume your duties. I'll supervise the Society of the Undead, as you have so ably done for lo, these many years," he said, careful to keep the sarcasm from his voice. "After I've helped the mortal woman--if can--

I'm yours to command." He strained to keep his voice and expression neutral. And forget about the elixir, he lamented, stifling the tears of rage and disappointment that threatened to spill.

For a tense moment of silence, Moloch's face remained impassive. "Very well," he said with a nod. He pointed a long finger at him. "But if I find you've gone back on your word--"

"I intend to keep my promise."

"--If I find you've broken your promise--and remember, I have my spies--I shall destroy you. Do I make myself clear?"

"Very clear. And while we're expressing doubts, what assurance do I have that you'll keep your word?"

A sly smile twisted his aged face. "None whatsoever."

Anguish added a new dimension to Galan's inner turmoil. "Then I beg of you, as I have never asked you before--let me visit this mortal woman. Let me discover the nature of her suffering and help her. Then I shall stay away from her forever. And you will have me, for all eternity." His heart was breaking, but he'd lie beneath the midday sun before he'd let the fiend know his feelings.

Moloch nodded. "Agreed, you have my word on it."

For whatever that's worth. Galan left him then, giving rein to the many doubts and anxieties that tormented him. He needed all his mental faculties to cure Stevie of her illness. But how?

* * * *

A fierce night wind rattled the windows as Stevie sat at her tiny kitchen table, eating a late snack of an English muffin and strawberry yogurt. Showered and ready for bed, she dipped a spoon into the yogurt. She chewed on a sweet, crunchy strawberry, trying to forget the pain and fatigue that were her constant companions. Behind her, the CD player carried the taunting, sensual strains of Ravel's Bolero, the very kind of music Galan liked.

She sighed. How long since she'd last seen Galan? Weeks. She realized now--she loved him beyond reason, loved him so much it tore her in half to be parted from him. No matter who he was or what secrets lay hidden in his heart, she loved him and always would.

Awkwardly, she gripped a mug handle and sipped chamomile tea sweetened with honey. Her finger joints ached, but she drew comfort from the warmth of the mug, the spicy aroma of the tea. Setting the cup down, she took a deep breath. Had Galan found another woman? God, no! Dread sent a fresh shaft of pain through her body.

A knock on the front door startled her. Glancing at the microwave clock, she forced herself to rise. Nine thirty-four. Who could be visiting at this crazy hour? Please let it be Galan. She brushed crumbs from her fingers and wiped her mouth and hands on a paper napkin, then headed for the living room. First checking to see who it was, she opened the door, not even trying to hide her happiness.

"Galan!" Here, with her now. She stopped herself from pressing her hand to her thudding heart, afraid she'd give herself away.

He paused in the doorway. "I fear it's late, your bedtime no doubt," he said, his eyes taking in her nightclothes. "I should have come sooner, but...." The sentence remained unfinished as he spread his hands in a helpless gesture. He wanted to take her in his arms, kiss her to drive them both insane, but caution held him back. Surely she must think he'd neglected her, if she thought about him at all, since he'd erased the memory of the revenant from her mind. "You must tell me if I've come at an inopportune time."

"Hey, it's okay. Come on in."

She adjusted her bathrobe and tightened the sash, every movement endearing to him, to be remembered in the long, lonely centuries ahead. Too, he felt her pain, wincing as he noted her swollen knuckles.

As he stepped inside, a multitude of sounds and fragrances tantalized his senses, an enchanting medley that only deepened his despair ... a reminder of what he must sacrifice until the end of time. The aroma of lilac soap predominated, mingling with traces of strawberries, honey, and chamomile. Tendrils of damp hair clung to her forehead and brushed across her shoulders, heightening her allure, prompting a fierce desire to touch her, hold her close.

"Wait until I turn the CD off." She headed for the kitchen.

"Please leave it on," he called after her, knowing he would forever associate the sensual music with Stevie and this moment. "Bolero is one of my favorite pieces."

"Mine, too." She paused at the kitchen entrance. "Can I get you anything to drink?"

"Nothing, thank you." He wanted only her.

"Wait a minute while I get my tea."

Never taking his gaze from her, Galan sank into the leather chair, his legs spread apart. Observing her painful steps to the kitchen and back, he searched his mind for the most tactful way to broach the subject of her health, finally deciding the direct approach was best, as usual.

"How have you been?" he asked as she settled herself on the sofa and positioned her mug on the end table.

She studied her crippled fingers, then folded her hands in her lap. "Um, a little tired lately. Nothing serious." She reached for the mug. "A few aches and pains."

If only he could help her. "What has made you so tired, I wonder--overwork?" And why were they talking like strangers, when all he wanted was to take her in his arms and make love to her all night long? Dear God, how I love this woman.

"Not overwork, no." After a long moment, she stretched her feet out. She wore fluffy pink slippers with rabbit ears and eyes and a black rabbit nose, another enchanting memory to add to his mental collection. "I ... something's been giving me a lot of pain lately...." She bit her lower lip.

"Tell me about it, Stevie."

She twisted her fingers in her lap. "The doctor doesn't know! It's something like rheumatoid arthritis, only different ... if that makes sense. A mutation, the doctor said."

"And there is no cure?" By all the saints, he would take her pain to himself, if he could.

"No cure." She brushed her hand across her eyes, then reached for the mug again and took a slow sip. "The doctor prescribed some medicine for pain. Hasn't helped at all. Kinda hard to find a cure when he can't identify the illness."

"Yes, of course." He tapped his fingers on the arm of the chair. How in God's name could he help her? Playing for time, he kept her talking. "Have you tried other medicines, even simple aspirin?"

"Ten aspirins at a time, for all the good they do me."

"Take care. Stomach trouble."

"At this point, I don't give a darn."

"Well, I care, for your sake. You don't want to add stomach or liver trouble to your other ailment." A period of silence stretched between them as he desperately sought to console her, a hundred different inspirations crowding his mind.

Go to her, his heart commanded. Surely, she wouldn't spurn him. Surely she wanted his touch as much as he longed to hold her. He looked into her eyes and saw all he'd ever wanted in life, all he'd never have, from now throughout eternity.

Without a word, he rose from his chair to sit beside her and took her in his arms. "It grieves me to see you suffer," he murmured, cradling her head against his chest. "I would buy you all the medicines in the world, if I thought it would help."

She looked up at him, her long hair brushing against his chest. "A lot of money, all those medicines. What did you say your last name was--Trump?" she asked with a teasing smile.

He returned the smile, kissing the top of her head. "Shall we say only that I want to help you, more than anything in the world?" He raised her hand to his lips and kissed each swollen knuckle. Shamefaced, she eased her hand from his grasp.

"Please let me touch you. It's been so long, so very long." He drew her closer, running his hand up and down her arm, reveling in her warmth and softness. "You have come to mean so much to me.

"Sweeting!" He pressed his lips to hers, kissing her as he'd wanted to all this time away from her, like years. He ran his hand through her hair, letting the strands fall between his fingers like warm satin. From the kitchen, the dramatic strains of Ravel's Bolero provided a passionate backdrop for their lovemaking.

Desire raged inside him, hot, compelling, more potent than anything he'd ever known, a longing to make this woman his, a dream that would forever remain unfulfilled. A fresh barrage of sensations besieged him, of sight and sound and taste, but especially of feeling. His kiss deepened as his fingers grazed her face, tracing a path from her cheek to the curve of her jaw and on to her neck.

She was so good, he thought as his lips tasted her sweetness. She was innocence and light, everything he'd ever wanted in a woman. Everything he could never have.

Inexorably drawn to her carotid artery, he heard the blood gushing through her body, like the raging waters of a river. Fingering her pale, delicate throat, he smelled her blood, more aromatic than the finest perfume. And her skin--softer than the finest cashmere. Hunger roared inside him, a burning, aching need, threatening to consume him. By St. Aidan, he must not do the very thing that would frighten her away. How easy it would be to drink of her sweet nectar, to join her body to his for all time, and make her one of the undead.

He struggled to dismiss his vampire yearnings, but oh! he wanted her beyond reason. His teeth grazed her neck, his tongue licking her exquisite skin, his body fighting this wild craving. With an inward sigh, he drew away from her neck and returned to her lips.

Easing her bathrobe open, he found her breast, tempting and warm. He caressed her, wanting her more than anything he'd craved for all these centuries, more than sustenance or even mortality. He needed to lie with her, bare skin to bare skin, warm womanhood against hard masculinity. Aching to bury himself in her soft, warm folds, he fought his burning attraction, his need to make love to her.

Instinctively, he knew she was a virgin, and he must not violate her chastity. Above all, he must not bind her to him when nothing but hopelessness stretched ahead.

* * * *

Stevie forgot her pain, forgot everything but the passion that overwhelmed every part of her body. His lips, hard and demanding against hers, aroused heat and desire like nothing she'd ever known, like nothing she'd ever imagined. She pressed closer to him, wanting him, needing him, as she needed food and drink, air to breathe. Their tongues touched, probing, and he teased her mouth open, sending a fresh burst of pleasure from her head to her toes.

Galan, she silently cried. Her hands roamed his body, from hard-muscled arms to his broad back, then to the base of his neck, where she ran her fingers through the thick mass of dark curls.

She reveled in his faint scent of sandalwood, clean and masculine. She wanted him so much, wanted to--

"My dearest!" Galan eased away. "I fear I must leave you, although I wish I could stay," he said in a strangled voice, feathering kisses on her cheek. "No doubt you must arise early tomorrow."

His words cut through her like a knife. She struggled to compose her features. He was leaving her, just like that? She shoved a loose lock of hair from her forehead. Galan, please don't leave me now. If only he would stay with her tonight. What if they made love, as she'd dreamed of doing with him for a long time? It would be the first time for her, but with Galan, it would be worth it. Somehow, she knew lovemaking would be wonderful with him.

A pleasantly persistent ache settled in her feminine core. Determined to calm her erratic heart, she tried to act casual, as if he hadn't driven her out of her mind with his touch, his kisses.

"Right." She adjusted her bathrobe, keen disappointment welling inside her. "Have to get up at six." She tucked strands of hair behind her ears and waited long, silent moments for her heartbeat to return to normal, for her passion to subside.

"I want to see you again," he said, "and very soon."

His voice, hypnotic and sensuous as always, wrapped around her like a warm blanket. She could only nod, as if he'd just explained the mysteries of the universe.

"Best I leave now," he repeated, rising to his full height. "Don't bother to get up, dear Stevie. I can see myself out. I shall call you later."

"Hey, I'm not helpless." She walked him to the front door, her body still on fire for him.

At the door, he drew her into his arms and gave her one last lingering kiss, then stepped back, a look of longing on his face. "Au revoir." He turned and headed for the street.

She watched from the living room window as he strode toward his car and drove off. She'd go to bed now, since tomorrow--

There, behind the grapefruit tree! That old man again, the one with long, bushy hair. She leaned closer to the window, pressing her head against the glass. Her heart thudded against her ribs. She'd call the police, and this time--

He disappeared! One minute she saw him, and the next minute he was gone. Her hand trembled as she drew the deadbolt in place. What was he doing here, and where had he gone? Was he after her, and if so, why?

Another question froze her insides. Was there a connection between him and Galan?

Chapter Thirteen

How come I never see Galan in the daytime? On a cool and breezy Sunday that carried a hint of spring, Stevie attended the Miami Shores Presbyterian Church with the Shipleys. The morning light beamed through the stained glass windows, casting a pale glow over the sanctuary. While the minister made announcements, she studied the stained glass windows, thinking about Galan, a too common occurrence lately. Why not ask him to church? She fiddled with the church bulletin, unsure what he'd think of her suggestion. Funny she'd never seen him in the daytime. Well, it wouldn't hurt to ask.

Her joints screamed as she rose to sing the opening hymn, In The Garden....

I come to the garden alone, while the dew is still on the roses....

Was Galan sleeping now? He sure did keep odd hours, she mused as she reviewed the times they'd shared, including the first night they met. Unwilling to dwell on the past, she brought her mind back to the present.

> And He walks with me, and He talks with me
> And He tells me I am his own....

When the song ended, she returned to her seat and shifted her position again and again, trying to get comfortable.

"You okay?" Melissa whispered during the offering.

Stevie smiled weakly. "Just a little tired."

The service continued with the Apostle's Creed and a baptism until the minister gave the sermon, and in no time, Stevie's mind wandered again, every thought on Galan. Something nagged her, like a painful toothache. What was it? The restaurant! She remembered his standing next to her by the glass cabinet, but she hadn't seen his reflection. Why not? Had to be a logical explanation.

With the conclusion of the sermon, the minister gave the benediction, then the congregation filed out of the pews.

Melissa squeezed her hand. "Now you can go home and take it easy for the rest of the day."

"Wish I could, but I have to help serve dinner at Camillus House this evening." Stevie sighed.

"Can't you call them, tell them you don't feel good?"

"Uh, uh, I promised them I'd do it."

She eased out of the sanctuary with hundreds of other congregants, her every thought on Galan. The scene in the restaurant still hounded her, but she figured it must have been a trick of the light.

\* \* \* \*

While the rest of the city slept, Galan sat in his dark living room, with Stevie a continual ache in his heart. How in God's name could he make her well again? A long-forgotten memory crept through the corridors of time, a recollection that hovered at the edge of his consciousness. He closed his eyes, thinking, thinking, thinking. Ah, yes, he had it now. Venice, 1452. His good friend Antonio had fallen in love with a beautiful mortal, a lady who had reciprocated his affection.

Shortly after their avowal of love, she'd developed a painful disease, now known as cancer. Over time, the affliction had ravaged her left breast. With only a faint hope of success, Antonio gave her a few drops of his blood, and the rich, restorative fluid drove the disease from her body. Much to Antonio's surprise, it also created a spiritual bond between him and his beloved, each being attuned to the other's thoughts and wishes and aware when the other was in need.

Dared he try that vampire cure with Stevie? But she didn't even suspect his true essence, and surely that suggestion would frighten her away. She'd think he was a nutcase, as the mortals would say. Nevertheless, he'd store the inspiration in his mind. And later? If Stevie's condition didn't improve, then by God, he'd try this remedy.

He paused, pressing his hand to his head, wondering what else he could do to make Stevie happy, help her forget her pain. Orchids! She loved those flowers; why, just think of the many blossoms hanging all over her backyard. His Mercedes wouldn't hold all the orchids he wanted to buy, so he'd simply fetch a bigger vehicle, certainly no impediment. A glance at his watch revealed the time--1:33.

After checking for orchid nurseries in the telephone directory, he wished himself onto the next block, where a search on both sides of the street led him to an unlocked Ford Explorer. He felt under the seat for the keys, but came up empty. Climbing onto the driver's seat, he stared at the ignition in absolute concentration, finally rewarded as it slowly turned and the engine came to life.

Less than an hour later, Galan arrived at a spacious orchid nursery, a locked gate denying admission to any human. He parked the car about ten yards from the gate and stepped out, then closed the door quietly. Alert to every surveillance method, he stood by the vehicle for countless minutes and sniffed for guard dogs, but he caught only the intriguing scent of exotic flowers. A wave of his hand opened the gate, and he entered the nursery with confidence, secure in the knowledge that he could make his selections undisturbed.

So many flowers to choose from, thousands! A medley of colors and aromas tantalized his senses, and he walked past rows and rows of potted plants as he looked for the prettiest ones to please Stevie.

Not wasting time, Galan gathered up forty orchids, adding the prices as he went and making several trips to carry them to the SUV. There, he arranged them so they wouldn't tip over. Back inside the nursery, rows of hangers caught his attention, and he grabbed so many handfuls, he soon depleted the racks. From his pocket, he withdrew a wad of bills and peeled off $1,500 that he left by the cash register, including a generous tip.

An hour's drive brought him to Stevie's street, where he left the orchids by her front door and stood back to admire the selection. Just knowing they'd make Stevie happy brought a smile to his face.

He returned the Explorer and headed back to his house, checking his watch. Stevie would arise soon.

Before the sun's rays lightened the eastern horizon, Stevie's telephone rang. Dripping wet from the shower, she quickly wrapped a towel around her and headed for the phone, anxious about a telephone call at this hour.

"Sweeting, I didn't waken you, did I?"

Her heart beat faster, hearing Galan's voice. She forced herself to speak calmly. "No, I just got out of the shower."

"Ah."

Her cheeks warmed. "Are you okay?" she asked to cover her embarrassment.

"I am well," he said in his bedroom voice. "And you--how have you been?"

"I'm okay, too," she replied, not wanting his pity. "Getting ready for work."

"Then I mustn't keep you--"

"No, I didn't mean it that way." She gave herself a mental kick. "I got loads of time before I go downtown."

"The reason I called--please take a moment to check outside your front door. I left a surprise for you."

"A surprise? But what--?"

"Please, only go see."

"Sure." Tucking the towel in place, she headed for the front door. Wow! Look at all the orchids! Scads and scads of orchids stood at attention, awaiting her silent admiration. So many brilliant colors and pretty fragrances teased her senses. She fingered a yellow phalenopsis, delighting in its velvety soft petals. After one last glance, she returned to the phone.

"Galan! How--how did you get so many? They must have cost a fortune. How'd you do it?" she asked, aware she was babbling.

"Made a trip to an orchid nursery. I hoped they'd make you happy."

The towel slipped, and she adjusted it. "Yeah, but so many! I don't know what to say."

"A simple 'thank you' will suffice."

"Absolutely! I do appreciate them. When did you buy them--yesterday?"

A brief hesitation. "Indeed, yesterday."

"Well, it's just the nicest thing anyone ever did for me. If there's any way I can thank--" Another warm rush to her cheeks made her backtrack. "I mean, it was really nice of you. Honest."

"I appreciate your appreciation. Now, I must let you prepare for work. One other thing--if you can wait until this evening, I shall carry them into the backyard for you."

"Thanks, but it's no trouble for me to carry them," she lied. The sun-sensitive ones shouldn't be out in the bright sunlight all day, but she couldn't ask him to do any more for her.

"Very well. I shall come see you soon, but rest assured, I shall call you first. Au revoir."

"'Bye, and thanks again."

She hung up the phone and stepped outside again to survey the beautiful blossoms, already planning where she'd put them. By the bright outside lights, she studied the wooden fence and the spreading grapefruit tree. For now, she'd move them all under the trees in the backyard, so they wouldn't stand in the sunlight all day. Back in the house, she slipped into her bathrobe, then returned outside.

About a half-hour later, she'd transferred the flowers, happier than she'd been in a long time but aching from bending over and carrying the pots and baskets.

As she dressed for work, she paused while she buttoned her blue chambray shirt with embroidered daisies on the collar. Galan's gift to her must have cost him a lot of money, but she didn't see any way she could have refused.

Still, she wondered--why had Galan bought her such lovely but expensive flowers? He'd told her she meant a lot to him, but what did that mean?

\* \* \* \*

Galan visited her that evening, about a half-hour after she arrived home work. They kissed at her front door, a long, slow kiss that left her wanting more. After an intense moment when she couldn't think of anything but him, she eased from his embrace and leaned against his shoulder, waiting for her heartbeat to slow down. She looked up at him, caught in the lure of his dark, unfathomable eyes, those eyes that held a thousand mysteries. She tried to speak in normal tones.

"Before you come inside, let me show you how I arranged those gorgeous orchids you gave me. The outside lights are on. I think you can see well enough."

"I assure you, I have excellent night vision." With his easy stride, he followed her through the backyard, where dozens of orchid pots hung from the limbs of the grapefruit tree or dangled from the wooden fence.

Smiling, she touched a delicate dendrobium aggregatum, whose scads of little yellow flowers drooped over the pot like a vibrant waterfall. "All these beautiful orchids--I'm floored!"

"Let us say only that I am one of your admirers." His gaze took in the flowers, then quickly returned to her. "I knew they would make you happy, and I dared hope they could make you forget your pain, if only for a while."

"Sure," she lied, "it's easy to forget my aches when I have such pretty orchids. How can I ever thank you--" She stopped, her face warming. There she went again.

"How about another kiss?"

"Yes!" She was in his arms again, his lips on hers, their bodies fused as one. His kiss deepened, chasing all her doubts and worries away. How she wanted him, this man she'd known for such a short while. If only she knew more about him, their relationship would be perfect. But how could she think when he was kissing her like this? When his touch alone made her forget everything but him?

"Now, let us go back inside," Galan said after they drew apart. "Mustn't have you on your feet so long."

"Right."

Hand-in-hand, they walked back inside and settled on the sofa.

"I hope you're taking care of yourself," he said, his arm around her shoulder. "Been taking your medicine?"

"For all the good it does me. I have an appointment with the doctor at the end of the week. He told me on my last visit there's a new arthritis medicine that should be on the market soon. Supposed to do wonders. He'll write me a prescription whenever it's available. Like I said, though, I have something more than just arthritis, so I don't want to get too optimistic. We'll see."

"Let us hope it helps you. You mean so much to me," he murmured, kissing the top of her head.

"You've said that before, but...." She bit her bottom lip.

"But--what?"

She turned in his arms to look at him, taking in every feature of his face, his dark hair, straight nose, and square jaw, but more than anything, his pale skin. "I don't know much about you," she blurted.

"What would you like to know?" he asked in his deep melodic voice.

"Well, your family, for instance."

"I told you before, they're all dead."

"All of them? You don't have any living relatives?"

"So long ago," he said, as if to himself. "They all died a long time ago."

"How long ago?"

"Sweeting, has it never occurred to you that perhaps it hurts me too much to discuss my family?"

She lowered her eyelashes. "Sorry." A brief pause. "I've noticed your accent, so different from mine. So did you live in England?"

"Ah, that was long ago, also."

"Whereabouts in England did you live?" she asked with the uneasy feeling he wasn't being entirely honest. What was he hiding?

"Kent, near the coast."

"Kent! That's your last name." She shifted her position on the sofa, concealing the pain that gripped every joint in her body.

"Not an uncommon custom, to take a place name as a family name. Such names go back hundreds of years."

"Hey, you're right. By the way, my last name is Czech. My ancestors came to this country in the 1890s."

"Part of the Austro-Hungarian Empire in the nineteenth century, and a lovely part of the world."

"You've been there--to Czechoslovakia?"

"Yes, I've been to every country in Europe. Prague is a beautiful city."

"You've seen a lot of places, haven't you?"

"True enough." He hesitated. "It would be my pleasure to take you to many of these places if--"

"If I felt better," she finished for him. "There's a lot of cities I'd like to see--Paris, Vienna, Rome. Prague, too."

"All lovely cities."

She studied her swollen fingers, no longer ashamed that he should see them. "Well, it'll be a long time before I feel like traveling. But something I've been thinking about--would you like to go to church with me?"

He jerked back. "Church?"

"If you don't want to go, just say so," she snapped. "You don't need to act like I'd suggested we rob a bank together."

He turned away for a moment, then swung his gaze back to her. "Sorry, I didn't mean to sound so, uh, adamant. But you see, I sleep late and--"

"But there are two services, an early one and a later one."

"Sorry, but I sleep very late every day."

"So you're a night owl?"

He nodded. "You might say that."

"Okay, so ... Would you like to meet me for lunch sometime? Lots of eateries at Bayside, and we could--"

"Dearest, I'm sorry, but I absolutely can't."

What was his problem? She shrugged, aiming for humor. "I never see you during the day. What are you, a creature from the dark side of the moon?"

A fierce look crossed his face, and if looks could kill, she'd be headed for the morgue. After a moment, his face cleared, and he spoke slowly and distinctly, as if explaining a simple situation to a child.

"I've already told you I'm a night owl--your words, incidentally. But true, just the same. Why can't you accept my explanation?"

She slid back on the sofa. "It seems odd to me that once in a while we can't do something during the day. All the things to see and do in Miami--daytime activities, like the zoo or Fairchild Tropical Garden--well, I think you're missing out on a lot."

"Please, I don't need a rebuke."

"Hey, just listen a minute. Let me say what I've had on my mind. You should get out in the sun more. I told you that once, remember? No, let me finish," she said as he opened his mouth to speak. "It's not good for you to spend so much time in bed. Why, if you were any paler, you'd be a ghost."

A long moment of silence stretched between them.

"Are you quite finished?" he asked in a voice as cold as a Siberian winter.

"For now. Maybe I'll think of something later."

"You've said enough for now ... or later." He gave her a long, steady look, and she sensed she'd pushed him too far. Too late to swallow her words, and she wouldn't want to anyway. What was he hiding that couldn't bear the light of day?

"I had thought," he said in his low voice, "that it was enough for us to attend nighttime activities together and--"

"--and don't get the idea I haven't enjoyed myself and all the things you've done for me--the Nutcracker and everything, not to mention the time it must have taken you to buy all those lovely orchids. Honest--"

"--and I think you could accept my explanation that I prefer to socialize in the evening."

"Well, sure, I understand if that's how you want to do things. I was mainly thinking of you--you know, getting out in the sun more." Not entirely true, since she still thought there was something peculiar about someone who never ventured out during the day, or not until afternoon, for all she knew.

"Stevie, I've taken care of myself for quite a long time without anyone else's advice. I believe I can continue to do so."

"Well, why does everything have to be a secret with you? I mean, this business about church--"

He scowled. "And that's my business."

"There! You see what I mean? Don't tell me you sleep so late every Sunday that you can't even attend a church service. Or that you can't even have lunch with me one time. You know, I have a sneaking suspicion you're not being honest with me, and I think you owe me some answers."

His expression hardened. "I don't owe you anything."

"Well, pardon me for thinking you do. I thought that after all the time we've known each other, you could at least be open and honest with me." She drew her knees up to her chin, hugging her legs.

"I have never lied to you."

"Funny, that's not the impression I get."

He sighed, his voice gentle now. "Please let it go for now. I promise you that very soon I shall give you answers, and I won't hold anything back." He splayed his fingers through his hair. "The truth of the matter is, I've had many worries lately, more than you can imagine. For now, let's leave matters as they are. Please wait and be patient."

What was the matter with him? Did he have skin cancer or some other terrible disease? Maybe he had an ailment that kept him away from the sunlight. She'd read about such an abnormality. Then why didn't he just say so? And maybe she was only adding to his worries by her questions. Okay, for now, she wouldn't ask any more, but he'd better give her some answers soon.

A smile crept over his face, making her feel a lot better. She didn't like to have angry words with him.

"You're not satisfied with my answer, are you? Haven't you heard the expression, 'Oh, God, give us the serenity to accept what cannot be changed, courage to change what should be changed, and wisdom to distinguish one from the other'? Reinhold Niebuhr.""Uh, uh, I never heard that. You must read a lot."

He tapped his head, a grin on his face. "I'm smart." He sighed. "And you would do well to remember that quotation. Now, no more lectures for today." He reached for her again and held her close to his chest. "Let us not have any disagreements between us," he murmured, nuzzling her ear. "Rather, let us make the most of every minute together, for you never know...."

A chill raced over her body. "Never know what?" She let her legs slip to the floor.

"Never know what tomorrow may bring. And I really don't want to talk anymore." He smoothed her hair away from her face and angled his lips onto hers, his fingers tracing a path from her cheeks to her neck and on to her breasts, hips, and thighs.

Entranced by his touch, she wrapped her arms around his waist, pressing her breasts against his solid chest, loving his hard strength. Galan moaned, his hands roaming her body, arousing her, helping her forget her pain. She wanted to give herself to him, but how could she when there was no commitment from him?

He feathered kisses on her face, behind her ear, and across her jawline, stopping at her neck. Breathing hard, he licked a spot there, softly nibbling the skin. With a low groan, he released her, his face heavy with passion and something more, something she couldn't define. A look almost like ... hunger.

"We must stop," he gasped. "I ... I could stay with you forever, but the world intrudes, I fear. You need adequate sleep for your job." He eased away from her. "I must leave you now, although I would wish it otherwise."

"Right, it's getting late," she agreed, afraid she sounded like a broken record, she'd said those words so many times. Throbbing all over, she wanted him to stay with her all night long, wherever the night would lead them. And where would the night lead them? One guess was all she needed.

She tightened her bathrobe sash. "I'd better get to bed. As you say, I need my sleep."

"Yes, of course." After a quick kiss, he stood, looking down at her with those eyes that missed nothing. "I shall call you later this week."

And then he was gone, leaving her with more worries than ever, more questions than before. Something told her that soon, he'd be out of her life forever, this mysterious man with secrets he refused to share. She leaned her forehead against the door for the longest time, an ache deep inside her.

* * * *

Galan closed Stevie's door and walked out into the dark night, the darkness that was so much a part of him, as much as his arms or legs or atrophied heart.

Fool! Why hadn't he told her what he truly was? All those questions she'd asked, her curiosity about why he wouldn't attend church with her or take her to lunch--surely that was the time to let her see his true essence--a monster of the night.

Coward. Yes, he feared to tell her the truth, feared losing her forever. But the time for subterfuge was past. Next time he saw her, he'd reveal his true nature ... and suffer the consequences.

* * * *

Beneath the ground, Rosalinda lay in a crypt, brooding and vengeful. They thought she was dead--Galan, Octavius, Moloch ... and no one cared. No one had looked for her, even while she lay with a stake through her chest, not half a mile from the chateau, where Lilith had taken her and left her for dead ... where she pretended to be dead. Lilith--the imbecile!--had missed her heart by an inch.

After she pulled the stake out and allowed a few hours of recovery from her wound, Rosalinda had transported herself to this crypt, where she lay for a long time, recovering. But a day of reckoning would come. For now, she'd lie low, lick her wounds, as the mortals would say. She needed time.

And then--oh, then!--she'd have her retaliation. She'd show them all she couldn't be killed or forgotten so easily. Later, she'd deal with Lilith, but for now, she'd get even with the others, starting with Galan. Anticipation swept all resentment aside. Revenge would be sweet, for she knew how to make Galan suffer, knew how to inflict a pain worse than the most exquisite torture.

She would kill the mortal bitch, and she would do it slowly, so that it took her days to die.

Soon, very soon.

Chapter Fourteen

There goes another book! After she retrieved Dean Koontz's latest thriller from the floor, Stevie caught Julie's attention across the room and motioned her over to the shelf. She winced with pain as she struggled to her feet, finally managing a smile as Julie joined her.

"Julie, how about if you finish shelving these books and I'll handle the cash register when the store opens." She tried to flex her fingers, a rush of alarm zipping through her, sending her heart down to her stomach. "A little stiff today." She kept her smile, determined not to show her trepidation.

Julie frowned. "Okay, but that cash register's kinda stiff, too."

"Yeah, but anything's better than trying to stock these books. I end up with more books on the floor than on the shelves. Besides, the doctor told me I should exercise all my joints, so here's my chance!" She laughed, then shifted her position again, taking pressure off her left knee.

I plead temporary insanity, Stevie lamented later, working the cash register after the store opened. Julie was right; just touching the keys was like trying to swim through tons of thick molasses. Customers grumbled in the long line that stretched far back from the counter, some tossing their books aside and storming out of the place.

A familiar face in line brightened her morning, the same man who'd helped her pick the books from the floor several weeks ago. Tall and good-looking, he waited patiently, two books and several magazines in his arms, a slight smile on his face. What was his name? Slipping a book into a plastic bag for a customer, she thought hard. Oh, yes. Mark Farrell.

Within a few minutes, his turn came. "Another busy day, I see." He grinned, setting his books and magazines on the counter, then reaching into his jacket pocket for his wallet.

Struggling to make the impression with his Master Card, she smiled back. "Every day is busy. Good thing, too," she said as she rang up his books and magazines. "Store would have to close if we didn't have customers." She slipped his purchases into a plastic bag. "Thank you," she said as she handed the bag to him.

"You're welcome." His smile cheered her as he walked out, making her job a little more bearable.

With another glance at the long line, Stevie realized it would make for better public relations if Julie manned the register and she returned to stocking books, and never mind what agony that was.

* * * *

Hooray, closing time! Doors locked, the sales tallied up, Stevie spoke to Julie by the cash register. She darted a glance outside at the dark, deserted street, dreading the long ride home, wanting to rest with her feet up and have a hot cup of tea. Despite the many aches from her neck to her toes, she mustered a firm voice. "I've been fighting this for months, but I give up ... for now, anyway. So I'm taking a temporary leave of absence and--"

"Geez, I hate to see you in such pain," Julie said, lightly touching Stevie's arm. "We all do. But I guess you know what's best."

While Stevie pushed a few papers to the side, a burning pain shot through her elbow, but she put on a brave face. "Looks as if I don't have much choice. So I'm asking you to take over for two weeks or so--hopefully no longer--and whenever I feel better, I'll be back." She winked, then reached under the counter for her purse. "You can't get rid of this ogre for long."

\* \* \* \*

What was she going to do now? Ensconced on the sofa with a hot cup of chamomile tea, Stevie gazed out her living room window as the sky turned from lavender to sapphire, and the noises of the neighborhood quieted on her street. With darkness, the temperature fell, and a cold gust of wind riffled the pages of a magazine on her coffee table and sent a frigid draft of air rushing through the room.

Groaning, she eased her feet to the floor, then plodded over to close the window. She buttoned her sweater as she returned to the sofa, telling herself she had to face facts. Could she go back to work after only two weeks at home, as she'd told Julie? Hardly. So what about money? The government loan she'd recently received would fund her college education, but she still had her living expenses, and even though she scrimped on food and everything else--even discontinuing cable TV--her expenses weren't el cheapo. Her savings would pay the rent for the next couple of months. And after that? Zilch. Nada.

She rubbed her fingers across her eyes, so afraid she'd have to apply for unemployment compensation. No matter what, she refused to even consider asking her father for a loan. She'd managed fine so far, and somehow, some way, she'd continue to get by on her own. But how? Rob a bank?

Her throat clotted, and she brushed a tear from her cheek, ashamed of her vulnerability, furious because of her pain and weakness. She'd manage, and if she only gave it more time, she'd get better. Maybe--

"It saddens me to see you in such despair."

Stevie's head jerked up, and she pressed a hand to her pounding heart. "Galan! How'd you get in?" Her gaze flew to the front door, deadbolt in place. The back door? No, she remembered locking it, too. "How did you get in?" she repeated.

Galan sat next to her, sliding his arm around her waist. "Shall we make a deal? I'll tell you how I got in if you tell me first why you are so despondent."

"Had to take a temporary leave of absence from the bookstore. Can't handle the job." She studied her swollen fingers. "Just can't do it." She turned away, fighting tears, fearing she'd break down in front of him.

He gathered her in his embrace. "Oh, my sweet one." His arms comforted her, but depression still left her in the dumps. Of course she was happy to see him. But how had he gotten in? Like a magician. Poof! Just like that.

"And you need money," he said in his low, soothing voice, a voice that could melt all the ice in Antarctica. "Gladly would I give you whatever you need, no matter the amount."

She drew back, her gaze meeting his. "I couldn't take money from you. It wouldn't be right."

"Why not, if I'm willing to give it to you?"

"Just wouldn't be right."

"Then a loan?"

She flicked her fingers, wincing with the pain. "I don't know when or how I could pay you back. But you haven't answered my question. How'd you get in? Or do you count lock picking among your many talents?"

"A locked door simply poses no impediment for me." Galan opened his mouth, then closed it again, and for the first time since she'd met him, he looked uncertain.

"I still don't see--"

"Sweeting, have you never wondered why you see me only at night?" He tilted his head, his gaze probing.

"Yeah, we were just talking about that the other day. So tell me why."

"I cannot go out during the day. The sunlight would burn me up."

She nodded, full of sympathy. "Oh, you have one of those skin diseases I've read about. Some people can't be out in the sun, or it does something harmful to their skin. So why didn't you say so in the first place? And what does that have to do with getting inside my apartment when the door is locked?"

"It's more than the sunlight." He sighed deeply, as though he carried a world of worries on his shoulders. He touched his face. "Look at my skin. So pale!"

"Well, sure, if you don't ever go out in the sun."

For a brief moment, he turned away, then met her look again. "Let me say it clearly. Let there be no more pretense, no more evading the truth." His hands rested on his thighs as he stared down at the floor, his mouth twisted in a grimace. He opened and closed his mouth, looking as if he'd lost every cent in the stock market. She'd never seen him so rattled.

"I am a vampire," he finally said.

Oh, oh. She searched his face, checking for a trace of a smile, anything to show he was joking. But no, the man was serious. *What kind of a guy have I been dating? He thinks he's a vampire, and it's not even Halloween.*

Stevie laughed. "Come on now. You got a weird sense of humor." She gave him a close look, playing along with his 'joke'. "Okay, show me your teeth."

"Don't tell me you believe all that silly Hollywood nonsense." He smiled widely, revealing white, even teeth. "See? No fangs. Only in the movies and insipid Gothic literature."

Right! She remembered the TV program that said the same thing about vampires, but so what? That didn't prove a thing. "And I suppose you're going to tell me there's a Santa Claus and an Easter bunny, too?"

"Not at all. I assure you, this is no jesting matter. You must believe me." He cracked his knuckles. "Remember when I took you to the restaurant, and you stopped to admire the porcelain?"

"Yeah, I remember," she said with a sick feeling deep in her stomach. She pressed her hands to her hot cheeks. "But there's a logical explanation ... something about the light...."

"You know it's more than that. Come with me." Galan rose, gently taking her hand to ease her from the sofa. "Let's go to the mirror in your bedroom."

There, they stood next to each other, facing the cheval mirror. She could see herself, but she couldn't see him. She glanced at her side to make sure he hadn't moved. "Hey, how'd you do that?" She peered behind the mirror to check the backing. "Neat trick! I didn't know you were such a good magician, although I always suspected you knew some magic."

He raked his fingers through his hair. "What can I say to convince you! Don't you understand? I-am-a-vampire."

"Sure you are. And I'm the Wicked Witch of the West."

"Then let me show you something else." He closed his eyes and frowned, as if in concentration. Then he disappeared.

"Do you believe me now?" he called from the kitchen.

"Oh, my God!" She sank onto the bed, holding her head in her hands, wanting so badly to refute everything she'd seen. The room swam around her, a buzzing in her ears. Grabbing the edge of the bed, she fought her dizziness, her anguish. God, please let this be a nightmare.

In a split second, he returned and stood before her, hands on his hips, speaking with calm precision. "Now what do you think?"

She wrung her hands together. "Oh, my God." She lowered her head and breathed deeply. "Ohhh." Sour bile rose in her throat, and she swallowed hard, willing herself not to throw up.

"Quite so," he replied with calm assurance, as if he hadn't turned her world upside down. "So you see me for what I truly am--a vampire, one of the undead."

Stevie gathered her strength about her, as a mother duck would enclose her ducklings. Sorrow and despair roiled inside her, but anger trumped all other emotions. "You're the one who's been killing the homeless! All those men with their blood drained--"

"No! I swear by all that is holy, I did not kill those unfortunate men. I feed on criminals, but I don't kill them."

"Well, what do you want? A medal for just feeding on them? Who's killing them, then? I suppose you're going to tell me there are dozens of vampires in Miami."

"A fairly accurate guess."

"How can I believe you?" She gripped the bedspread in both hands. "You've lied to me so--"

"No! Never have I lied to you."

"Come on, get real. Let's put it this way--you haven't told me the truth, not until now."

Galan sat down on the bed next to her, but she slid away. He spoke in a low voice, barely above a whisper. "If only you knew how I wanted to tell you, how it hurt me not to reveal what I truly am."

"Yeah, I'll bet that just broke your heart."

"Dearest, you are breaking my heart now."

"You don't have a heart."

He nodded, pain and misery on his face. "My heart is not like yours. But this much I tell you, and I beg you to believe me. I never sought my vampirism. It was forced on me whilst I lay drugged and unconscious."

"And you expect me to believe that?"

"No matter, it's the truth."

Stevie shook her head, unwilling to accept all she'd seen and heard this night, scared out of her wits that Galan spoke the truth. But, wait! Maybe her pain medicine gave her hallucinations. Yeah, that was it ... her medicine.

But if he really was a vampire? Pity for him brought tears to her eyes. If what he said was true about his vampirism being forced on him--and she had to take him at his word--what a horrible burden to bear until the end of the world.

She had to be by herself. It was all too much to take in. No matter that she loved him, she saw no future for them. Better if she broke off with him and never saw him again.

She raised a forefinger to catch a tear sliding down her cheek. "You'd better go now, leave me alone. And I think"--her voice caught--"I think it would be best if we stopped seeing each other. I ... see no point in it."

"You need time to get used to the idea. I understand. I'll call you later this week."

"No! You don't understand. This is good-bye. I don't want to see you again." She choked on her words, hating herself for speaking to him like this, for hurting him, but she couldn't accept his vampirism. It was all too much. Too much.

The pained look on his face tore her apart, but she faced him unflinchingly, never wanting him to see her heart was breaking.

His face revealed nothing but sadness, his eyes downcast, his mouth contorted with sorrow. After a long moment when charged emotions crackled between them, he spoke, his voice barely above a whisper. "All the good times we've shared, all those orchids I bought you--they don't count for anything?"

Silence was his only answer.

"I see." A lengthy pause ensued, her heart pounding so hard the beats echoed in her ears. "Good-bye, dear Stevie."

He left then, as quickly and mysteriously as he'd come. One minute he sat next to her, and the next minute he was gone. She glanced up, anguish and shock clashing inside her, a combination that stiffened her body and made her wonder if she could ever move from the bed.

An eternity passed before she flopped back, wishing she could cry her heart out. It was all a nightmare. If she just pinched herself, she'd wake up. Easing onto her side, she drew her legs up, a tangle of emotions driving her crazy as every thought, every feeling, led to Galan. She'd never stop loving him, but he was out of her life forever.

                              * * * *

A light rain tapped against the window as Stevie tossed in bed. Looks as if I'm not going to get any sleep at all, she lamented, flopping onto her back and staring at the ceiling. Would she ever forget this day ... and night? Never, not if she lived to be one-hundred. First, her arthritis forced her to quit her job, and then the man she cared for-- She groaned and squeezed her eyelids shut. Galan is a vampire, Galan is a vampire. Don't let it be true. But it was.

She should have known not to trust him, not after all the disappointments in her life, when she'd loved and trusted others who had failed her.

Pain and money worries forgotten, she could think of nothing and no one but Galan. Memories of him flooded her mind, all the good times they'd shared in the weeks and months since their first meeting. She remembered his rescuing her from the mugger and driving her home, walking her to her apartment. All those flowers he'd given her came to mind, not to mention the orchids. He was everything she'd ever wanted in a man, but he wasn't human.

Tears flowed down her cheeks as she recalled his kisses, his touch, his whispered love words. Oh, God, she loved him. Nothing would ever change that. Then why had she spoken to him in such a mean way? His hurt look taunted her, and she'd give anything to take back those awful words she'd flung at him. But what else could she have done? Accept him for what he was? Pretend he was like any other man? If they married--a condition he'd never mentioned--what would he do while she grew old and gray and feeble and he stayed young, as handsome as ever? Sure as anything, he'd tire of her and find another woman to love, a probability she didn't want to consider.

He'd told her he hadn't killed those men, but how could she believe anything he said? She had to believe him, because otherwise, she couldn't handle his guilt. Couldn't take it.

Reaching for a Kleenex to blow her nose, she stopped, an idea tugging at her mind. She had his phone number. Funny, she'd forgotten that. She'd call him tomorrow night and apologize for her words, not tonight, though. Her feelings were still too raw. Could they take up where they'd left off, put all these bitter words behind them, pretend everything was normal again?

She could dream, couldn't she?

A million heartbeats later, her tears dried, and she fell into a restless doze. Her sleep deepened, an eerie dream forming in her mind, then--What?! A touch on her shoulder jolted her from a groggy sleep. Galan! He'd come back after all.

She forced her eyes open. "Oh!" Terror paralyzed her.

A woman with a pearlescent face and long, black hair bent over the bed, her claw-like fingers jerking the blanket back.

"No!" Stevie bolted upright. Who was this creep?

Never mind, get out of here!

The woman laughed, sending shivers down Stevie's arms and legs. "Don't try to fight me, for it will gain you nothing." She smiled, a wicked, evil grin. "I have the power of life and death over you. No one escapes Rosalinda."

## Chapter Fifteen

"No one will find you here, not even Galan. No doubt he's forgotten you already." Her captor's voice echoed within Stevie's cell, where pitch blackness surrounded her, showing nothing, not even the walls.

Stevie's pulse pounded in her ears so hard she thought her head would burst. She shuddered inside her thin blanket as she strained her eyes to see her prison. How had she arrived in this hellhole? God, how? The last thing she remembered was a raven-haired woman by her bed. Then ... nothing.

"And did you get my name?" The harsh voice tormented her. "It's Rosalinda." With long, claw-like nails, she tapped Stevie's arm, a gesture that made Stevie jerk back. "I'm a vampire, like Galan." She laughed, a piercing, brassy laugh, a shriek that sent chills racing over Stevie's body.

The cell reeked of mold and dead animals, of things Stevie didn't dare think about. Slippery slime coated the stone floors, prompting Stevie to keep her hands in her lap.

The vampiress' pungent scent of musk mingled with the other smells to produce a nauseous mixture that made Stevie gag. Water dripped from overhead, a continual discomfort that added to her misery, chilling her skin and dampening her blanket. Iron bands encircled one wrist and ankle, connected to a long chain that extended to a massive pin on the wall.

"This cell is called an oubliette." Rosalinda's grating voice continued. "Do you know what that means?"

Nausea churned in Stevie's stomach, and she swallowed again and again. Her skin turned hot, then cold. She could only stare, not even able to see her captor.

"I asked you a question!"

The harsh voice jolted Stevie. As if she gave a damn about a French word. "No, you tell me."

"Oubliette comes from the French word for 'to forget'. A long time ago, prisoners were left in this castle dungeon and simply forgotten." She laughed, an eerie sound sending shivers down Stevie's arms and legs and making her stomach churn with fear. "As Galan will forget about you, if he hasn't already. Oh, incidentally, I'll let you keep your blanket. Wouldn't want you to freeze to death." Her voice oozed with sarcasm.

"Let us have illumination," the vampiress said, "so you can see my features. I need only touch this torch on the wall, and voila! light!" She cackled with satisfaction as a fire came to life, blazing from the torch. "After all, it's only fair that you should see the one who captured you, the one who will ensure that you die in this prison."

The smoke burned Stevie's eyes, making them water, but the light revealed her captor's features--the albino skin, long black hair, her hands with their claw-like nails. Diamonds glittered on her ears, neck, and wrists, like gems on a ghoul.

"What do you want with me?" Stevie struggled to ask.

"It's my way of getting even with Galan. We were lovers once, did he ever tell you that?"

Lips clamped tight, Stevie refused her the satisfaction of an answer. Lovers? Galan and this fiend? It couldn't be true.

"No, of course he didn't tell you, but I have always had a special place in Galan's heart. Oops! My mistake. Our kind has no normal heart, nor do we need one. But you get my meaning. He'll be so happy to see me again." She ran her fingers through her long strands of hair, thrusting out her full breasts. "The men all adore me, and I've spent far too much time with others. It's driven Galan wild with jealousy."

She adjusted her gown's low bodice and flung her hair behind her shoulders. "I shall depart now, and when I come back-- maybe in a century or two--you'll be nothing but dust." She screeched, a sudden, unexpected sound that made Stevie jump.

"Farewell!" The witch extinguished the light, leaving the cell as dark as before, with only the stench and slime to remind Stevie of her surroundings.

Shudders shook her body from her neck to her feet as her gaze covered the four pitch black walls of the dungeon. Nausea roiled in her stomach, and she continually swallowed, forcing down sour bile.

Stevie's head sank onto her chest. How had she gotten here? She delved into her brain, tracing every minute from the time she'd gone to bed until now. But she couldn't solve the puzzle. The most important question--how would she get out? Would she get out? She raised her head and glanced around with only a faint hope that a glimmer of light would shine into her cell, but there was no light, not even a damn window. The shackle held her tight, the rusty metal scraping against her skin, already making it raw. With her one free hand, she tucked the blanket closer around her, the hard stone floor intensifying the pain in her joints. God, she had to get out of here!

"Help!" A scream tore from her throat, almost inhuman in its intensity. "Someone help me!" Please, please, she prayed, fighting tears, someone help me.

No answer.

With quivery fingers, she reached down to grasp her shackle and jerked it, trying to loosen it. No luck. Stifling her disgust, she felt around on the icy stone floor for a pin, a piece of metal, anything she might use to unlock the shackle around her leg ... and came up empty. She twisted around and yanked hard with both hands, trying to pull the chain loose from the wall, but it held fast.

Despair froze her blood. She'd die alone in this dungeon. God! She'd starve to death if she didn't die of thirst before then.

She screamed again, screamed to burst her lungs. "Help! Get me out of here!" The sound echoed off the walls, as if to say, You'll never escape.

Tears suppressed, she shifted her position on the frigid floor and tried to think of other matters, anything to get her mind off the prison.

Galan. Only a miracle would bring him back to her. She'd never see him again, never know his passionate kisses, the comforting strength of his arms, the seductive pleasure of his low, melodious voice. She had to admit she loved him, and if she could do it over again, would she have refused him? She didn't know! One thing she did know--she should never have spoken to him so sharply.

Images of him teased her--his chiseled features, the wavy coal black hair and obsidian eyes, but especially, his pale skin. Tall and broad-shouldered, he exuded raw power and pure masculinity ... but he wasn't a mortal. And he was gone from her life forever.

Painful memories of her father surfaced, of his illegal dealings and their years of estrangement. She wished that somehow she could reconcile with him. Now she'd never have the chance to make up for his misdeeds. She remembered Galan's words at the restaurant. You are not responsible for your father's sins. Easy for him to say.

Her thoughts rambled, her depression deepening.

She'd never again get the chance to help others, never attend the university and earn a degree in social work, never do all the things in life that meant so much to her.

Never see Galan again.

No, don't think like that!

She had to get out of here. She grasped the shackle, but it didn't budge.

She jerked at the chain on the wall. No luck.

God, please save me. I don't want to die.

\* \* \* \*

Pacing the carpeted floor of his living room, Galan kicked a footstool out of his way, cursing his foolish dreams. How could he blame Stevie for her revulsion, not to mention, contempt? What had made him think she could ever love him, that they would have a future together?

Stevie, I miss you so. There would never be another woman for him. He knew that as well as he knew he'd stay a vampire for the rest of his days.

If only he were human again, to walk in the sunlight and breathe the fresh morning air, and yes, if only he could have Stevie as his wife, father their children, love her as a man was meant to love a woman. To join his life with hers throughout eternity--ah, that would be bliss. If only he had the elixir....

* * * *

He had to see her one more time. In the early evening darkness, Galan rose from his coffin, every thought on Stevie, each memory a torment. Three nights had passed since he'd revealed his vampirism, hours of painful memories, a time of recriminations. Far better if he hadn't betrayed his essence, let her think he was mortal like any other man. But no, he had aimed for honesty. He had wagered that she'd still care for him ... wagered and lost.

Later tonight, he'd visit her clandestinely, as he had in the past. Hours to wait....

The moon rode high in the sky when he finally arrived in Stevie's bedroom ... and found her bed empty! By St. Aidan, where was she? Staying with a friend? Another man? God, no! If she had found another man to love, he'd hunt him down, then tear him apart, limb by limb.

The next night was the same, and the night after that. Worry gnawed at his insides, as a rat chews on a rope, rendering him confused and helpless. If only his brain were clear, if only painful anxiety didn't cloud his thinking, he'd know immediately where she was.

Moloch. Why hadn't he considered him sooner? The fiend had gone back on his word and captured Stevie, damn him to hell! What if the whoreson had already transformed her into a vampire, or worse still, a revenant? He pictured his beloved Stevie as a revenant, a soulless, mindless creature, with no thoughts or emotions of her own, but a robot, made to obey Moloch's orders.

Confront the demon! No time to lose!

* * * *

Near death, Stevie languished in her cell, as still as a cadaver. Thirst tortured her. Like a clump of dried leather, her tongue stuck to the roof of her mouth, her lips dry and swollen. Every part of her body throbbed with pain, a deep, stabbing agony like nothing she'd ever known. Too weak to scream, she couldn't even part her cracked lips. Listlessly, she tugged at the chain and grasped the shackle, determined to make one last effort to break free. Both still held fast. Tears streamed down her cheeks, and she sobbed dry gasps of pain and despair.

She had to escape.

Galan, she silently cried, please come save me.
But how could he find her?

## Chapter Sixteen

"What have you done with her?" Galan stared at the fiend, every muscle tense.

Enthroned at the long trestle table, Moloch toyed with the stem of his goblet, his look cruel and cunning, his gaze boring into Galan. "If you're speaking of the mortal woman, I haven't the vaguest idea where she is, and furthermore, I don't give a damn. It's up to you to surveil your Godforsaken woman. Why should I--?"

"You son of a bitch!"

Moloch jerked to his feet, sending his chair crashing to the floor. "You dare to speak to me with such disrespect? I could destroy you--" He snapped his fingers-- "just like that!"

"But you won't," Galan said. "You need me, don't you? Who else can you groom to supervise the Society of the Undead? What other nightwalker would want to assume your duties? Not a one. So there you have it. Now, if you'll tell me where the mortal woman is--"

"For the last time, I don't know!"

"Bastard!"

Is he lying? Careful to mask his dejection, Galan stalked out of the hall. Return to Miami, find Stevie!

A silent plea penetrated his consciousness. Galan, save me!

In a split second Galan disappeared from the room, then reappeared below ground.

* * * *

Galan, please save me!

Within the dank, gloomy dungeon, Galan stopped to concentrate and finally homed in on Stevie's presence. Water dripped from the ceiling, the walls slimy with green mold. A powerful stench assaulted his nose, a smell that made him choke.

"Stevie!"

Galan!

A rush of happiness clashed with deadly anger when he found her chained to a wall, covered only with a thin blanket. Who had done this to her? If not Moloch, for God's sake, who?

"Stevie, my darling!" Galan knelt beside her and gingerly drew her into his arms, feathering kisses from her forehead to her neck. Alarm jolted him as he held her frail, unresponsive body in his arms and noted her closed eyes, her faint heartbeat. A frisson of fear raced through every cell in his body, finally settling in his heart, freezing all rational thought except one. Was it too late to save her?

Her lips moved, but no words came. Like a wilted rose, she lay immobile in his arms, as cold as the snow that blanketed the Alps. Mindful of the need to warm her, he ran his hand across her arms and down her legs. In absolute fury he found the rusty shackle that bound her to the wall, the manacles that fettered her hand and ankle. Thankful he'd recently fed and now had the strength of twenty men, he jerked at the shackle and tore it loose. The massive pin on the wall fell to the floor with a loud clatter. He tugged at the manacles and broke them.

"Now you're free." With gentle fingers, he smoothed lank strands of hair from her face while he murmured endearments to comfort her. More worried by the minute, he sat down next to her and felt her carotid artery. So weak. So very weak.

"My dearest," he whispered, "I'm going to take you home now." Eyes closed, she lay as silent as a corpse, her lips blue with cold. Dark circles shadowed her eyes, her skin stretched taut across her face, as if death had already claimed her. When had she last eaten or drunk? God, it might have been days ago since she'd consumed food or water.

A fresh spurt of anger erupted inside him. Who had done this? God, who? When he found out, he'd kill the bastard. Moloch had denied knowledge of her imprisonment, but the fiend was a crafty bastard and a skilled liar, a monster with no scruples. Later, he'd ask Stevie, but he feared she wouldn't know.

Giving up his quandary for now, Galan saw his chance to cure her of her horrible affliction, now while she lay near death. He'd give her his blood, for the rich, red liquid had recuperative powers beyond anything the blood of puny mortals contained. He'd do it now ... no hesitation, no equivocation.

He raised his wrist to his mouth and bit down hard on the radial artery, watching the blood flow and drip onto the stone floor.

"Stevie." Gently, he shook her and held his wrist to her mouth. "Drink my blood. It will revive you." With infinite care, he lifted her head and pressed his wrist to her mouth. "Please, my darling." After several entreaties, the pressure of her lips on his wrist told him his offer had found acceptance.

He monitored the amount until he judged she'd drunk enough to ease her thirst and cure her illness. Satisfied, he withdrew his hand. In no time, his bleeding stopped, the skin mended.

Clasping her slender body in his arms, he pulled a handkerchief from his pocket and dabbed it across her mouth.

Her eyes blinked open, a frown creasing her forehead. "Galan? How ... how did you find me? How did you know I was here?"

"Sweeting, you should know by now that an invisible cord binds you to me. You are a part of me, and whether or not you accept me for what I am, I want you to know I'll always be near whenever you need me." As if she were a fragile porcelain vase, he lifted her in his arms, tucking the blanket close around her, holding her close to his chest.

"Now I'm taking you home."

\* \* \* \*

"Here we are, sweetheart ... home again." Galan's voice, as sensuous as an ocean breeze, aroused Stevie from her slumber. Still clad in her flannel nightgown, she blinked her eyes open and looked around in hazy recognition. Settled on Galan's lap, she nestled against his hard chest, drawing comfort from his strong arms holding her and the smooth cotton of his shirt grazing her cheek. Back home again, in her own bed!

After another dazed glance around, she asked, "How'd I get back here?"

His arms tightened around her. "I transported you, darling, first putting you to sleep."

She moistened her lips. "But the dungeon ... how--?"

"Don't you remember? I rescued you from your cell, where I found you near death." An expression of tenderness gentled his sculpted features as he kissed her on the cheek. "Can you tell me how long you were imprisoned?"

"I lost track of the time ... several days, I'm sure."

She shuddered. "The cell--" She rubbed her arms and shuddered, as if she'd never get warm again. "Galan, that cell!"

"Please put it from your mind," he said with another light kiss on her cheek. "You're home now, safe again."

She raised her head to gaze at his ebony eyes, those eyes that held a thousand secrets but revealed nothing but love. With only a dim light by her bed, his dark eyes appeared even blacker, as if all the mysteries of the cosmos had gathered in their depths. The lamplight cast a silvery sheen on his hair and gave his face a distinct hue, masking its usual pallor.

She stretched her arms and legs, another question puzzling her. "How can I feel so much better after being in that crazy cell for so long? My arthritis--it's gone." She flexed her fingers, opening and closing them. Pure joy made her want to dance, sing, fly around the room! She ran her hand from his chest up to the nape of his neck, tangling her fingers in his curly hair. "I don't need to tell you how happy I am, but I still don't understand about my cure."

A long pause ensued, then he clasped her hand in his strong one and bent to feather a kiss on her lips. "I gave you a few drops of my blood. It was the only way--"

"Your blood?" She jerked back. "But how can that make me well again?"

"My blood has healing powers. While you languished in the dungeon--and frankly, starving to death--I saw my chance to cure you of your dreadful affliction." He kissed her again, harder this time. "Now, we will say no more about it, only that it gladdens me to see you healthy again, as you were when I first knew you." His gaze flew to the curtained window, where a slow dawn lightened the east, and the chirping of robins announced the dawn. Time for one last embrace. "I must leave you now, but I shall come again tonight. There are things I want to know."

* * * *

After Galan left, Stevie stood under the shower, luxuriating in the warm spray of water that sluiced onto her head and down her body, washing away the dungeon filth. Even now, in this short amount of time, she missed Galan, missed his sexy voice, those dark, mystical eyes of his, everything about him.

In familiar surroundings again, she felt better than she had in months, and tomorrow she'd return to her job at the bookstore. She could resume her karate lessons, too, something she definitely missed.

Thankful for all Galan had done for her--he'd saved her life and made her well again--she realized she couldn't base a lifelong commitment on gratitude. If he asked her to marry him, there was only one answer to give. Tell him "no", even though it would break both their hearts. No matter how much she loved him--and she did love him, no question about it--she wouldn't marry him. She wanted a normal life and children, and how could she have that if she married a vampire? Imagine telling her dad about Galan. Dad, I'm in love with a wonderful man. Only one problem. He's a vampire.

* * * *

"We have much to discuss," Galan said that evening after a long, sensual kiss she wished would go on forever, a poignant kiss, too, because she knew she had to end their relationship. She wasn't the kind who played with a man's feelings ... even if that man wasn't mortal.

They sat on the sofa, his arm around her shoulder. "One thing I must know--who in God's name kidnapped you? If not Moloch--"

"Moloch?"

"Forgive me for throwing that name out when you are not familiar with this, uh, person. Moloch heads the Society of the Undead--vampires, in other words."

A chill raced across her arms and legs. Was this the same creep who'd scared the daylights out of her? "An older, skinny ma--, er, vampire with long, bushy hair?"

"The same," Galan said with a puzzled look. "But how do you know of him?"

"If he's the one you're talking about, I've seen him a couple of times when I was out on my nightly run, and other times outside my apartment. He looked as if he wanted to kill me! But Galan--"

"Why have you never told me about him?"

"How was I supposed to know you knew him? But he's not the one who kidnapped me. It was a woman, called herself Rosalinda."

"Rosalinda? She's dead." For a brief moment, he looked uncomfortable. "I mean, truly dead."

"That's the name she gave me. She's got long, black hair and her nails--" Stevie shivered-- "her nails were like claws."

"By St. Aidan! Either Lilith lied, or Rosalinda didn't truly die."

"I'm not following you."

"A thousand pardons, sweeting. This must all seem bewildering to you, especially after your recent ordeal. Lilith and Rosalinda are two vampiresses who hate each other. Lilith supposedly killed Rosalinda, or so she said. Apparently, she was mistaken, for she had no reason to lie." He scratched his chin, looking worried. "So--"

"Rosalinda! She told me you were lovers once."

He turned away for a moment. "A couple of centuries ago." He faced her again, his voice low and reassuring. "But no longer. Please dismiss the thought," he said, squeezing her hand. "Now, let us continue. You are still in danger, once that vampiress discovers you didn't die in the dungeon. We must take you to where Rosalinda can't touch you."

"Where would we go?" She sighed. "So many things I wanted to do, now that I'm well again--return to the bookstore, do all the things I couldn't do before." She traced her finger down his cheek, storing all his features in her memory. "I'll always remember that you rescued me and made me well again, but I hate to leave here." Another sigh. "Are you sure Rosalinda would look for me again?"

"Let me put it plainly," he said, harsh lines etched on his face. "If Rosalinda finds you're still alive--and that may well happen--

what she'll do to you will be infinitely worse than leaving you to starve in a dungeon."

"What could be worse than starving to death?"

"You really want to know? She could torture you--burn you to death or put you on the rack. That same prison you languished in has a rack, didn't you see it? Other possibilities--she might turn you into a vampire or worse, transform you into an empty creature with no mind or soul. Do you want to hear more?"

"No, that's enough!" She peered into his face. "You got any ideas? Where can I go so Rosalinda won't find me?"

"The question is not only where, but when." He reached for her hand again, his voice low and soothing. "I intend to take you back to the fifteenth century--"

She jerked in his embrace. "What?"

"Take you where Rosalinda can't get you," he said, an expression of calm assurance on his face. As if his expression assured her!

"You've got to be kidding!" This was all getting crazier by the minute.

"Time travel poses no problem for me. However, Rosalinda can't go back to the fifteenth century because she wasn't born yet."

"Neither was I, obviously."

Galan spoke with cool nonchalance. "Ah, but since I was born before that time, I can take you back with me. I need only to hold you in my arms--an exercise I greatly enjoy--and transport you."

She shoved a lock of hair from her forehead. "This has got to be the craziest travel idea since the Children's Crusade."

"A viable idea, nonetheless," he said, smiling. "The only viable one."

At a loss for words, she studied the avocado vase on the end table. With so many questions that nagged her, she didn't know where to begin, so ... start at the beginning. "Something I've wondered about--when did you become a vampire?"

"I suffered a mortal wound at the Battle of Hastings, an arrow in my stomach. That same night, I became a vampire." A world of sadness defined his face and voice, but then he spoke on a forceful note. "Truly, I will tell you more of my transformation another time. For now, we should be on our way. We must arrive in England before dawn."

"We're going to England? Well, at least I'll be able to speak the language."

"I think not. English as spoken then was much different from the language now. But do not worry, you won't come into contact with others."

"So what are we going to do?" she asked, not even trying to keep the sarcasm from her voice. "Make hotel reservations?"

"Hardly, but finding a place to stay should present no problem." He wrapped his arm around her waist. "Now, let us go."

"Wait! If we can go back in time, can we at least arrive in the summer? It's going to be real cold there now."

"Even better. I know of a house we can stay at."

"How do you know this?"

"Because I lived in England then." He took her hand and stood, drawing her up with him.

A hundred problems zipped through her head. "Clothes! All the things I'll need--toothbrush and toothpaste."

Galan flicked his hand. "You will find clothes there. Please fetch your toiletries and let us leave."

Not given much time, Stevie hustled to her room and grabbed her overnight case from a shelf in the closet, deciding on the spur of the moment she would take clothes with her. She threw toiletries into the bag, along with T-shirts, paperbacks, and quickie snacks she retrieved from the kitchen.

"Okay," she said after a few minutes. "I'm ready."

With her hand enclosed in his, he frowned in fierce concentration, his eyes closed, his fingers gripping hers. A rushing sound bombarded her ears, like waves upon a seashore, becoming louder. An unseen force was drawing her back, back, back....

Chapter Seventeen

*England, 1486*

Clutching her overnight case as if it were the winning lottery ticket, Stevie stood with Galan outside an English manor house, too shocked to say a word. A jutting window--an oriel window, Galan called it--added local color to the front of the house, but the early morning darkness made it difficult to see anything else.

She finally found her voice. "What do we do now?" she whispered. "Just barge in?"

"I wouldn't put it that way," he said in an even tone. "We are merely taking temporary custody of the house."

"What about the owners? Something tells me they won't welcome us with open arms," she said with another questioning glance around.

"The house is empty. Ownership of the house and the surrounding land are in dispute. The people who claim it--a wealthy wool merchant and his wife--have gone to London to argue their case to the king."

"The king?"

"Henry VII, on the throne for less than a year." He took her hand. "Come now, let's settle in."

She gave the house another doubtful glance. "What about servants? There's no one here now?"

"As I said, the house is empty."

"I'll bet the place is locked up tight as a bank vault."

He grinned, his teeth shining white in the moonlight. "That presents no difficulty." With a wave of his hand, he opened the front door.

"Wow! There's no limit to your talents, is there?" She stepped into a narrow entrance hall, feeling her way along the wall. In absolute blackness, she bumped into a high-backed chair, and Galan took her arm to guide her.

Past the hall, moonlight streamed through the multipaned leaded windows, leaving a silvery path along the tiled floor. She blinked her eyes in the dark as she tried to focus on the huge room--living room?

"Rushlights," Galan said as he walked from one waist high iron sconce to another and lit each with a touch of his finger.

No longer surprised by anything he said or did, Stevie kept silent, her attention focused on the first floor, whose ceiling rose majestically, like a cathedral. A large stone fireplace dominated one wall, and enough armor to start a canning factory decorated the space to the right of the fireplace. Wood paneling filled with rosettes bordered the ceiling, and stained glass heraldic devices on the windows added a certain dignity to the house.

A tapestry on the opposite wall caught her attention, but she couldn't make out its design even with the flaming rushlights, whose pungent smell made her wrinkle her nose.

Galan placed his hand under her elbow. "Upstairs. Better sleep while you can. We still have much to discuss when it becomes dark again."

"Where will you sleep?" she asked as they mounted the slippery stone steps.

"Wine cellar--no light." On the second floor--or did the English call it the first?--he led her to a spacious bedroom where an ornately-carved bed commanded the greater part of the room, and a large wooden chest hugged a near wall. Draperies decorated the lead-paned square windows.

"You know something?" she said with a dubious glance at the huge bed. "I don't think I'll get much sleep this morning. I usually get up about this time." She threw him a wistful look. "So you'll be sleeping while I'm awake?"

"I fear so. That is the way of vampires." He ran his fingers through his thick mass of hair. "Dearest, I realize what a strange experience this is for you--a different century, different food, so many aspects of life that will seem strange to you. These are matters we must talk about this evening. In the meantime, to be safe, please stay inside the house on the very slim chance that one of the neighbors might ride by. Read or do whatever you wish. Young ladies of your time don't do needlework, do they?"

"Needlework? Are you kidding?"

"Pity. Possibly women of long ago had more resourceful means of keeping busy. No TV, after all," he said with a teasing smile. "Sleep as late as you can, and in the evening, I shall come to you again. Don't forget, though, darkness comes much later here than in Miami during the summer." With a heavy sigh, he cast a long look toward the bed. "I can think of better ways to spend my time with you, but I fear dawn will arrive soon."

Even as he spoke, the first pale rays of sunlight chased the shadows from the room and cast a golden glow on the purple velvet bedspread, turning it to crimson.

He drew her into his arms and kissed her long and passionately, then released her as daylight found its way into the corners. "Try to sleep. I'll come to you when it's dark again," he said with one last embrace. "Sleep well."

Shoulders thrown back, he strode past the thick wooden door and on down the steps. Flummoxed by all that had happened this night but determined to brazen out this weird experience, she looked around the room and reminded herself she had plenty of time to get used to her surroundings. She stripped down to her underpants and pushed the bedspread back, sneezing in a cloud of dust. Sliding into bed, she knew she'd never fall asleep....

Hours later, she awoke, jerking upright, her gaze covering the strange room. Where was she? She sank back down as memories flooded her mind: her trip back in time with Galan, their arrival at the manor house in the early morning. With a wide yawn, she glanced at her watch, already reset by English time. After eleven! She must have fallen asleep as soon as she crawled into bed. Surprising. Had Galan cast a sleepy spell on her? She wouldn't put it past him.

Stevie stepped out of bed and pulled on her jeans, then slipped her bra and T-shirt on. One thing for sure--she had to pee. She had no idea where the bathroom was or if the house had one. She had a sneaking suspicion the place had no indoor plumbing. Galan had told her to stay inside, but apparently he didn't understand the female bladder. A glance out her bedroom window showed tall trees and clusters of bushes at the side of the house. That would have to do.

Within minutes, she returned to the house, where her growling stomach sent her rushing back upstairs to rummage through her overnight case for a banana and a cherry pop-tart. That and a lukewarm lemonade had to last for several hours, but she'd sell her soul for an ice cold coke.

* * * *

"How have you spent your time?" Galan asked in the late evening after he emerged from the wine cellar, looking well-rested, as handsome as ever in black jeans and a gray T-shirt. How did he spend his leisure time? she wondered as he sat on the wooden bench and beckoned her to join him. "Did you sleep well?"

She turned from her study of the heraldic devices emblazoned on the windows and came to sit beside him. "Believe it or not, I slept okay." She paused. "But I've got to ask you, 'cause it's been on my mind--how long will we stay here? I want to return to my job and get back in the swing of things. This isn't my idea of a vacation."

"You're going to stay here until I find Rosalinda and kill her, however long that takes."

Confusion swamped her. "But you told me Rosalinda can't come back to this century, so how will you find her?"

"I want you to stay here whilst I--"

"Me stay here? By myself?"

"To put it bluntly, I must hunt her down until I find her. Otherwise, she'll remain a continual threat to you." He took her hand, wrapping his fingers around hers. "I'm doing this for your sake, so you'll no longer be in danger. Believe me, I don't like to leave you, but I have no choice. Please accept the circumstances," he said with a persuasive smile that didn't persuade her.

"Okay, while we're being blunt, let me ask you a question. What if you don't come back?" She immediately regretted her words. God, what if he didn't? The possibility sent her mind reeling, and she pressed her hand to her stomach. What would she do if he didn't return?

He drew back. "Of course I'll return. Do you think I would leave you here for all time?"

"Not intentionally, but let's look at this from all angles. What if she kills you?" She twisted her hands in her lap, one quick breath following another.

"She won't kill me," he said without hesitation. "I'm much stronger than she, and if I may say so, more resourceful." He hugged her to his chest. "I'll return to you, I promise."

Arms folded across her chest, she turned to face him. "If you don't come back, and if I have to, I can learn to adjust to life in this century. I won't like it, but I'll do it. But aside from worrying about you--and honestly, I can't help it-- why in the world would I want to stay in this crazy century? You already told me I wouldn't understand the language. And when the owners come back, I'll have to move on. Or--"

"Stevie, it will not come to that."

"Let me finish. If I'm still here when the owners return, should I say, 'Excuse me, but I come from the twenty-first century, and I just happened to use your house as a hotel?' But the main thing," she said, placing her hand on his shoulder, "is that I'll miss you ... very much."

He laid his hand on top of hers. "Dearest...."

"And no matter what you say, I'm still scared that you might not find Rosalinda right away, or at all." In distraction, she got up to study the tapestry on the wall, but she could hardly appreciate the decoration when she had so much on her mind.

Galan came to stand behind her and wrapped his arms around her waist. She leaned back against him, breathing in his sandalwood scent, absorbing the full force of his masculinity, never wanting to leave his arms. He eased his hands up to cup her breasts, sending all her anxieties flying across the ocean.

He pressed his lips to her neck. "Please, dearling, don't make this difficult for me. How can I concentrate while you are tempting me so? As for leaving you, I don't want you to worry about me. It will do you no good. This I promise you, if I don't find Rosalinda within a month--"

"A month!" She escaped his hold and swung around to face him. "What if the owners of the house come back next week?"

"They won't. I remember they stayed in London for several months. 'Twas November before the king settled in their favor and they returned." He gave her a tender smile, one meant to reassure her ... but it didn't. "You are in no danger. The nearest village is miles away. No one will see you. But if someone should come by--highly unlikely--you can wear the lady's clothes she keeps in the chest upstairs."

"Wow! You sure have a lot of nerve, I'll say that for you. Not only do I sleep in their bed and make free use of their house, but I wear the lady's clothes besides." Another concern grabbed her attention. "Let's assume that a neighbor or peddler comes by, no matter how farfetched that seems. What should I do if I don't understand their language?"

"Pretend you're a deaf mute. That is the only answer. But the possibility of meeting someone is so remote as to be virtually nonexistent. This house is isolated on many acres of land with only cows and sheep in the vicinity. You can even go for walks, if you want, as long as you dress according to the times."

Reluctant to worry him further, she suppressed her misgivings. "I'm going to miss you very much." She took in all his features, studying his face as if seeing him for the first time. When he came back--and he had to!--what then? What kind of a future would they have? She chased that speculation from her mind, afraid to deal with it now--if ever. "I'll miss you," she repeated.

"The same with me." He enclosed her in his arms again, binding her to him, as if for all time. "Oh, God, I'm going to miss you!" He kissed her again and again, pressing her to him, as though they were part of the same whole, with one body, one heart, one being. She returned his kisses, tangling her fingers through his thick locks, her hands playing across his back.

Gently, his fingers traced a path from her cheek to her throat and down to her breast, his hand molding her curves. A rush of warmth made her weak, and she couldn't think for wanting him so.

With a low moan, he stepped away to look long and fully into her eyes, as if to imprint her features in her memory. "I'll come back to you as soon as I can, and that shouldn't be too long." His expression hardened. "Never doubt that I shall find Rosalinda, and when I do, I shall kill her."

She kept silent; no point in repeating her fears.

"You know I want to return to you, more than anything," Galan said, looking so dejected she wanted to hold him close, never let him out of her sight. "But I fear I must leave you now."

"Already?" I'll miss you so much.

"We'll be together again soon. Only remember that." He smiled his blue ribbon smile. "And then I shall take you back to your own city, your own time."

After one more deep kiss, he disappeared.

* * * *

Stevie's worries about Galan increased with each day. Memories of his kisses, his caresses brought a rush of warmth to her body, a surge of hope to her heart. She missed him more than she'd ever thought possible. Resolved to convince herself he would come back, she explored the house and grounds, where she found a vegetable garden behind the manor. Cabbages, carrots, beets, and so many other vegetables flourished there, and those, added to the foods she'd brought, kept her from going hungry.

The land behind the house stretched over one-hundred yards to the river--the Thames, she guessed, since Galan had told her the house was about forty miles northwest of London. In lieu of a bath, she swam in the river every day, hoping the water was free of pollution this far from the capital.

Every hour of every day, she thought about Galan, praying for his safe return to her. When he came back--and she had to believe he would--what would they do then?

Forget about him, her brain warned her heart. There was no future for them. But could anyone else take his place? No need to ask.

As usual, Moloch and Rosalinda lurked at the back of her mind, keeping her awake at night and nagging her during the day. Galan had told her Rosalinda couldn't travel to this century, but what if she sent someone else after her? What about Moloch? If that creep came to kill her, what could she do?

Galan, please come back to me.

\* \* \* \*

Where is the witch? Galan strode the length of his spacious living room, clenching his fists, aiming a vicious kick at a table leg. He must find Rosalinda. By the wide front window, he stared out at the night's stygian darkness, as if he'd see her lurking in the shadows.

There! Something moved by the allamanda bushes. Rosalinda? No, damn it, only a tree swaying in the breeze.

Weeks had passed since he'd left Stevie in fifteenth century England, since he'd begun his search for Rosalinda. Still no sign of the crafty vampiress. How in God's name would he ever destroy the slut when he couldn't even find her?

But first, he had to feed, then--

"Going somewhere?"

"Octavius! You do have a way of catching a body unawares."

His visitor grinned. "Part of my charm. Why advertise my visit when I never know from one night to the next where I'll be?" He settled himself in an easy chair, adjusting the folds of his toga. "Thanks, I believe I will sit down." He frowned anxiously at Galan. "I meant this only as a social call, but I'm glad I came. You look worried, my friend."

Uneasy, Galan sat on the sofa opposite him. "As well I should be." He cracked his knuckles. "Did you know Rosalinda is still alive? She captured the mortal woman, cast her into a dungeon."

"By Apollo, no! So what--?"

"I rescued the mortal woman and took her back to the fifteenth century, but I must find Rosalinda." Galan leaned forward, hands resting on his knees. "I want to know your feelings for the vampiress. I suspect you still harbor a tendre for her."

Octavius snorted. "No longer. Lilith and I have renewed our relationship, and I flatter myself that she returns my affection. So if you want to find the other vampiress and eliminate her--"

"That's the problem! I can't find her. I've hunted her for over two weeks."

"I'll look for her, help you all I can. If I find her, I'll tell her how much you miss her. Won't bother me if you get rid of her. In fact, I wish you would." He stood, skimming his fingers through his golden locks. "Now I must return to Lilith. She misses me very much when I'm away. And I shall certainly apprise her of Rosalinda's resurrection. She might know something."

"Indeed, yes!"

After Octavius left, Galan raked his fingers through his hair as his promise to Moloch returned to taunt him.

He must forget mortality, pretend he never knew Stevie, but was the fiend keeping his promise to leave his dear one alone?

He wouldn't count on it.

* * * *

In his bedroom, Galan stepped into his black loafers and ran a comb through his thick, unruly hair, then drew his car keys from his pants pocket. Another night's search for the vampiress. Another night away from Stevie.

Hunger pangs tortured him, and if he didn't eat soon, he'd have no strength, no power. Once satiated, he'd search for Rosalinda, and when he killed her, he'd bring Stevie back to this century.

And live without her until the end of time.

"Galan!"

"Rosalinda!" Absolute shock chased all other thoughts from his mind. By St. Aidan, she'd come to him again, a vision of cruel beauty with her pearlescent skin and glossy raven hair coiled atop her head. In a red velvet gown trimmed with black soutache and diamonds that flashed from her ears, neck, and wrist, she looked as seductive as ever. But soon, she wouldn't seduce anyone. She'd be dead.

She glided over to him and placed her hands on his shoulders, a blood red ruby sparkling on her ring finger. "Miss me? You thought Lilith had killed me, didn't you?"

Too bad she failed. Relief impeded his speech, and he hoped she'd mistake his silence for joy in finding her alive. "Rosalinda, I can't tell you what it means to me to see you again," he declared. "When I heard you were dead...." He placed his hand over his heart, affecting an anguished look.

"You missed me?"

"If only you knew how much."

"Speaking of Lilith, have you seen her? I'd like to, um, pay her my respects. She must be evading me." An expression of pure cunning crossed her face. "I wonder why."

"Lilith? Haven't seen her in ages. Never mind about Lilith." He reached for her. "We're together now and--"

Without a word, she turned from him and snapped her fingers.

Puzzled shock froze his movements.

"What?"

Too weak to vanish, unable to escape, Galan saw two revenants approach, their faces set with grim purpose. One beast held manacles.

"What the hell--?" Galan threw a glance at Rosalinda, a smug leer plastered across her face. Currents of fear zipped through every cell of his body. His pulse thundered in his ears. He couldn't think, couldn't move.

Clad in coarse burlap robes, the revenants stank of rotten meat and stale urine. Plodding steps shook the floor, a porcelain vase toppling onto the carpet.

"No!" Galan stepped back, summoning his vanishing powers ... to no avail. Weak from hunger, he was as helpless as a twig caught in a raging river.

The monsters grabbed him in their filthy, sausage-like fingers. Galan stared in horror at the manacles.

"Damn you!" He struggled against their grip, knocking over a table lamp, cracking the shade, shattering the bulb. "You bastards!" Fists flying, he struck out at them, but he was no match for their doltish brawn.

Galan twisted in their grip. "God, no!"

He spat in their faces. "Ugly dogs!"

Rosalinda stood to the side, smirking. "Dear Galan, is that the best you can do? What a limited vocabulary you have."

Neither speaking, the empty-faced revenants pinned him to the floor and clamped iron bands on both wrists and ankles. Glowing yet empty eyes stared at him, lolling tongues hanging from open mouths. Thick, beefy hands ended in sharp claws, like tiny knives that scraped and scratched his skin.

"You sons of bitches!" He writhed and twisted, kicking out at them, blows that bounced off, like trying to knock over a boulder with a balloon.

"Whoremongers!"

Rosalinda's shrill laughter echoed off the walls. "I have you now."

Within seconds, he landed in a dungeon, amidst the dirt and slime that fouled the stone floor, the stench that polluted the air, the silence that presaged solitude for eternity. Sporting a proud grin on her pallid face, the vampiress preened before him.

Galan uttered one word. "Why?"

"You won't leave the mortal woman alone. I captured her, but you already knew that, didn't you? I told her I'd come back to check on her in a century or so. But something--call it womanly intuition--prompted me to return a week later, and lo and behold, I find she's gone. Well, it didn't take too many guesses to tell me who rescued her. As long as she's alive, you'll remain my prisoner." She giggled. "I brought you to the same cell she occupied. Rather a nice touch, don't you think?"

"You bitch!"

"Oh, my, such ungentlemanly language." She patted her upswept coiffure, her sharp nails gleaming like daggers in the dark. "I'm truly ashamed of these bonds," she said with a dismissive nod, "but they were the only ones I could find at present. I took them from another cell, since you apparently broke the mortal woman's manacles," she said with an accusing look. "Have to fetch new ones, and soon." As if to tease him, she took a few steps closer, peering down at him. "I'll release you if you tell me where the human is."

He shifted his position on the hard stone floor. "She's where you can't get at her."

"So that's the game you're playing, is it? Well, then, I'll leave and come back to check on you in a century or so."

"Moloch--"

"--still thinks I'm destroyed, and it suits my purposes to let him think so. He brags about all his spies, but they're a disloyal group. I bribed them not to tell him I'm alive, and I'll leave it to your imagination to guess how I accomplished that feat. We'll just say I haven't lost my bedroom charms."

She cackled. "Moloch doesn't even know you're here, right in his own residence. Now it looks as if you won't be doing anything ... except die." With one loud screech, she disappeared.

Galan strained at the clamps that bound his wrists together. He jerked his feet, trying to break loose. It had been a snap to break

Stevie's bonds after a recent feed, but now hunger debilitated him, draining him of all hope.

What was Rosalinda's purpose in capturing him? Did she think that if she eliminated Stevie, he'd love her again? Foolish, demented vampiress. Evil Rosalinda.

Was Moloch truly unaware of Rosalinda's machinations? The head vampire was far craftier than any other nightwalker, and surely Moloch knew of his imprisonment. Why, then, did Moloch not save him? If ever he escaped this cell--and by God, he would--he'd discover why that fiend did nothing to help him. But how would he get out of this Godforsaken pit? How?

Try one more time. If the vampiress intended to fetch new bonds, he must work quickly. He jerked and pulled and twisted, straining at the rusty bonds, never accepting defeat. Drawing on his power, he stared hard at the manacles, willing them to break. He was too weak, too weak! After a brief rest, he gathered strength for another attempt, then tried again. Still no luck.

His mind flashed a warning. Hurry before the witch returns!

He rubbed his wrists against each other, his aim to wear away the metal. Time lost all meaning as bits of rusty metal flaked off the manacles, until only a thin band of iron remained. Soon he'd free his wrists, then loosening his ankle bonds would present no problem. He breathed a sigh of relief. Not long, then--

"Well, what have we here?"

Like a satanic apparition, Rosalinda flowed into the cell, shining new shackles in her hands.

"Dear Galan, did you actually think you could escape? I had an idea you'd try a little trick like this. My womanly intuition again."

A snap of her fingers brought the two revenants back. "Boris, hold him down! Caractus, bind his wrists!" She gestured disdainfully at Galan. "This foolish man wanted to leave us. My, my. We can't have that."

"Damn bastards!" Galan shot Rosalinda a look of pure ridicule. "You puny, Godforsaken bitch!"

Rosalinda snickered. "'Sticks and stones may break my bones, but words will never hurt me.'"

The revenants' task completed, Rosalinda gestured toward the new manacles. "There now, that should do the trick. Let's see you try to escape now." She shook her head, an expression of mock distress on her face. "Poor man, we all know how you want to return to your mortal lover. But you're my prisoner for as long as it pleases me."

Aiming one last smirk at Galan, she left. Galan leaned back against the wall, every muscle aching, a painful, debilitating hunger torturing his insides.

He needed a miracle to escape this prison, but far worse, Stevie needed a miracle to escape the fifteenth century, to return to her own time. He'd never see her again.

By the blessed Virgin, how would she manage?

She was gone from his life forever.

\* \* \* \*

"You think he believed you?"

"You know what a good actress I am, a good liar, too." Rosalinda faced Moloch in the great hall, where an intricate spider web adorned a far wall, draping from the ceiling to the floor and stretching from one window to the next. A stiff wind gusted through the open windows, molding her gown to her body and whipping her hair across her face, but the spider web remained intact, a durable work of art.

Moloch sipped his wine, his gaze leveled on her.

She shrugged. "With Galan, you never know what he accepts as truth. He keeps his thoughts to himself. But I think I convinced him that I'm acting on my own."

Moloch narrowed his eyes. "For your sake, he'd better believe you. I don't want him to discover that I'm behind these kidnappings."

"But you realize he rescued the mortal woman?"

He grimaced. "Of course I know. And he will pay for his betrayal." A sly grin crept across his face. "Or perhaps I should say the mortal woman will pay."

\* \* \* \*

Inside Galan's cell, one night drifted into the next until he lost track of time. Hunger prowled his insides, such a desperate need for sustenance he could think of nothing else ... but Stevie. Like red hot pokers, pain skewered his belly. He moaned, weak and out of his mind with his need. He stared at the four stone walls and the slime that coated their surface, trying to ignore the stench. Too weak to transport himself, despair sucked all the spirit from his body. He'd expire in this Godforsaken dungeon, never able to rescue Stevie, to embrace her once more, to kiss her and know the joy of her presence.

And if he managed to escape, what then? Give her up, let her find a mortal man to love, for surely they could never achieve permanent happiness together. He would love her forever. But he'd never expect her to spend all her tomorrows with him, even if he could escape, even if he were free of Moloch. The fiend owned him body and soul. His promises returned to taunt him, bitter reminders of his fate throughout eternity.

God, how it hurt.

What if Rosalinda sent one of her admirers to fetch

Stevie ... and kill her? Tears slid down his cheeks, and he pressed his hand to his head. God, he prayed, please take care of Stevie. Nothing must happen to his beloved.

A strong scent of musk and the rustling of silk announced Rosalinda's presence. Had she changed her mind and decided to release him? In your dreams!

Finely attired in a fiery orange silk gown, she stood by the cell door, her emerald eyes glowing with satisfaction, her body twitching with suppressed excitement. Gold and diamonds glittered from her ears, wrists, and fingers, the slut!

She jabbed his leg with her slippered foot. "I'll release you if you tell me where the mortal woman is."

"Not a chance!"

"Still the stubborn hero? Let's see if I can change your mind." She raised her hand, her bold bracelet slipping along her arm. Reeking of decay, a revenant shuffled inside the cell, his fetid breath fanning over Galan like lethal gas.

"Take him outside," she ordered.

By all the saints, no! Not outside, where the sunlight would find him! Panic froze his blood. Fear raced through his body. But he refused to beg for mercy. God, he couldn't even kick at the beast, couldn't raise his leg.

"Son of a bitch!"

The revenant tore the chain loose and lifted him effortlessly. Galan squirmed in his clutches, feeble movements that proved no match for the monster's strength.

Rosalinda sneered. "Daylight will come within a few hours. Let's see how obstinate you are when the sun's rays begin to burn you to cinders. Call me if you want me. You need only tell me where the mortal woman is, and I'll release you."

"Go to hell!"

"No," she cackled. "You will, and very soon."

Within moments, he found himself alone on the hard, snowy ground outside the castle walls, with only the pine-covered hills and the snow-capped Alps in the distance. A fierce wind whistled through the trees, its keening sound reminding him of death. He remained fettered to the manacles, the chain wrapped around a tree. Soon, the stars above him would fade, heralding the deadly dawn.

To burn alive! Fear paralyzed him. He had to escape. In desperation he wiggled his arms and legs on the frozen ground, trying to loosen his bonds, but the shackles held fast.

For hours, he twisted and thrashed, strained against his manacles. With the last vestige of strength, he tugged, gritting his teeth, exerting every muscle. Despite the freezing temperature, sweat poured down his face and soaked his clothes.

Too soon, the stars faded, one by one, and the sun's torturous rays began to tint the horizon. Too soon, oh, too soon! A fiery glow defiled the eastern sky, like flames that licked at his skin and devoured his body until he became nothing but ashes.

"Please, God, no!" He begged for deliverance, prayed as he'd never prayed before.

He had to rescue his beloved Stevie. By the blessed Virgin, what would happen to her? *Stevie, I love you so much.*

Already, the sun's lethal rays scorched him, a precursor of the horrible death to come. Tears streamed down his cheeks. Fire erupted in every cell in his body, a burning agony that made him wrench and jerk and moan with pain. His outer skin turned red and peeled, soon sloughing off his body. Smoke drifted skyward, his singed hair heating his scalp.

No hope. No escape. He was doomed to burn to death.

## Chapter Eighteen

*Galan, I miss you so much.* In faded jeans and a T-shirt, Stevie brooded on the bank of the Thames and gazed across to the other side, where the light of the setting sun sparkled like gold on the water, the tall trees along the opposite bank reflected on its surface. The scent of lavender and wild roses drifted her way, carried along by a light summer breeze. How she wished Galan were with her now to enjoy all this English countryside. With her legs drawn up and her arms crossed over her chest, she closed her eyes, wanting to forget her worries, to pretend Galan was with her now.

But wait-- She blinked as vague, hazy images filled her mind, drifting among smoky mists, weaving in and out of her consciousness.

A vision of Galan materialized, then vanished.

Braced on her elbows, she raised up, her heart thudding against her ribs. She eased back on the grass, trying hard to grasp these images, to make sense out of her visions. She'd seen Galan, but where? She had to think, to concentrate.

How could she see these things? Like an earthquake in a phone booth, the answer exploded in her brain and sent heat rushing to her face. The blood he'd given her in prison had created a spiritual bond between them, the only logical explanation. Her breath caught, her heart beating fast. It couldn't be true. But it was.

She closed her eyes again, more visions emerging. There! She saw Galan, bound and feeble in prison, the same cell she'd languished in, with its pitch blackness, its slimy mold, its atmosphere of hopelessness.

She jumped to her feet and hugged her arms, then paced back and forth along the riverbank. No other images came to her, but that vision alone was enough to send shivers racing from her head to her toes, cold fear churning in her stomach. Did this picture mean he'd never return?

How could she rescue him? She was stuck in another century, as helpless as a fly caught in a spiderweb.

Galan had to escape, had to! What if he died alone in prison? God, she prayed, please bring him back to me.

* * * *

"Galan, quickly!" Staccato fast, Octavius beat out the sparks in Galan's hair and unlocked the manacles that bound his wrists and ankles. With infinite care, he helped him to his feet.

At Octavius' touch, Galan groaned with pain.

The maverick threw him a look of apology. "Sorry, mon ami."

"Not your fault. After all, you are rescuing me." On wobbly legs, Galan sighed with relief, trying to maintain his balance. "Rosalinda?" he croaked.

"Dead, sans doute. I killed her and burned her body. I shall tell you more later. Come, we must hurry! The sun...."

The sentence remained unfinished, the sun's burning rays leaving no doubt of his meaning. "I know of an abandoned coal mine close by. Do you have the power to transport yourself?"

Galan struggled to get the words out. "May need help."

"Very well. I shall carry you...."

Weak and starving, Galan awoke hours later within the troglodytic confines of the coal mine. Raising up on his elbows, he looked around in confusion. He ran a hand through his hair as everything came back to him: Rosalinda and the revenants, his imprisonment, Octavius' rescue. With his acute night vision, he saw his friend sitting across the train track from him, the maverick vampire viewing him with concern.

In one fluid movement, Octavius rose and brushed the coal dust from his hands. "So you're back in the land of the living, or should I say returned to the world of the undead."

Galan forced a laugh, his mouth raw and sore. He pushed himself upright and leaned against the wall, shifting his position as an outcropping of coal gouged into his back.

"Returned, thanks to you, my friend. You have done much for me. How can I ever repay you?"

"Tut, tut." Octavius waved a languid hand. "Think nothing of it. Remember all the things you've done for me throughout the centuries. It all evens out."

Questions crowded Galan's brain. "The key to the manacles? And how did you kill Rosalinda? How did you know I was outside the castle?"

Octavius held up a hand. "One thing at a time. Killed Rosalinda first ... in the early hours of the morning, shortly before I came to you. On a tip from Morcar, I found her in a Paris cafe. Told her how much I missed her, how I wanted to be her lover again." He snickered. "You know how conceited she is, so she fell for the bait. With my inimitable charm, I enticed her to a chateau I own in the Loire valley. Drove a stake through her evil heart. Then I took her body outside and burned her, to ensure she was truly destroyed this time." He smiled with satisfaction.

With long, delicate fingers, Octavius smoothed the folds of his toga. "When we first arrived at the chateau, would you believe she actually bragged about capturing you. Even showed me the key to the manacles she wore around her neck. Naturally, I grabbed the key before I disposed of the body." He snorted. "Stupid, wicked woman. But she is gone for good."

Galan nodded, dizzy with the movement. "Thank God! As soon as I gain my strength, I must fetch the mortal woman." The prospect alone was enough to make him forget his imprisonment, his weakness, his hunger. How could he bear the wait? He struggled to rise, bracing his hand against the wall of the mine. "First, I must feed."

"I fed before I uh, did away with Rosalinda and came to you, so I'm not hungry. But you will need assistance."

"Again, I fear."

"No matter. There's a serial rapist in Frankfurt you can feed from. Lures the prostitutes of the city to a dark alley and ravishes them there, then chokes them to death. Should have taken care of the bastard myself, but Lilith and I usually feed together. Didn't want her to know about the scum." He giggled. "I try to protect her from the harsh realities of life."

Galan straightened to his full height. "Lead me to him...."

After he fed, Galan arrived back in Miami shortly before daylight. Several more hours remained until he could fetch Stevie, too many! By then, he'd recover from his burns and his hair would return to normal, for the undead heal quickly.

After he rescued Stevie, he must leave her and eventually succeed Moloch as leader of the undead. God, why did it hurt so much?

\* \* \* \*

Inside the manor house, Stevie paced back and forth from one end of the great hall to the other, her footsteps slapping along the tiled floor. Sick to her stomach, sleepless from worry, filled with hopelessness, she knew there was nothing she could do, no way on earth she could rescue Galan.

Her family! They'd get desperate when she didn't write or call. Okay, so she had an uneasy relationship with her father and stepmother, she still kept in touch with them. Now, there'd be no "keeping in touch."

Her frantic thoughts returned to Galan. Assuming he'd come back for her--and he had to!--could they work something out between them? She had to face facts. She loved him, this vampire. Always would.

Every wonderful thing about him came back in a flash--his low, sexy voice, the tender expression on his face when he held her tight in his arms, his loving touch. All his special qualities came to mind, his kindness, his consideration of her, his courtliness, a trait you didn't see much anymore.

Could she come to terms with his vampirism? No point in asking. She'd take him any way she could.

\* \* \* \*

"Galan!" Stevie rushed into his arms, covering his face with kisses, pressing him close to her heart. "Galan, you came back to me!" Tears misted her eyes, and she brushed the back of her hand across her face.

"Stevie, my Stevie!" He returned her kisses, his body hard and strong against hers, the most wonderful sensation in the world.

Her hands on his shoulders, she drew back to look into his face and saw his own eyes moist with tears. "I thought ... I thought...." She swallowed and shook her head.

Galan smiled down at her, his eyes so full of love it chased every worry from her mind. "You thought I wouldn't come for you?"

Tears streaming down her face, she choked on her words. "I didn't know ... what had happened to you. But I'm so glad you're back." She hugged him fiercely. "So glad." Several moments passed before she could talk again. "What ... what happened to keep you?" Her fingers traced a path from his forehead to his neck, lingering on his hairline, smoothing across his unruly curls.

"Rosalinda gave me a bit of trouble. Later, I shall tell you more. Suffice it to say she is truly dead now, no longer a danger to you. A friend of mine killed her."

Stevie wiped her hand across her cheeks, trying to speak in a level voice. "Looks like she made a lot of enemies."

"True, but enough about Rosalinda." Galan embraced her again, feathering kisses on her forehead, her cheek, behind her ear, his hands playing across her back to ease her ever closer. "My love, I have missed you so." He looked longingly into her eyes and ran his finger along her cheek. "Now we can put all this trouble behind us and return to Miami."

She smiled dreamily. "Then what are we waiting for?"

* * * *

Returned to Stevie's apartment, Galan enclosed her in his embrace as a wave of despair halted his speech. He kissed her long and lingeringly, too well aware of the little time they had left between them. Too well aware he must let her go ... for all eternity.

"Galan," she murmured in her husky voice, "I was wrong when I said I never wanted to see you again--remember, the night when you told me what ... what you were." She sighed. "I've never been so wrong in my life."

He turned away, his mouth working. What could he say?

She lay back on the sofa, drawing him with her, her arms wrapped across his back. "We don't have to stop at kisses," she murmured. A smile of embarrassment skimmed over her face. "I'm usually not this bold. I've never ... never suggested this to any other man before. But with you...."

"Oh, my darling!" How easy it would be to give in to her, to disavow his promise to Moloch. But he couldn't take her to bed, couldn't bind her to him when he must leave her for all time.

She feathered kisses across his cheek. "Hours before daylight," she said, her breath warm on his skin. "No excuses."

Her body was sweet torment, a temptation near impossible to refuse.

Galan rested his head by her beautiful throat and breathed a deep sigh. "You know I want you." He nuzzled her neck. "But perhaps we should deal with this some other time. You are vulnerable now, I fear, after your recent capture and then your sojourn in England. Best to wait." He didn't want to wait, he wanted her now. God, how it hurt.

"Don't think I'll change my mind about you ... or us." Her fingers traced the harsh lines and angles of his face.

Quiet for a moment, a look of understanding came over her. "You're scared you'll forget yourself while we make love, is that it? You're afraid you might, uh, feed on me. That's it, right?"

There! She had just presented him with a perfect reason, albeit a false one. Take it. "Now you know how it is with vampires. I would never forgive myself if I took your blood. So best I avoid temptation."

"But it wouldn't matter to me," she said, her lips placing light kisses down his cheek. "I'd stop you in time."

Drawing on all his willpower, he sat up and eased away from her, then rose from the sofa. "But it would matter to me." Unable to remove his gaze from her, he tucked his shirt in his pants. "I must depart now," he murmured, the words choking him. His gaze lingered on her, to every dear feature--her blonde hair, rose-tinted cheeks, her full, lush breasts, slender waist, and long legs. But more than that, he caught her very essence, her easy laugh and warm smile, all the qualities that made her the woman he loved.

She sat up, too, brushing her hair from her face. "When will I see you again?"

"I shall come to you soon." And then leave you forever.

\* \* \* \*

A few days after her return to Miami, Stevie knelt on the floor of Bookworm's Delight, shelving books in the Architecture section, a pile of volumes beside her.

Why hadn't she heard from Galan? A week had passed since he'd brought her back to Miami, and she hadn't had a word from him. Sighing, she rested her hand on the bookrack, trying not to worry, telling herself there had to be a logical reason for his neglect. Sure, any number of reasons, she mused with false optimism. Maybe he was sick. Did vampires suffer illnesses, like mortals? She'd never heard of such a thing, but that didn't mean it couldn't happen.

Finished stocking the books, she rose to her feet and adjusted her cotton pants.

"Hey, it's good to see you back."

A tall, nice-looking guy with light brown hair and blue eyes stood next to the bookrack, a biography of Anne Boleyn in his hand. She thought hard, trying to place him. Now she remembered--he was the same man who'd helped her pick the volumes from the floor only a few weeks ago, a steady customer.

"Were you on vacation?" he queried. "Or shouldn't I ask?"

Stevie stifled a laugh. What if she told him where--and when-- she really was. "Right, I took a few weeks off."

He looked around the bookstore, his gaze settling on her again. "I'm a regular here, you know. Love to read when I have the time. Only TV I watch is the History Channel. But I see you're busy, so I won't take up your time. By the way, I'm Mark Farrell, a history professor at the University of Miami," he said with a slight nod. "And you are...?"

"I remember your name, and you can call me Stevie." She liked his boyish looks; hard to believe he was really a college professor.

He shifted the book in his hand. "Okay, Stevie, how about having lunch with me? Bayside is only a few blocks away," he said, referring to the downtown shopping center with its many eateries.

"We're very busy, and I've got a lot of books to take care of." She needed more complications in her life like she needed a broken toe.

He threw her a teasing smile. "But they give you a lunch break, don't they? Or do they starve you here?"

Starve! Her days in the dungeon came back to haunt her. If only he knew! Well, why not have lunch with him? She'd had enough exotic experiences to last her a lifetime, so a switch to the mundane might be good. Never mind her earlier pronouncement against complications. Becoming a hermit wouldn't bring Galan back to her, and she could use a little fun in her life.

"Since I'm the store manager, I usually take off for lunch at one."

"Just for today, do you suppose you could take off a little before twelve? That way, we'll beat the lunch crowd and have a more relaxed time together."

She nodded. "Ten 'til twelve. No problem."

\* \* \* \*

"You said you were on vacation?" Mark asked. He sat with Stevie at a table in El Gaucho, a cozy restaurant located on the ground level of Bayside. Several tables away, only a few other people occupied the Spanish restaurant at this early hour, so she and Mark virtually had the place to themselves.

"Vacation? Um, yes." Reluctant to elaborate--he'd think she was nuts--Stevie glanced around the place, a much fancier restaurant than the other eateries at Bayside.

"Three weeks in England," she said, fiddling with the napkin in her lap, wanting to end this conversation, afraid he'd trip her up on something.

"England! Place is cold this time of the year. Where did you stay--London?"

As a matter of fact, I stayed at a manor house in the fifteenth century, in the middle of summer. "No, north of London, near Oxford. You're right, it was cold," she lied. Frantically, she searched her mind for a fresh topic. "What history do you teach at the University?"

"English history. And yes, I know the usual argument. How can you make a living teaching history? Well, I make a pretty good living at it, besides enjoying the profession." He looked up as the waiter brought their orders. "Now, tell me about your trip. Of course, England is chock-full of things to see and do. Been there a few times myself."

"It was an unusual vacation, I'll say that much." She pushed the paella around on her plate and licked her bottom lip. "I lived at a manor house, learning how people lived in the fifteenth century."

"Oh, a study program! Now, that is interesting. I've participated in study programs, also. Spent several weeks in England and Scotland. Now--"

"Are you from Miami, Mr. Farrell, or should I say Professor Farrell?"

"Just say Mark. No, I'm from Cincinnati. But--"

"Do you miss Ohio?" She dipped her fork into the rice, glancing up at him.

"The cold and snow? Not on your life. And give up trying to change the subject, because I want to hear about your vacation, especially this manor house."

"Well, I guess the house was typical of the fifteenth century, made of creamy stone with a pretty oriel window in front, a tiled floor downstairs, stone steps...." She sipped her iced tea, then set the tall glass down....

"So," she said a few minutes later, "I enjoyed my stay in England--" A lie; she was worried out of her mind the entire time--"but it's good to be back in Miami." She spoke quickly. "You like your job at the University?"

"Wouldn't teach if I didn't enjoy it." Mark set his glass of burgundy back on the table. "One more question. Do you have a boyfriend?"

"No, what about you?"

"No boyfriend for me, either."

She laughed. "You know what I mean."

"Let's just say I have no entangling alliances. So why don't we do something this weekend. You don't work on Sunday, do you?"

"No, not on Sunday." Now that she gave it some thought, it might be good for her to see this man now and then, if that's what he wanted. Galan hadn't made any commitment to her.

"--lots of things to do on Sunday," Mark was saying, "Movies, the beach...."

"Does the zoo sound too crazy? I always enjoy seeing the animals."

He looked surprised. "The zoo, then. Sounds like fun. Now give me your address and telephone number...."

Back home that evening, Stevie had second thoughts about accepting a date with Mark Farrell. In her bedroom, she undressed, tossing her cotton blouse, bra, and panties into the clothes hamper, then made her way to the bathroom to take a shower. It was only a date, after all. She didn't intend to marry the guy.

What if Galan discovered she was seeing another man? She paused as she lathered soap on her right arm. Hey, a little bit of jealousy might be a good thing. Right, she thought, soaping her left arm, working on down to her stomach and legs. Jealousy might be a very good thing.

\* \* \* \*

For days, Galan had purposely stayed away from Stevie, missing her so much, aching to see her again. She was safe now, and he must let her go, but he had to see her one more time, if only to say good-bye. Good-bye. The word resounded in his brain like a death knell. While darkness hung over the city and a breeze lifted his lace curtains, he stalked his living room, every thought, every wish, every dream of her.

During this time away from her, he'd visited vampire friends and acquaintances throughout the world, trying to discover--in a devious way, of course--if any of them knew of an elixir that would restore one of the undead to mortality. And found nothing.

Let Stevie go, then, and God forbid that she should feel duty-bound to stay with him out of gratitude. Best to convince her he'd found another woman to love, one of his own kind. He paused, gazing out the window, a knife twisting inside him.

He'd call her tonight and visit her. After that, he'd be out of her life forever.

\* \* \* \*

"Funny, you've been to my place lots of times, but I've never seen yours." Stevie sat next to Galan in her living room, breathless after his kisses, wanting only to stay in his arms but wondering if she could ever have a real, lasting relationship with him. On the edge of her consciousness, she thought about Mark. Could he ever replace Galan?

"You would like to see my house?" Galan said, drawing back in surprise.

"If it's no trouble."

"No trouble, and I assure you," he said with a wry smile, "I have no dead bodies in the closet."

"Well, I never thought that!" Not true. Since learning he was a vampire, she'd filled her mind with questions and weird images about him. Most important, where did he sleep? In a coffin, no doubt.

Over five minutes later, they drove up to a two-story stucco house in an old, pleasant neighborhood with oaks, palms, and ficus trees lining both sides of the street. Stevie made a mental note of his address, glad that most Miami suburbs had an easy street identification system, numbering each street instead of naming them.

"My home," he said as he helped her out of the car. "No ghosts, no monsters."

A brick walk lined with variegated lariope led to the front door, and he opened the door with just the wave of his hand.

She looked at him in shock. "You don't lock your door?"

"It was locked, but I don't need a key to open it." Galan smiled. "I have magical powers, remember? My part-time housekeeper is the only person who has a key." He indicated a pile of bricks at the side of the house. "Except for a spare key the previous owners gave me, which I keep under those bricks."

Darkness enclosed the house as they entered, but a flick of the wall switch produced a mellow glow from a Tiffany stained glass table lamp. Stevie's gaze covered the large living room with its enormous beige sofa and two matching chairs, plus a long glass-covered coffee table and a couple of end tables with lamps on each.

Envy made her catch her breath. She wished she owned a place like this.

"I bought the house several years ago," Galan explained by her side," and the furnishings came with it." He nodded toward a Monet. "The paintings are mine, all original."

"Wow! They must be worth a fortune."

"Indeed."

Her gaze made another sweep of the room. "Very nice." And it was. What had she expected--a haunted mansion with cobwebs in the corners and a decayed body in a rocking chair, a la Tony Perkins?

"Sit down, won't you. Can I get you something to drink? Wine?"

She sank onto the sofa, loving the deep cushions, its luxurious feel. "Beer?"

"Tuborg. Only wait whilst I fetch it from the refrigerator, then I'll get my wine from the bar."

He returned a few minutes later with a mug of foaming beer and handed it to her, then headed toward his bar between the living room and dining room.

Wine glass in hand, he sat beside her. "Merlot," he said, raising the glass.

Galan cleared his throat. He must lie to her now, tell her he no longer cared for her, that he'd found a vampiress to replace her. With no hope of mortality--for he knew finding the elixir was a lost cause--he must walk out of her life, never to see her again, to touch her, hold her in his arms, cover her face with kisses. His heart was breaking, but she must not see his sorrow.

With gentle fingers, he brushed a strand of hair from her cheek and studied her face, storing each feature in his memory. "Stevie, I've been thinking about us, and--"

Her face lit up. "Oh?"

He spoke in a rush of words. "I think it is best if we stay apart, only mingle with our own kind."

"What are you saying?" She jerked back, wringing her hands.

Her pained expression tore at his insides, but he plunged ahead. "You know we could never achieve lasting happiness, never have children or a real marriage."

She sat up straight, a look of hurt bewilderment on her face. "That's what you really want--never to see each other again?"

"It's for the best. Besides, I should tell you I have found one of the undead to love, a vampiress I have known for several hundred years, and--"

"You what!" Her flushed face devastated him, and he knew this scene would torture him for the rest of his life.

"Let me finish. Does that give you some idea of the differences that separate us? I am almost one-thousand years old, and this woman is nearly as old as I. It is only recently that I came to appreciate her charms--"

"So all the time I was in England, out of your way, when you were supposedly hunting Rosalinda--"

"I was hunting Rosalinda, and my friend killed her, as I told you." His stomach knotted, her agonized look tearing him to pieces. "But lately I renewed my relationship with this vampiress and realized how much she means to me."

He gazed at her lovely face, hating himself for causing her such distress, hating himself for what he was. "So this is good-bye."

Chapter Nineteen

The frosty morning air sent shivers along Stevie's arms and legs as she headed past her living room sofa, then on outside to get the Miami Herald. The grass was wet and cold beneath her slippered feet, and she shuddered, tightening her terry cloth robe around her. Her gaze drifted upward, where Orion glittered like a diamond bracelet in an amethyst sky, and a quarter moon hung low in the west. A strong wind rustled the leaves of the grapefruit tree and sent her orchid baskets swinging on the branches.

Thoughts of Galan brought a lump to her throat, an ache in her heart. What was he doing now? Sleeping with his newfound lover, no doubt. She wished it didn't hurt so much.

Never depend on anyone. When would she ever learn her lesson?

Back inside, she slipped the newspaper from its cellophane bag, glancing at the headlines as she padded toward an easy chair in her fluffy bedroom slippers.

MORE VAMPIRE MURDERS, the headline blared.

She flopped onto the chair and lowered her head to fight her dizziness, the room spinning around her. Her hands shook as she pressed them to her hot cheeks. Galan had said he didn't kill criminals, but how could she believe a word he said? For months, he'd deceived her, pretending to be mortal. Vampire. Like a curse, the word richoted in her brain, making her clutch the armrest until her fingers turned white.

Memories of Galan swamped her, his ebony eyes, his mysterious half-smile, but more than anything, his kisses and caresses, his love words. She'd never forget him, no matter how long she lived, even if she married another man.

\* \* \* \*

After another lonely night of wandering the streets of Miami, Galan drove up to his house as the rising sun lit the eastern horizon with a fiery glow. The Robellini palms thrashed in the wind, and a discarded paper cup scudded along his concrete driveway, resonating like cannon salvos to his extra sensitive hearing. Merde! He kicked the cup aside. Slovenly mortals! A neighbor's windchimes clanged in the wind, sounding as if all the cathedral bells of Paris were ringing at the same time, prompting him to cover his ears to shut out the horrendous noise.

Hours later, as darkness crept over the city, he descended the carpeted stairs to the living room, his steps slow and halting. Images of Stevie taunted him, like a moth that continually beats against a lampshade. Everything about her returned to torture him--her flowing blonde hair, those lustrous topaz eyes, her sweet yet husky voice, the beguiling touch of her hand that could make him forget everything but her.

From his bar, he fetched a bottle of Merlot and poured himself a glass, then returned to the living room. Trying to expel Stevie from his mind, he sat in a wing chair and opened the Herald. MORE VAMPIRE MURDERS. By all the saints, no! The newspaper fell to the floor, forgotten, as he sat forward with his elbows on his knees to rest his head in his hands.

Who was behind all these killings? No need to ask. Moloch, damn the son of a bitch! Galan clenched his hands at his side. By St. Aidan, he wanted to destroy the bastard! Now Stevie would think he, Galan, was killing these unfortunate men, and he wanted--no--needed her to have only pleasant memories of him. Anger pulsed inside him, like a thousand pounding drums, reaching an explosive crescendo. He gulped his wine, his fury fiercer with each passing second.

Damn it! He grabbed a book from an end table and hurled it across the room, where it hit a far wall and bounced back onto the floor with a hard thud. He waited countless seconds, then gulped the remainder of his wine as he tried to rein in his temper.

Empty wine glass in hand, he paced the floor, determined to assure her of his innocence, too well aware he was using a convenient excuse to see her again. By the blessed Virgin, he couldn't stay away from her, this woman who haunted his dreams, each night without her a torment. He'd visit her this night, counting the minutes until he'd see her again. See her again ... and then spend eternity without her.

His mind made up, he drove to her apartment. An unfamiliar car in the driveway ignited a fresh rush of fury inside him. Possibly the family she rented from had a visitor, but every sense within him refuted that wish.

If it were a man, he'd kill him, rip into his subclavian vein and drain all the blood from the bastard's body. Inside the car, he gripped the steering wheel as his anger became a tangible entity, pounding inside his brain, urging him to kill, kill, kill!

He slid out of the car and slammed the door shut, then strode toward the apartment.

* * * *

At the small kitchen table, Stevie set a piece of chocolate cake and a cup of coffee in front of Mark, then took a seat opposite him.

He sampled the cake, smiling in appreciation. "A great ending to a delicious meal. Did you bake this yourself?"

She laughed. "From a mix. Does anyone bake a cake from scratch anymore?"

"Well, it sure tastes good, no matter--"

A knock at the door stopped him in mid-sentence. Her face set in a neutral mask, Stevie placed her linen napkin by her plate and slid her chair back. "Go ahead and eat. I'll be only a minute. Might be someone from church."

First checking through the peephole to see who it was, she gasped before opening the door. "Galan, what a surprise." Of all times, why had he come now? What about the vampiress he professed to love? She stood back for him to enter, fixing a look of indifference on her face.

Without a word, he stepped inside, his mouth twisted in a grimace as his gaze lit on Mark.

She motioned toward the other man. "Mark, I'd like you to meet an acquaintance." She stressed the last word.

Her gaze shifted from one to the other as Mark rose from the table and came forward, looking hesitant, as if unsure whether to greet the visitor or shove him out the door. She made the introductions, well aware each man sized the other up.

Mark winced as Galan shook his hand, making her wince. Damn Galan! What was he so mad about? His eyes radiated malice, a muscle jerking at his jaw. Raw anger and energy vibrated from him, like a tiger poised to pounce on its prey. He finally released Mark's hand, and a whoosh of relief escaped her mouth.

"Mark's a history professor at the University of Miami," Stevie said, trying to relieve the tension.

Galan's expression was glacial. "I see."

Stevie observed the look of shocked puzzlement on Mark's face and knew repercussions would result from this night's encounter.

With one last glare, Galan spun on his heel and strode toward the door. "I shall come at another, more opportune time."

She glanced from one man to the other. "Oh, but don't think you have to--"

"I said, I shall come some other time."

\* \* \* \*

Which he did, the following night.

He burst into Stevie's apartment. "Who is he?"

"Who do you think you are, barging in here like this?" she snapped. "Some avenging angel? Or devil," she muttered under her breath. But he heard her words. And ignored them.

"Just answer my question."

"Don't you remember?" she said with acid sarcasm. "I introduced you to him."

He splayed his fingers through his hair. "Yes, yes, I know. But what does he mean to you?"

"What's it to you? You've found someone else, and it's just as well we stay with our own kind--your words, in case you forgot." She indicated an easy chair. "Come on, let's sit down. If we're going to argue, we might as well make ourselves comfortable." She plopped down on the sofa across from him, arms folded across her chest, a scowl on her face.

"I'm not arguing," he insisted.

"You could've fooled me."

He rested his hands in his lap, hoping to present a placid appearance, although he seethed inside. "How do you know he's a university professor? He may be a rapist or murderer, for all you know. This city is full of evildoers."

"Well, look who's talking."

"I have committed no evil, and I have ever been honest."

"Sorry, my mistake," she said with a derisive smirk. "You only feed on innocent people."

"Not innocent. Criminals, every one of them."

"That's not for you to decide," she replied with a shake of her head. "A man is innocent until proven guilty. I seem to recall we had this discussion once before at the restaurant."

"You don't see the things I see--the murders, the rapes, the child molestation."

Stevie frowned. "How do you see all these things?"

"I am a vampire, remember? I can come and go as I please with no fear of retaliation. Remember Nick, the homeless man who used to sleep by the New World Tower?"

She sat upright. "So you did kill him! I should have known you--"

"No, truly I did not kill him. But I saw him murder an old man for a few dollars the unfortunate victim carried in his pocket."

"I don't believe you."

Galan shrugged, resolved she wouldn't see how her mistrust hurt him. "Don't believe me, then, but I assure you it's true."

"Let's drop that for now." She paused, drawing her legs under her. "Something I've wondered about ever since you told me you're--" Her voice caught--"that you're a vampire. Why don't you feed off of animals?"

"I tried that at first. But I found I gained no strength or power from animal blood, that I barely existed. It would be akin to your living off of bread and water, only worse. I could not transport myself, and I lived in constant fear of detection." He clenched his hands as painful memories shuffled through his mind.

"Something else I must tell you, and you may find this difficult to believe, but there have been many vampires who so tired of immortality that they've committed suicide by exposing themselves to sunlight. A terrible way to die, I do assure you."

"What about you?" Stevie asked. "Do you want to become mortal again?"

"Once, but no longer," he lied. "The situation has changed, now that I have found one of my own kind to love."

"You two go feed together?" she asked with a bewildered expression.

"But of course! We must live off the blood of mortals."

"No!" She shook her head vigorously, her hair flying across her face. "No matter what you say, you don't have the right to feed off of people. You can still drink animal blood. So you lose some of your powers, so what? Why do you have to transport yourself from one place to another?"

Indignation welled inside him, but he forced himself to speak with cool precision. "You forget that's how I saved you from Rosalinda."

"Oh." She remained silent for a moment. "But if I'd never met you, I wouldn't have been in danger in the first place."

"So you are sorry you met me."

She rose from the sofa and paced the floor, a troubled expression on her pretty face. "Galan, we could argue about this forever and not get anywhere. The fact remains, you are what you are--a vampire. You've found someone else, someone of your own kind. Good. I'm happy for you. But don't expect me to approve of your ... your lifestyle."

He gazed up at her, aware she would never find lasting contentment with him, a vampire. Torn between love and desire for her happiness, he said nothing, for there was nothing to say.

She glanced his way. "So tell me something. Why'd you come here tonight? Your girlfriend's not available?"

Inwardly, he winced, never wanting her to see how her words pierced his soul. In her white jeans and light blue sweater, her blonde hair rippling down her back, she'd never looked so lovely, so desirable, the only woman he could ever love.

He found refuge in silence, for words became stuck in his throat.

She waved her hand at him. "And quit thinking you can pop in and out of my life whenever it pleases you, because I've got better things to do with my time...." She continued talking, each word a stake through his heart.

Galan wanted her now, this minute, as he'd never wanted anyone or anything in his long ill-begotten life, yes, even more than mortality. Willingly would he give up his wish to be human again if he could only make her his own. He trembled with his need for her, this woman he loved more than life.

The wounded look in her eyes, the sorrow etched on her face, told him her heart was breaking, as his was. Silent for a moment, she picked up an avocado vase and stared at it, as though she'd never seen it before; then she looked his way again.

"A bit of advice for you," she continued, aiming another disdainful look his way, "if you ever tire of your vampire girlfriend--and I'm sure you will, sooner or later--leave the mortal women alone. Better for everyone if you stay with your own kind...."

Her words struck him like lance thrusts, yet he couldn't remove his gaze from her. As if she were the most exquisite diamond, he studied her hand movements while she talked, those long elegant fingers, tipped with a rosy polish, every gesture elegant but controlled. She tucked her hair behind her ears, a familiar gesture of hers, graceful in its simplicity. Two bright spots of pink tinged her cheeks, evidence of her agitation. Even now, her voice had a sensual quality, low and husky. Her sweet-spicy scent tantalized him, reminding him of meadows and wildflowers of England, of everything he'd known and loved so long ago.

She was all he'd ever wanted in a woman.

But she wasn't his.

Never his.

All the beautiful things in life resided in her, her warmth and goodness, everything that made Stevie the woman he loved, the only woman he could ever care for. All he'd ever dreamed of but could never have was embodied in this unique woman, one he'd foolishly thought might want to share her life with his.

Her jeans hugged her body, revealing her slim waist, the curve of her hips, her tight derriere. His imagination soared in a hundred different directions, every byway leading to Stevie. Her cotton sweater revealed the tempting swell of her breasts, and passion flared inside him, a searing heat that swept over his body.

She stopped pacing and settled her gaze on him. "And I don't know why you came back to see me, because your presence--and your arguments--haven't accomplished anything. You won't convince me it's right to take human blood. You have your life and I have mine. So go back to your vampiress and leave me alone. I never want to see you again."

Chapter Twenty

On a balmy evening, Stevie returned with Mark from a dinner, and hand-in-hand, they strolled toward her apartment. Overhead, a quarter moon floated in a clear, starry sky, a light breeze whispering through the trees and bushes. She glanced sideways at Mark, and he met her look, a quick smile on his face. His good looks had an engaging quality, and his infectious grin was enough to tempt any woman ... almost any woman. She wished she could think only of him, but memories of Galan hounded her--his kisses, those obsidian eyes and warm smile, all the wonderful things that made him a man she could never forget.

Mark stopped by her front door and drew her toward him. She pressed closer in his embrace, hoping his kisses would blot out memories of someone else.

They didn't.

Easing away, he gave her a troubled look. "It's that other man, isn't it?"

"Who?" she asked, pretending ignorance.

"You know who--the guy who came to your place when I was there for dinner."

Stevie flicked her hand. "Take my word for it, he doesn't mean a thing to me. Oh, I'll admit we went together at one time, but we broke up because ... because our lifestyles were so different." She fingered the lapels of his brown wool jacket, giving him an appealing look. "Mark, these last few weeks with you have meant a lot to me. You're the nicest guy I've met in a long time. Can't we continue as we are? We're not making any lifelong commitment. So let's enjoy each other's company. Who knows? Maybe we just need time."

He captured her hand and squeezed it. "I'll settle for that."

After she said good-bye and stepped inside her living room, she tried to make herself believe her words to Mark. He was a nice guy; she was lucky to have met him. If they merely stayed friends, that was okay with her. In only a few months, she'd start at Barry University to study sociology, and for all she knew, she might not have time for any serious relationship.

Love and marriage were both far in her future.

So I'll just forget I ever knew Galan, she vowed as she unbuttoned her white rayon blouse and headed for her bedroom.

* * * *

As dusk cloaked the city and Venus heralded the night, Galan found a letter from his editor waiting for him. Striving for nonchalance, he sat down beside his coffee table and slit the letter open.

"...an eminent writing style," the editor wrote. "You make the battle scene and the events preceding the battle come alive, as if you'd actually fought at Hastings."

Legs stretched out, Galan read on. "...an advance of $100,000. Both The Book-of-The-Month Club and its subsidiary, The History Book Club, want to feature your book, and their sponsorship should greatly increase your sales."

He studied the check: one-hundred thousand dollars, an amount that meant nothing to him. Money can't buy happiness, as the mortals always said. If he had Stevie with him--ah, what he would do with the money. He'd take her to London, Paris, Rome, and Prague. They would stay at the most exclusive hotels, eat at the finest restaurants, and yes, she could shop at the finest boutiques, an activity he knew all ladies enjoyed, whether vampire or mortal.

He tossed the letter onto the table and stared out the window.

Why wish for the impossible?

Clenching his hands, his mind switched to Moloch. The fiend had summoned him to Schloss Omerau, a message delivered by one of the demon's creatures. It was a demand he couldn't ignore, for if he did, it would only endanger Stevie. Galan felt sure the command dealt with her, and he agonized over what evil Moloch was devising now. God, please protect Stevie.

\* \* \* \*

"You betrayed me. You agreed to stay away from the mortal woman once she recovered from her affliction." Moloch pointed a skeletal finger at Galan. "You went back on your word."

"She was in danger and still suffering from her illness when I rescued her," Galan said, facing the demon across the trestle table. "I had to save her from Rosalinda." And now he must save Stevie from Moloch. But how?

Outside, a winter storm raged, and dry snowflakes blasted through the wide open windows. A stiff wind whipped the tapestry on the wall, all but tearing it from its hanging.

Moloch's eyes shone like black daggers, probing, seeking, never leaving Galan's face. "You think I didn't know that Rosalinda had captured the mortal woman. Of course I knew. If she had died--and I wish she had--it would be no great loss."

"You bastard!"

Moloch slammed his hand on the table. "I've had enough of your impertinence. Don't try my patience too far." He gave Galan a hard look. "As for your own imprisonment, I knew about that, too."

"Then why--?"

"Because I wanted to test your mettle, see how much suffering you could take. I won't consider a coward to head the Society."

His mind reeling, Galan stared at him. "So you left me in the dungeon, later exposed to the sun, to die a horrible death."

"If Octavius hadn't saved you, I would have," the fiend said with a negligent wave of his hand. "You weren't out in the sun very long, scarcely long enough to burn your skin." He scowled. "As for the human, this is your last warning. I'm ordering you to stay away from that woman."

"Not if she's in danger."

"Who cares if the slut dies?"

"You son of a bitch!" Galan kicked a table leg. "Damn you, I care! We made an agreement--did we not?--that I would leave her alone if no danger imperiled her."

Moloch smiled, thin lips pushing back his cheeks into deep wrinkles. "I've not imperiled her. But if others want to harm her, I'll not stand in their way." He sat back in his chair and folded his arms across his gaunt chest, looking for all the world as if he were discussing a business arrangement, or giving a benediction.

"Then the hell with you!" Galan scoffed. "Find someone else to supervise your Godforsaken Society of the Undead. I'll have no part of it." His jaw clenched as he spun away to leave the hall, striding along the stone floor past the open windows.

"...all manner of hideous deaths," Moloch called after him. "How would you like to see her suffer on the rack, to have her body torn apart until she's a helpless mass? Or to be burned at the stake, where you can smell her roasting flesh?" He chuckled. "I assure you she'd take hours to die. You understand me?"

Slowly, Galan turned around, his shoulders sagging. Misery stalked every cell of his body, but he must protect Stevie with his life. "Very well. It shall be as you say. I'll stay away from the mortal woman."

Galan's despair deepened. Would the fiend keep his word? No need to ask.

* * * *

As he observed Galan leaving the hall, Moloch remained at the table, drumming his fingers, his long sharp nails tapping on his wide belt. Click, click. Despite pretending otherwise, he liked Galan's impertinence, his grit, his determination. Galan had guts, a necessary qualification for dealing with the nightwalkers throughout the world. The young man had tenacity, too, a trait not to be disregarded. If only he would forget this stupid mortal woman...

Moloch reached for a crystal flagon to pour a glass of red wine, fed up with the mortal woman, a constant disruption to his peace of mind, like a stake aimed at his heart. He would destroy her himself, but not now ... later. Let Galan be lulled into a false sense of security. Let him think she was safe. Then her destruction would be so much more satisfying.

Soon, he'd get rid of her, torture her while she begged for mercy, watch with pleasure as it took her hours to die. But how? Thinking hard, he rested his head in his chin. Should he stretch her on the rack until all her bones broke and she screamed in agony, or should he hang her upside down while he held a flaming torch to her face?

A speck of dust on the table irritated him, and he brushed his fingers across the table, then returned to his joyous musing. His hand trembled with anticipation, the wine spilling down the side of the glass, onto the table. He could hardly wait to kill the mortal woman.

## Chapter Twenty-one

The last deadly rays of sunlight thrust through the window blinds as Galan slept in his coffin, oblivious to the sights and sounds of the mortal world.

He awoke, and after pushing the coffin lid up, he stepped out and opened his closet door as darkness covered the room and sounds of the mortal world blasted in his ears. Two foxes prowled a porch three houses down, their footsteps on the wooden planks sounding like a herd of elephants to his acute hearing, their squeaky squeals thundering like a foghorn in his ears.

Smells, too, became magnified within his bedroom. The fragrance of smoke and barbecued beef floated his way while someone down the street presided over an outdoor barbecue. Hunger roared inside him, a powerful reminder he must go feed this night.

He clutched the doorknob as impossible dreams and futile wishes raged within him. Like a comatose human, he slumped against the closet door, his need for Stevie a burning ache, infinitely more intense than his hunger for sustenance, yes, even greater than his desire for mortality.

A long sigh of despair escaped him as he sank onto the bed and leaned forward, his hands locked between his knees, too well aware he must never forget Moloch, a continual danger to his beloved.

Enough brooding. Now he must--

Galan sat upright. "Octavius!"

"Lilith is visiting friends, so I thought this would be a good time to visit you." In his long white robe, the maverick drifted across the room and sat in an easy chair next to the bed, crossing his legs. "You've been much on my mind lately."

Galan smiled. "Is that meant as a compliment, or am I about to get a lecture?"

"Neither, but...." He paused, a grin brightening his face. "Is it still true you wish for mortality?"

Galan sprang from his chair. "Octavius, what have you heard?"

Octavius spoke with exactitude, as if imparting a secret, which he was. "After all this time, I finally have some good news for you. Word has reached me--never mind the source--of a former vampire who, like you, hates Moloch for what that fiend did to him. He is human now, has a wife and family. Another thing-- and this is what you wanted to know--he holds the secret of mortality. Not very many of our kind know about him."

Opening and closing his fists, Galan gave him a steady look, his voice rising. "What is his name? Where does he live?"

Brow furrowed, his visitor pressed a hand to his forehead. "Name's Roger Dorsey, lives in New York City. Number Five Empire Towers. Here's his phone number," he said, handing him a paper. "Oh, by the way, don't worry about Moloch following you. He's busy initiating a neophyte vampire, which is why I came to you now."

"Does Moloch know about this man?" Galan asked.

Octavius shook his head. "Much as Moloch likes to think he can control all the undead of the world, there are a few that fall through the cracks, as the saying goes. But believe me, Dorsey is aware of Moloch."

Galan paced the length of his room. Happiness welled inside him, more potent than an army of vampires, more beguiling than a lover's smile. Mortality! He stopped by his friend. "Octavius, should I become mortal again--and I pray that I shall--let that not end our friendship. I would hope to see you from time to time."

A stunned look came over Octavius, then a slow grin took its place. "Friendship between a vampire and a mortal? Nothing surprises me anymore." Octavius stood, fingers combing his golden locks. "I must leave you now. Time to fetch Lilith so we can feed together."

Galan smiled. "Thank you, my friend. I can never tell you what this means to me."

But he was speaking to an empty room.

Euphoria welled inside Galan, his hunger forgotten. But wait--what would Moloch do to Stevie if he gained mortality? The fiend's ghastly threats surfaced, a continual torment. He shook his head, unable to think clearly, his main consideration to protect his beloved. Go visit this man first, he decided, and see what he says.

That settled, he closed his eyes in deep concentration, and within seconds, he arrived in New York, amid the razzle-dazzle of Times Square. Reluctant to appear at the man's doorstep unannounced, he decided to phone him first, and within minutes, found a phone booth.

Three rings later, a man answered the phone. "Hello."

Galan scratched his chin. How best to introduce himself? "Sir, you don't know me, but we have a mutual friend--Octavius."

An indrawn breath, then silence. Finally: "Who is this?"

"My name is Galan Kent, and I assure you I mean you no harm. Rather, I have a favor to ask of you. May I visit you to discuss this favor?"

"I want nothing to do with you," the man replied in a voice full of anguish. "I put that former life--or death--behind me."

Galan paused. "Yet I understand you have certain knowledge that may prove beneficial to me, a secret you must share with others who want to follow in your steps."

Another long moment of silence. "Very well. You may visit me, but I make no promises. I shall inform the security guard you're coming. Do you need directions?"

Galan managed to keep his voice even. "That won't be necessary."

More seconds later, he reached the man's apartment on the fifth floor of a magnificent red brick building, twenty stories high. He knocked on the front door, preferring to approach him the mortal way, rather than make a sudden appearance, vampire style, inside the room.

The door opened. "Mr. Kent, come in." Tall, with gray hair and a trim build, Dorsey looked to be in his late forties. He had a low, pleasant voice with a slight French accent, prompting Galan to wonder why he resided in the United States. In a slate blue cashmere sweater and charcoal wool gabardine trousers, he exuded an air of wealth and distinction.

Galan stepped inside a spacious apartment, decorated in shades of rose and aqua, with here and there a dash of yellow. A lovely abode, tastefully done. Not bad for a former vampire.

"Mr. Dorsey, I can't tell you how much I appreciate--"

"Sir," Roger Dorsey said, raising his hand, "you must understand that it is only because of Octavius that I agreed to see you. You spoke of knowledge I have, knowledge that may prove useful to you. But for all I know, you may have come under false pretenses. Perhaps the leader of the undead--"

"Moloch? Believe me, Mr. Dorsey, he has no idea I'm here. I do assure you once more that my interest is sincere. I shall tell you frankly that I want to become mortal again. That is my greatest wish."

Dorsey gestured toward a chair. "Sit down, won't you, and may I get you a drink? Wine, perhaps?"

"Nothing, thank you." About to sit down, Galan paused as a pretty woman of forty or so walked into the room. Clad in beige linen slacks with a matching silk blouse, her light brown hair drawn into a chignon, she looked every bit as sophisticated as her husband.

Roger Dorsey slid his arm around the woman's waist. "My wife," he said, "and the reason I turned away from ... from all that I was."

After the introductions, Galan settled himself in a wing chair, Dorsey and his wife sitting opposite on the sofa. "The same with me," Galan said. "I have yearned for mortality for a long time, but it is only recently, since I met a human woman, that my wish has taken on an urgency."

"Which brings us back to my doubts," Dorsey said. "Why should I believe you? Moloch--how I hate that fiend!--has his spies. You may well be one of them. I'm sure he'd do anything to obtain the secret of mortality, if only to destroy the concoction."

"Sir, I--"

"So how do I know you can be trusted?" he asked on a desperate note. "Going on the assumption you mean us no harm, I agreed to see you. Yet you must realize I'm taking a big risk."

Galan spread his hands wide. "What can I say to convince you? All I can tell you is that I mean every word I say ... from the bottom of my heart."

For the first time, Dorsey's wife spoke up. "Darling, have you forgotten that you've retained your psychic powers? Surely you can tell if you can trust our visitor--"

Dorsey waved his hand dismissively. "I've tried to put every aspect of that previous life behind me. My psychic ability causes me more misery than joy. I want only to live a normal life." He nodded toward Galan. "As for this gentleman, already I'm wondering if we may have to move, to escape Moloch's clutches once he discovers where we live."

Galan held his hands out. "Sir, I swear to you that I mean you no harm. I hate Moloch as much as you do. You must believe me!"

Touching his arm, Dorsey's wife spoke again. "Honey, please, just this once."

He sighed heavily. "Very well. Mr. Kent, hand over your keys, anything of yours that I can touch and hold."

"Of course." Galan dug into his pants pocket and handed over his gold pocket watch.

Eyes closed, Dorsey held the watch for a long moment, turning it over in his hand, his fingers covering the entire surface. A myriad of expressions played across his face, then a slow smile appeared, and he opened his eyes again. "Ah, yes, we can trust him. Very good." He handed the watch back to Galan. "Mr. Kent, I see now you're not lying, that you truly wish for mortality."

"I can't tell you how much it means to me that you put your faith in me," Galan said, returning the watch to his pocket.

"Sorry I doubted you, but you have to understand why I must be cautious." Dorsey tapped his fingers on his thigh. "One mission I shall ask of you first which is no easy matter. Destroy Moloch, eliminate him once and for all so he can no longer endanger another mortal."

"But--"

"Mr. Kent, let me finish. Should have done this long ago. Always regretted that I never eliminated the fiend."

"What does he matter to you now?" Galan asked. "I mean, if you are mortal, and you know I won't betray you--"

"Revenge, mainly, for what he did to my loved ones and to me," he said, his voice choking. "Killed my first wife and young son before transforming me into a vampire. There! First time I've used that word 'vampire' in a long, long time." As if lost in memory, he stared off into space, then slowly returned his gaze to his visitor. "For the present, I am safe from him. He doesn't know where I live. Even though I became mortal twenty years ago, it's been a constant worry how long I'll remain safe, for, as you know, time means nothing to the undead. Others, too, might betray me."

He cast a loving glance at his wife. "If he ever found out about me, it would be just like that demon to go after the very ones I hold most dear--my wife, two sons, and a daughter. I could not bear it if any harm came to them. But more important, we must protect other humans from his evil influence. So get rid of that demon and come back with proof of his destruction. Then, and only then, will I give you a potion that will restore you to mortality."

Galan suffered a barrage of doubts and emotions. "You are asking me to destroy--"

"--a monster! Moloch has ruined so many lives. He must not be permitted to exist."

Galan switched topics. "This potion...."

"The effects of this elixir are truly painful--mortifying, if I may use that word. Many who have taken it have not been able to bear the pain, finally driving a stake through their own heart to end their agony. And once you swallow this concoction, you cannot undo its effect. There is no antidote."

"I see." Galan clenched his hands in his lap. He considered the enormity of all he must do. Eliminate Moloch. Thou shalt not kill. For centuries, he'd refrained from killing any beings, mortal or vampire. Now, in order to become mortal again, he must murder his nemesis. Kill him in cold blood. Cold blood, he repeated to himself. The irony of those last words taunted him, their veracity a painful reminder of his vampirism, of what he must remain if he failed to get rid of the monster.

No matter that Moloch was evil, that he deserved to perish, Galan didn't know how he could lower himself to the demon's level. But if he didn't get rid of him, he, Galan, would remain a vampire throughout eternity, destined to exist only in the world of the undead, never to see Stevie again.

By all that was holy, what should he do?

\* \* \* \*

Stevie sat with Mark on the sofa, his arm around her waist, his look deep with longing. He drew her closer to kiss her.

She tried, oh, she tried, to lose herself in his kiss, to enjoy the taste and touch of him, especially after the wonderful time they'd shared on their date this evening. But another man intruded on her efforts, a man with dark hair and ebony eyes, his face etched with harsh lines and sharp angles. A man who could tempt her with just a look.

After long moments, Stevie eased away, knowing she couldn't deceive Mark any longer, couldn't pretend something she didn't feel.

A look of hurt bewilderment crossed his face. "Stevie, what is it?"

"Mark, I...."

"No, you don't need to tell me." He gave her a sharp look. "It's someone else, isn't it? The guy who came here to your apartment." He smirked. "Barged in is more like it. Frankly, Stevie, I don't understand what you see in him."

I see his basic goodness, she wanted to say. I see the most wonderful man in the world, one I can never have, because he's not even human. A man I will always love.

She sighed. "Mark, I think it's best if we stop going together and--"

"God, is that what you really want? Never to be with each other again? Is that all I mean to you?"

She twisted her fingers in her lap. "It's because you mean a lot to me that I think we should break off--"

"You're not even making sense." With one quick movement, he pulled at his tie, jaw clenched, his hand shaking.

"Just listen to me." She ran her finger across his shirt collar, but he jerked back. Licking dry lips, she tried to hide her hurt. "It's not fair to you for me to continue to see you, when I lo--when there's someone else on my mind. Believe me, I appreciate all the good times we've had, and I'll always remember you, but--"

"Well, thanks a lot!"

"--but let's make a clean break of it, with no hard feelings."

"Right! If that's the way you want it." With one last angry glance, he sprang from the sofa and stormed out of her apartment.

After the door slammed behind him, Stevie remained motionless for a long time, pressing her hand to her throbbing forehead. She wanted to cry for all she'd lost, for a good man she'd never see again. Still, she knew she'd done the right thing, knew it wasn't fair to string Mark along when he'd never be more than a special friend.

She stared around the room, trying to absorb its restful atmosphere, to expel Mark's harsh words from her mind. Hoping to distract herself, she inhaled the nutmeg scent of a phalenopsis on the coffee table, one of the orchids Galan had given her. A hundred memories swamped her. Why couldn't she forget him? What would she gain by thinking about him all the time?

She slipped off her black slingbacks and stretched her stockinged feet out on the wide coffee table. Her glance flew to her porcelain rabbits--gifts throughout the years--that had finally found a home in a one-shelf pine bookcase she'd recently bought at a yard sale. Unable to shrug off Mark's bitter words, his hurt looks, she unbuttoned the tiny mother-of-pearl buttons of her blue silk dress, then pulled her gold-plated ear rings off, dropping them into her lap. She went through these movements with careful precision, as though to pretend everything was normal, as if her heart wasn't breaking.

Aren't you glad Galan's out of your life? her brain challenged. Liar! her heart cried. She missed him every minute of every day. He's out of your life, her brain repeated. Time she got used to his absence.

Carried on a wave of despair, she gathered up her shoes and ear rings and headed for her bedroom. It was getting late, and she was going to the early church service tomorrow, so--

The phone rang, yanking her from her reverie. Alarm froze her steps. It was after midnight. Something had happened to her father! More likely a wrong number, she prayed as she retraced her steps and set her shoes and ear rings on the coffee table. The phone rang again.

Her hands shook as she picked up the receiver. "Hello."

"Ah." A low, hissing sound came over the phone, like a snake that's zeroed in on its prey. The sound increased, as if a thousand starving snakes were trapped in a pit. The temperature in the room dropped, or was that only her imagination?

She gripped the receiver. "Who is this?"

Another hiss. "Don't you know?"

Chills raced down her neck and back, then along her arms, down to her fingertips. Warily, she looked around the room as her eyes focused on every corner. Her breath came in shallow gasps, her hand pressed to her stomach. A cold sweat broke out on her forehead. She exhaled slowly. She would not let the fiend sense her fear.

The hand that held the receiver trembled, but she spoke with determination. "Hey, you scumbag, why don't you meet me face to face?"

"I intend to. You won't get away from me now," the scratchy voice warned. "This time tomorrow, you'll be dead."

## Chapter Twenty-two

Send the mortal woman to hell--tonight!

Moloch raised the lid of his casket and climbed out, his fingers gripping the edges, skeletal feet touching the stone floor. He stepped into his short leather boots and strode toward the trestle table to pour a goblet of burgundy as problems crammed his mind, especially the mortal bitch. Galan had promised to leave her alone, but what assurance did he have the nightwalker would keep his word?

The wind tossed Moloch's bushy hair about his face as he drained his goblet, resolved to settle the matter of the mortal woman once and for all. Hunger stalked his body, a fierce agony that demanded satisfaction now. His deprivation weakened him unbearably, but he would soon assuage his need ... with the human slut.

He stared off into space, fearful he'd consume all his remaining power in his journey across the ocean. Ah, but the lure was too great, his goal too enticing. His painful hunger would render her blood all the sweeter.

Diabolical delight pulsated inside him as he shoved the goblet aside, his hand shaking and knocking the goblet over, where it rolled to the floor and shattered into a hundred pieces. He pushed away from the table, the chair scraping on the flagged stone floor.

Time to kill the woman!

\* \* \* \*

Alone in her apartment, Stevie moved restlessly from one room to another, each room brightly lit at this late night hour. Terror courted her each step of the way. Her gaze covered every square foot, every corner of the living room. She continually checked behind the draperies and stared outside her window.

A thick haze hung over Miami, spawned by a widespread fire raging in the Everglades. Even inside her apartment, she smelled the smoke. The smog hindered her vision, so that she could scarcely see outside her windows, which only intensified her fear.

Since last night's phone call, one idea after another raced through her brain. How can I defeat this monster? But maybe there was no danger at all. For all she knew, the call was only a malicious prank.

What if she phoned the police? Why, yes, she could hear herself now. "A man called last night and threatened to kill me. By the way, he's a vampire." Right.

No, face the fact that she must face the fiend. There was no escape. He would find her anywhere.

In her jeans and gray sweatshirt, she rubbed her arms and jumped at every nighttime noise--a neighbor's dog barking, loud music from a car whizzing past. A cold weight settled in her stomach. Chills raced down her arms, legs, and back. Perspiration sheened her forehead.

Well, no point in sitting around, waiting for the threat, she thought as she headed for the kitchen. After she slipped on plastic gloves, she grabbed bleach from under the sink and scrubbed the counter, pushing canisters, knife rack, and her CD player aside to sponge every inch of the kitchen space. The smell of the bleach made her eyes burn, and she rushed through the job, her hands shaking with agitation. Finished with the gas burners, she glanced at the wall clock. Hours remained before dawn.

She couldn't call Galan. He had his new love, no room in his life for her. On leaden feet, she made her way back toward the living room, where her gaze moved in all directions and focused on every corner. Would her skill in karate save her? She could hope. Without that skill, she'd be as helpless as a three-legged rabbit in a python pit. What about one of her sharp knives? She'd left a knife lying on the counter, just in case. A knife against a vampire? Hardly.

Forget the stupid phone call. Some people had a morbid sense of humor, and--

"Oh, no!" Horror flashed through her body when she saw the fiend. She raised ice-cold hands to her cheeks. "Please, God, no!" A tightness gripped her chest, sucking all the air from her lungs.

"You won't get away from me now." An old man in a long black robe approached from a far corner of the living room, his emaciated features chalk white, the same creep she'd seen before, the one who'd terrified her all these months. Here, in her apartment, now! A stench of decay clung to him, of sickness and death.

In an unconscious gesture of prayer, she pressed her hand to her heart. God, help me!

His face! Evil! His emaciated arm extended toward her, as if to gather her in a deadly embrace and crush all the life from her.

"You think you can escape me?" he snarled in his raspy voice. Long strands of tangled gray hair fell past his gaunt shoulders, like scraggly weeds on a mountainside. A large hooked nose jutted out from his narrow face, a face creviced with tiny wrinkles. His hands ended in talons, long, claw-like nails that made a clicking sound whenever he touched his fingers to his wide leather belt. Click, click. Gems studded his belt, flashing with every movement.

But his eyes, oh, God, his eyes! Narrowed and crafty, they were as black as the darkest night, his expression as brutal as a starving alligator. A pendant dangled from his neck, brilliant beams flickering in the bright lights.

She stepped backward, rubbing sweaty hands along her hips. Terror wrenched her stomach in knots. "You stay away from me!" His thin lips twisted into a sneer. "As if you can stop me!" Like a snake, his gaze slithered over her, teasing her, as though to say, I can kill you whenever I choose. He tapped his belt. Click, click.

Another step back almost tripped her over a magazine rack, but she caught herself in time. She had to reach the kitchen, had to get the knife.

Galan! she silently called. But she was on her own.

The fiend hissed, a cloud of steam exiting his mouth. "You have tried my patience enough." He ran a thick tongue along his bottom lip. Sharp teeth gleamed like daggers, his look like the bestial rage of an animal gone mad.

"What have I ever done to you?" she cried as she played for time. Desperation drummed inside her. If she could only divert him....

"Galan. You won't leave him alone." The words sprayed out like acid poison.

"I haven't seen Galan in ages."

"Don't lie to me." With taunting slowness, he inched closer.

"I'm not lying!" Another backward step, her aim to lure him into the kitchen. Her heart pounded against her ribs like a pile driver against concrete. Shivers shook her body, but she reached her destination, the knife in sight. She had to kill him, had to! She would not die, would not let him suck all the blood from her body.

She had so much to do, a life to live, friends and family she loved, people who loved her. This monster would not kill her. She wouldn't let him.

He laughed, that low, wheezy sound that chilled her like an ice cube against bare skin. "Don't think you can stop me."

"Oh, can't I?" she cried with false bravado. "Don't try me too far."

Shrieking with angry frustration, he lunged drunkenly for her, but she side-stepped and banged into the refrigerator, a hard jolt that sent mag notes tumbling to the floor.

Her breath came in gasps, every muscle tense. Nausea churned in her stomach, but damned if she'd let him see her fright.

"You stupid mortal woman, don't ever think I can't kill you. Soon you'll find you have no place to run to, no place to hide. You're no match for me."

"That's what you think." Strands of sweat-soaked hair fell in front of her eyes, hindering her vision. With shaky hands, she shoved the locks from her face. Please, God, give me strength.

The knife, get the knife! She rushed for the counter, her gaze on the back door. Let him think she was headed outside.

Almost there--

"You bitch!" The brute jerked her from behind, pulling her backwards. He sank his teeth into her neck, a sharp bite that sent alarm racing through every cell of her body. Skeletal hands held her in a firm grip. Scissorlike nails dug into her shoulders, scratching her skin. His fetid breath fouled the air, blowing across her shoulder like poison gas. Fear froze her reaction as he sucked on her neck and slowly drained the blood from her body.

Galan, please help me!

Desperation gave her strength. Raw power built inside her muscles and flowed throughout her body, growing stronger, stronger, stronger, until it reached a crescendo in which nothing was impossible. With the brazen assurance of a kamikaze pilot, she knew she would defeat him.

Karate class! Think, think! Frantic thoughts raced through her head. Heart thudding, she turned to her right. She pushed her hips back, and drove her elbow into his right side, forcing him to release her. Hurry, hurry, get him! She grabbed him by his right underarm and swung him past her hip, then onto the floor.

He jumped back up and spat at her face, bloody saliva scorching her skin like acid. Screaming with pain, she pressed her hand to her face. With a low growl of satisfaction, he took advantage of her weakness and clutched her again, twisting her arm behind her back.

Stevie raised her foot to wrap it around his leg, sending him backwards, forcing him to release her again. One foot flying out in front of her, she hit him full in the face.

He shrieked and reached for her again. "You little bitch! I'll get you yet."

"Oh, yeah? That's what you think!"

He headed for her, his hands shaking. She spun around, using the momentum to kick behind her again, this time knocking him to the floor, his head pounding against the hard tile.

Hands pressed to the floor, he tried to rise, but she kicked him again, in the face and the chest.

The demon screeched, a high-pitched sound that blasted from one end of the apartment to the other, louder than a thousand frenzied rats. Her hand trembling, she gripped the bottle of Clorox from the counter and splashed the liquid into his eyes, blinding him.

"Ahhh!" He writhed on the floor, banging his arms and legs on the tile. Gaunt fingers scraped at his eyes. Bloody saliva spilled from his mouth and stained his robe. Ear-splitting squeals came from his throat, like an injured animal.

Kill him now!

She seized the knife, but it fell from her slippery hands and clattered to the floor. She screamed with frustration.

Shivering all the way to her feet, she clasped the weapon again and plunged it into his heart. He lay still, the skin now burned from his face, revealing bony eye sockets, every skeletal feature. Had she killed him? She didn't know! She jerked the knife out and plunged it into his heart again and again, then dropped the weapon, certain she had destroyed him.

On her knees, she bowed her head while tremors shook her body. Her skin turned hot, then cold. Damp hair fell in front of her eyes. She raised a shaky hand to brush the locks away. She swallowed again and again, her stomach queasy.

Black shoes and dark trousers appeared within her vision, and a glance upward sent her heart leaping.

"Galan!"

He helped her rise to her feet, his look tender and comforting. "I heard you call me, but you've managed quite well by yourself." He gave her a puzzled look. "Tell me later how you defeated him. But he's not truly dead. Only an oaken stake through his heart will destroy him. Or burning. I'll take him outside to finish the job. You stay here," he said, glancing her way. "No reason for you to see. Best you lie down."

After he retrieved a box of matches from the counter and slipped it into his pocket, he dragged Moloch across the tile and headed for the back door.

Outside, he pulled the demon to a far corner of the yard, where the monster's body scraped against the grass, the pendant bouncing across his chest. With one quick look around, Galan glimpsed a tool shed behind the house next door. It took a scant moment to transport himself to the shed and fetch a gallon of gasoline, then return. Bending over, he jerked the pendant from Moloch's neck and pocketed it, then splashed the fuel on the fiend and lit a match. The vampire blazed and orange flames leaped to the sky, the stench of burning flesh filling the air, the smoke blending with the thick haze that hung over the city. Time lost all meaning as Galan waited, until only ashes remained.

He sighed heavily as he absorbed the reality of Moloch's demise. A medley of emotions roiled inside him, relief above all, but happiness, too, and especially such a fierce pride in Stevie. Reflecting on her courage, he could only shake his head in amazement. His Stevie. His dear one.

After he dispersed the pile of ashes with his foot, he returned the gasoline can and rushed back to Stevie. Inside the living room, his gaze covered the apartment, each room brightly lit. She sat on the sofa, her hands clenched in her lap, a stunned expression on her pretty face.

She glanced up as he approached. "Is he ... is he...?"

"Dead, thanks to you, sweeting. I merely finished the job." On a wave of tenderness, he stared down at her. "How in God's name did you overpower him?"

"Karate," she replied with a forced smile. "I always knew my lessons would come in handy some day."

Clad in jeans and a gray sweatshirt, she was lovelier than a queen in full regalia. His gaze roamed the length of her, to every feature he held dear, from the golden crown of hair, past the soft curves of her breast, on to moccasin-shod feet. He joined her on the sofa and took her in his arms, his fingers grazing her cheeks.

So proud of his beloved for defeating Moloch, he knew he must erase the memory of the fiend ... and of his own visit. God forbid that she should recall this confrontation for the rest of her life. Best she think he remained devoted to his--imaginary--vampiress lover, at least until he became mortal again ... if he ever did.

Whispered words and a light touch on her forehead removed all memory of the struggle. "Forget, Stevie ... forget you ever knew Moloch ... and sleep." Blue eyes fluttered closed, her head falling back. His heart swelled with love as he feathered kisses on her scratches, certain his touch would soon heal her skin. Gently, he lifted her from the sofa and carried her to the bedroom.

With every step, his heart cried out with love for her. A lilac scent lingered about her, an enthralling aroma that spawned a hundred memories of far-distant fields and meadows, of stately trees and meandering streams. Warm and soft, her body pressed against him, long blonde hair cascading over his arms. How dear she is, he mused, caught in the lure of her seductive face--the strands of silky hair, pink-tinged cheeks, inviting lips he ached to kiss again and again.

Unable to remove his gaze from her, he reached the bedroom and set her on the bed. Even then, he didn't want to leave. He wanted only to stay throughout the night and for all the nights to come. He sat beside her, staring at her for heart-filled moments, finally getting up to leave.

Reassurance that the danger was past--Moloch was destroyed!--overcame him, but sweet anticipation, too. The next time he saw Stevie, he would be mortal again.

God, he prayed, please let that happen soon.

* * * *

"The pendant," Galan said the next evening as he set the ornament on Roger Dorsey's oval coffee table. "I'm sure you remember Moloch always wore this around his neck." By itself, the pendant lay like a lump of glass, as lifeless as dirt.

"Ah, yes." The other man reached for it and held the pendant up to the light, then dropped it onto the floor as if it were red hot. He motioned for Galan to sit down. "How did you kill him?"

"Would you believe it was the mortal woman who overpowered him and rendered him unconscious," Galan said, settling into a wing chair. "Then--"

"How did she do that?" Dorsey asked in surprise.

Galan told him about Stevie's skill in karate, soon finishing the tale. "A remarkable woman," he murmured.

"Indeed she is." Dorsey threw him a sharp glance. "And you completed his annihilation? You're sure he's dead?"

"No doubt about it." Galan related the fiend's fiery death. "Eventually, only ashes remained, now carried away by the wind."

"Thank God!" Dorsey crossed himself. "I've waited centuries for his destruction." His eyes clouded over, as if a hundred sorrowful memories taunted him. "Blessed Virgin! I can breathe freely again. Never again need I worry about my family." He rose from the sofa, a smile creeping across his face. "Now I'll keep my end of the bargain." As he strode toward a short mahogany cabinet set against a far wall, he withdrew a key from his pocket. Crouched down, he unlocked the cabinet and seized a crystal bottle with a glass stopper, shaped like a cruet.

By the light of the crystal chandelier, the bottle sparkled in a dazzling array of colors--pink, blue, green, and gold, the hues coruscating in a hypnotic fashion. Dorsey held the container aloft, like a priest grasping a crucifix.

"The elixir!" His gaze lit on Galan. "It will make you mortal again!"

"But ... but it's empty." Galan wanted to cry from disappointment.

"Not quite." Dorsey smiled with encouragement. "This elixir has been passed down throughout the centuries. Each desirous vampire has taken the required amount. Now very little remains. But enough, my friend," he said with another hopeful smile. "I must warn you--wait until tomorrow night before you take it. Too late to drink it this night. Daylight may find you before the transformation is complete." He frowned, staring at the bottle. "I fear you will be the last of the undead to become mortal again. The necessary portion you must take will indeed finish the bottle."

He returned to Galan and carefully handed him the container, as a mother would transfer a newborn baby to the arms of another. "So take what remains of it--a combination of foxglove, strychnine, and a trace amount of other ingredients. Afterwards, you may discard the container." Beside Galan on the sofa, he laid a hand on his arm. "You will recall I mentioned the painful effects of this solution. But you can bear it. The promise of mortality is adequate reason."

Galan clasped the bottle and nodded, tears misting his eyes. A life with Stevie was more than reason enough. Afraid he'd break down in front of the other man, he fought the tears.

Dorsey eased away. "One thing I must tell you. When you feel no more pain, you will know you are mortal again. But then the soporific effects of the concoction will take hold, and an overwhelming sleepiness will come over you. But this is good, for you will need to rest after your ordeal." He draped his arm across Galan's shoulder and hugged him. "The pain will be great, but never doubt your ability to persevere. My thoughts and prayers will be with you tomorrow night."

Tears streamed down Galan's cheeks, and he spoke in a wavery voice. "My friend, I can't tell you how much--"

"No need to say a word. Your transformation will be my thanks." He looked out the window, where a bluish-gray tint colored the eastern horizon. "Hurry home, Galan, and later you must visit again." He winked. "And don't come alone."

\* \* \* \*

The first murky shadows stole into the corners of the room while Galan stood by his bed, clutching the bottle. Excitement warred with fear as he raised the container to his mouth and drained its contents, then winced at its bitter taste. After he tossed the bottle into a wastebasket, he waited a few moments and braced for the pain he knew would follow, but nothing happened. Not yet. No, not yet!

He shoved quivery fingers through his hair, then left the bedroom to head downstairs to the living room, past the glass door of the Florida room and on outside, to a light breeze and a plethora of pleasurable aromas. Among the trees and bushes, he prowled the backyard and stared up at the night sky, where a vast canopy of stars arrayed the heavens. A quarter moon floated in the east, flanked by Venus and Jupiter. Overhead, a plane roared northward, its lights flashing. On the street in front of his house, an ice cream truck rumbled past, playing--of all things!-- Beethoven's Fur Elise.

A hundred questions taunted him. Would he see the stars with different eyes this time tomorrow, or was the elixir only a hoax? What if it destroyed him? Anxieties tortured him, a relentless bombardment of worries that paralyzed all rational thought. Most of all, how would he adjust to life as a mortal after being a vampire all these centuries?

One wish and one person only gave him renewed optimism. When--not if--he became mortal again, he could court Stevie as a normal man, as one who loved her so much he would thrust all impediments aside to win her as his own. His wife.

Kicking a loose branch aside, he decided to return to the house, to read or watch TV, anything to get his mind off--

A stabbing pain gripped his stomach, a spasm so intense he gasped. The pain spread from his stomach down his arms and legs, pulsing, throbbing, burning, forcing him to stop and grasp an oak branch for support. Waves of dizziness washed over him. Nausea churned inside his stomach. He doubled over and fell to his knees, gagging with dry heaves, his body shaking uncontrollably. Sweat streamed down his face, dripping onto his shirt. The world spun around him.

After countless moments, he braced his hands on the ground and slowly straightened to his full height. On legs that shook like a high-rise in an earthquake, he shuffled across the lawn, each step an obstacle to overcome as he made his way to the glass door. Wet, slippery fingers shook as he slid the door back and stepped inside. A pain akin to a thousand knife wounds tore at his insides, making him shiver from his head down his chest and legs, on to his feet and toes.

The stairs loomed ahead of him, a thousand miles away. With drunken resolve, he plodded across the Florida room until he finally reached the living room. He grasped the banister and stumbled up the stairs, one leg dragging after the other. Sharp cramps accompanied him every step of the way. Could he make it to the top? He stumbled and fell, lying across the step, screaming with anguish and frustration. After long moments, he gathered his strength and grasped the banister again, then crawled upward.

"Stevie, I need you!" he gasped. If only she were with him now, he could endure his distress.

When his doorway came in sight, a series of convulsions wracked his body, one violent seizure after another, as though red-hot pincers tore his innards apart.

Agony slowed his steps as he toddled toward the double bed. He stretched out on the bed, moaning, groaning, tearing at his hair.

Unbearable pain. Relentless pain. Pain that touched every cell, every tissue, every organ of his body, an endless torture that nearly drove him insane. He tossed back and forth, grabbing folds of his bedspread, ripping the fabric. Tears streamed down his cheeks and dampened his pillow.

"Stevie!"

God, he prayed, please end this torment. Let me die, for I can't take it any longer.

Hour after hour, he suffered horrible misery. Stevie,

he gasped. Stevie, I need you. But why would she come to you when she thinks you love someone else?

Gripping the edge of the bed, he struggled to rise. He could not bear the pain any longer. He would go outside and kill himself.

## Chapter Twenty-three

Stevie, Stevie. A persistent plea roused Stevie from a sound sleep. In drowsy confusion, she turned onto her back and gradually became wide awake. She jerked upright, her stomach tense, her heart pounding with fear. Was someone in the room? Who was calling her? She pressed her hand to her heart, afraid to move, afraid to breathe.

Slowly, she sank back down, smiling at her foolishness. Only a dream. She pulled the covers up to her neck and closed her heavy-lidded eyes.

Stevie!

Galan! Wide awake, she threw the covers aside and slid out of bed. A glance at the bedside clock showed it was the middle of the night. Her fingers flew to the buttons of her pajamas, but halfway down, she hesitated. Why would Galan call her when she meant nothing to him, when he'd found someone new? She perched on the edge of the bed, shivering with the cold as she clasped and unclasped her hands.

"What should I do?" She'd make an ass of herself if she rushed over to his house and found him in bed with his new girlfriend.

Trust your instincts, every beat of her heart told her. A strong tie bound them in spiritual understanding, a link born the night he rescued her from the dungeon and gave her his blood.

But could she trust Galan? Hope blossomed inside her, spawning so many promising possibilities. Maybe he'd never had another lover. Perhaps he'd lied only to spare her, afraid she'd never want to spend her life with a vampire.

Things are not always as they seem. She'd learned that lesson a long time ago. And maybe, just maybe, she might find that there's more than one side to every story, more than one reason why people act as they do. Time she learned to trust others.

She lit her bedside lamp. Like a rabbit on PCP, she dashed about the room to dress, finally finishing with her jeans and a bulky sweater. She stepped into her running shoes and tied the laces, then grabbed the keys from her purse and headed for Galan's place.

After racing through the deserted streets, she reached Galan's house twenty minutes later. She tried the front door--locked! Where did Galan keep the spare key? Right--under the pile of bricks at the side of the house. She hurried over and lifted one brick after another, scarcely able to see a thing while ants crawled over her hands and up her arms. Frantically, she brushed the insects away. Minutes later, she found the key, then headed for the front door.

Inside, the house lay in darkness, blinds closed, not a lamp lit. Unsure what to do, where to go, she flipped the light switch by the front door, and a pale light blinked on from a table lamp. A series of low moans from upstairs jolted her and sent her headlong in the direction of the stairs.

Panic guided her steps as she rushed past the end table that bordered the wide sofa. Galan's cries sent a chill along her arms and legs, prompting countless questions. How could a vampire suffer pain? What was the matter with Galan?

Reaching the stairway, she bounded up the steps two at a time. At the top, she located the source of the cries and rushed for the end of the hall.

"Galan!" She stood in his doorway, her eyes focusing in the dark. Her heart slammed against her ribs as she pressed her hand to the door frame, her eyes searching the room, trying to locate Galan.

"Stevie?" Galan tossed and turned on the bed, his fingers digging into the covers. "I prayed you would come."

She hurried to his side and knelt beside him. "What's the matter?" she cried, running her fingers across his sweaty forehead. Heat emanated from his body, like a blast of hot air from a furnace. Her breath stuck in her throat, she waited for his answer. "Tell me!"

"An elixir," he gasped. "A ... a former vampire gave me...." He pressed his hand to his stomach and moaned--"gave me a mixture that will make me mortal again. He ... ahhhh! He warned me it would be painful, but I ... I had no idea...." He groaned, tears streaming down his face. "Don't know if it will work. Better to die."

"No! Don't say that!" She stretched out beside him and found his body drenched in perspiration. As gently as possible, she gathered him in her arms, his head on her chest. "I'm with you now. Don't even think about dying. I couldn't take it if anything happened to you!" If he were mortal again ... Her thoughts flew in a hundred different directions, every notion centered on Galan.

An elixir ... God, she prayed, please let it work.

"Only you, no one else," he murmured against her chest. "I lied when I told you ... told you I loved another. Thought it would be ... better for you. Can't expect you to love a ... a vampire." His hand gripped hers until she feared her fingers would break.

"But I do love you." She dug a handkerchief from her jeans pocket and gently wiped his face. "I've loved you for a long time. That other man you saw me with--he's a nice guy, but he can't compare to you." She tensed as convulsions shook his body, her sweater wet with his perspiration as she waited for the spasms to pass. "No one else for me, ever," she said. "And even if this elixir doesn't work ... Never mind, it will work. For sure."

Easing away, she rose from the bed.

"Stevie!"

"Be right back. Going to get a wet washcloth." A few minutes later, she returned and crouched beside him. She bathed his face, neck and arms, blowing on his skin to cool it. "I love you so much," she murmured as she unbuttoned his shirt and dabbed the washcloth across his broad chest.

"And I love--" He jerked and writhed on the bed as another spasm of pain wracked him. "Oh, my God, oh my God, oh, my God!" He screamed, an inhuman sound that sent chills racing over her body. "I can't ... can't take the pain. Let me go outside, drive a stake through my heart," he gasped. "Then you must burn me, make sure I'm destroyed."

"God, no!" She rose from the floor, then carefully lay beside him, drawing him into her arms again. "You're going to live, and you're going to become mortal. I won't let you kill yourself." Tears flowed down her cheeks as broken sobs shook her body. Ashamed of her weakness, she wiped her hand across her eyes, wanting to be brave for his sake, resolved to give him courage.

"Ah, Stevie, my Stevie."

Recalling their spiritual link, she fused her thoughts with his, giving him a glimpse of mortality, letting her strength and hope pour into him. Would this fusion work? She could only pray that it would.

She took a deep breath. "How ... how long will this last? Do you know?"

"He didn't say! But it's got to end soon. I can't take it any longer!"

"Oh, yes, you can! I'm here with you now, and if only I could take your pain from you, I'd suffer myself."

"Never! I would never wish that on you."

\* \* \* \*

Hours crept past, each minute a torment. Engulfed in pain, Galan prayed as he'd never done before, prayed for an end to his torture, even if only death brought relief. In his rare moments free of misery, he settled his gaze on his beloved, grateful she was with him, her comforting presence giving him the courage to persevere. She held him in her arms, murmuring words meant to comfort.

In the early hours of the morning, long before the sun rose, his pain eased, then gradually left him. He raised up on his elbows and stared around the room, one question taunting him. Was he mortal again?

Motionless, he waited precious minutes, fearful the pangs would return. God, he prayed, please let me be human again.

"Honey?"

"The pain," he whispered, "it's gone!"

She sat up to give him a close look. "What ... what does that mean--that you're mortal again?" She placed her hand on his chest to feel his strong heartbeat, her look full of love. "My God, are you really...?"

"I ... I don't know," he replied, afraid to hope, to dream of what might be. He waited a few moments, his breaths coming regularly. A slow warmth--sweet, blessed, wonderful warmth!-- seeped into his veins, his cells, his organs, nullifying the cold that had accompanied him for centuries. He stretched his arms and legs, hands and fingers as new life pulsed through his body. He stared at his hands and fingers, flexing them, turning them over, as if he'd never seen them before. Placing his palm on his heart, he felt its steady, even beat.

"Yes, oh yes!" He gathered her in his arms and kissed her fervently. He was mortal again! "Thank you, God," he breathed. "Thank you."

He sank back on the bed. "So wonderful ... I can't believe...." Too soon, the soporific effects of the elixir dragged him down. He fought his drowsiness, wanting to stay awake, to revel in his new life with his loved one. His eyes finally closed, joy in every cell of his body, every beat of his heart.

"My darling Stevie," he murmured in a slurred voice. "I love you so..." Then mercifully, he slept.

Stevie lay sleepless long after Galan had closed his eyes, countless questions and anxieties keeping her awake. Most important, how would Galan adjust to mortal life again, after being a vampire for almost a thousand years? Who was Linette, and what connection was there between that woman and her?

Galan was the link, Stevie felt sure, certain he would tell her soon enough.

A lesser problem, but still important--what about her family? Somehow, some way, she'd have to reconcile herself with her family, especially her father.

But Galan came first.

With dreamy eyes, she turned to gaze at him, this wonderful man who slept peacefully next to her. Love for him swelled inside her, almost painful in its intensity, prompting her to push her worries aside. Nothing was impossible when they loved each other so much.

She leaned over to kiss him on the forehead. "Galan, I love you." She could scarcely wait until he woke, when she would tell him again and again of her love.

One question still plagued her like a persistent headache.

Who was Linette?

## Chapter Twenty-four

Bright sunlight flooded the room as Galan roused from a sound sleep and yawned, staring around him in awe. Sunlight! By God, it was beautiful! Warm and soothing, it flowed over his body like water. For the first time in almost a thousand years, he'd slept at night, waking up to this glorious morning. He smiled as last night came back in full force, a night he'd remember forever, one that had changed his life, that had made him alive. A time in which his beloved had shared his metamorphosis.

A cool breeze wafted through an open window, bringing the scent of rain-washed grass. Next to him, Stevie lay on her side, eyes closed, a smile on her lips, as if she were having the most wonderful dream. Of him? He studied her for silent moments, unable to remove his gaze from her, this woman he loved beyond reason, whom he would cherish until death.

She mumbled in her sleep and stretched, then slowly blinked her eyes open.

"'Morning, sleepyhead." He gave her a light kiss on the cheek. "You came to me when I needed you. Just before I saw you, I was ready to go outside, kill myself."

"My God, what if I hadn't arrived in time!" She closed her eyes for a brief moment. "I don't even want to think about it."

"Having you with me made all the difference in the world. You know that, don't you?" Filled with love for her, he looked long and fully into her eyes. "I don't think I could have borne the pain without you."

She stared at him. "Your skin--it's not pale anymore!" Raising up on one elbow, she gave him a curious look. "But how do you feel?"

He met her look and smiled. "Like a mortal." Sighing, he squeezed her hand. "Things won't be easy, you know. After all these years as a vampire, when I lived by night and slept by day, when I had to ... to feed on others, so that I could exist." He shook his head as painful memories surfaced. "But I can face any problem, as long as I have you with me. And that reminds me...." He paused, unsure how to proceed, wondering if Stevie loved him enough to share the rest of her life with him.

"What, sweetheart?"

"Will you marry me?" he asked in a rush of words. "Please say 'yes.' You must know how much I love you, and I don't think I can live without you."

Her eyes shone with love. "Galan, I never dreamed I could love anyone as much as I love you."

"Then you'll marry me?"

"Did you ever doubt it?"

"Ah, Stevie, my dearest!" Eager lips traced a path from her neck to her mouth, his lips homing in on hers. He kissed her long and hard, so afraid the bloodlust would come upon him again. But no, this feeling was wonderful, glorious! as passion burgeoned inside him and became an all-consuming need to make this woman his own.

"Sweetheart!" She slipped her arms around his neck, and he reveled in her fierce embrace, her sweet lilac fragrance, the brush of her silky hairs against his neck--all these treasures that meant more to him than a fortune in gold.

His kiss deepened, his longing at the breaking point. Ah, to make her his own, here, now! To know all the warmth and sweetness that surely must lie within her. How he wanted to make love to her, but not now. Only as his wife.

Drawing on all his willpower, he found the strength to ease back. "How can you care for me," he asked, "knowing what I was?"

She ran her finger tenderly down his cheek. "I think I've always loved you, from the first time we met. Of course, I wasn't aware of it then," she said with a smile. "And how could I stop loving you, even after you told me you were a ... a vampire," she said, feathering kisses down his face. "You can't just turn affection off and on like a faucet. And even if that elixir hadn't worked--if you'd stayed a vampire--I'd still care for you."

"And still want to marry me?"

"Yes!" She kissed him again, a long, slow kiss that told him all he wanted to know. "Honey, don't ever doubt my feelings."

"We'll have to marry right away," he whispered. "Can't wait much longer."

"Is two weeks too long?"

"Two days is too long." He sighed. "But I'll try to bear it. After all, I've waited almost one-thousand years for you. I suppose a little while longer won't matter."

That settled, she lay silent for a long moment, her forehead creased, her fingers moving restlessly on the blanket.

He peered at her. "Darling, what did I say that bothers you?"

"Nothing you said now, but something I've wondered about...."

"So tell me."

"Linette," she said quickly, as if discarding a burden.

He shot up in bed. "How do you know about her?"

"I've had dreams," she began with a puzzled look, "about you and me, but sometimes--" She paused, licking her bottom lip-- "sometimes you called me Linette."

Gradually, he sank back down, his mind working, wondering what to tell her, how to tell her. "What are your thoughts on reincarnation?" he finally said.

"I have an open mi--" Comprehension showed on her face. "So you're telling me--"

"That you were Linette, a woman I loved almost a thousand years ago." He hugged her close. "Honey, didn't I just say I've waited a thousand years for you? I meant that in more ways than one. You are the woman I loved so long ago. And somehow, you absorbed that fact in your dreams." He thought for a moment. "Telepathy, perhaps?"

"But have we met in other lives?"

He shook his head. "Only in this one." He shook his head. "Don't ask me why, but I think ... I think...."

"Yes?"

"I believe it's because the time wasn't right before, that it's only now that we were ready to meet again. Call it fate or divine intervention ... who knows?" He smiled. "One of the mysteries of life."

She snuggled closer to him. "I'm glad I was the one for you. Can't imagine loving anyone else."

He kissed her again. "Nor can I."

* * * *

"Married? My little girl's getting married?" Stevie thought her dad sounded happy when she phoned him the next day, and she hoped this might be the beginning of a reconciliation between them. Still, they had a long way to go in mending their differences.

"At the risk of sounding trite," he continued, "who's the lucky guy?"

"Galan Kent, the most wonderful man in the world." She laughed, leaning back on the sofa. "And I guess I sound trite, too. But Dad, he's an awfully nice guy." She raised her hand to watch the light sparkle on her three carat emerald cut engagement ring Galan had bought this morning at Tiffany's. She never thought she'd own a such an exquisite ring. Must have cost Galan a fortune, but he'd told her money was no object.

"Do you want to get married in New York?" her father asked. "Naturally, I'll pay for the wedding."

"Dad, Galan and I decided to have a simple wedding here in Miami. I appreciate your offer of payment, but we can manage."

"Stephanie...." A trace of hesitancy tinged his voice. "What does this--Galan, did you say?--what does he do for a living?"

She should have known he'd ask that but supposed it was a legitimate question. "He's a writer. Non-fiction. Recently sold a book to a big New York publisher and got a large advance. Believe me, Galan's a guy who can do anything he sets his mind to. He told me he intends to make a living from writing, so I don't doubt he'll do just that."

"I see."

She twisted the telephone cord around her finger. Too bad if you don't like that idea, Dad.

A long pause, then she heard him sigh. "Stephanie, I know things haven't been as amiable between us as you or I would like--"

"And you know why, don't you?"

"Yes. So let me say something now, as long as we're being frank with each other. I want to apologize for taking that bribe all those years ago. Only time I've ever done such a thing. So happens I needed the money for your mother's medical expenses, but of course, that's no excuse. I wasn't thinking right, what with her cancer and all my worries. It's been on my conscience all this time. I know it's upset you."

"The understatement of the year," she replied. "How about making amends for that lapse in judgment? If you made a donation to the homeless, that would make me very happy."

"Since when have you taken such an interest in the homeless?"

Since you accepted that bribe, she wanted to say. "I've worked with them here in Miami for a long time. So, what do you say, Dad?"

A pause, then he spoke. "I'm due a payment from a wealthy land developer, a German fellow who bought a large tract of land west of the city. When I receive the money from him, I'll give a substantial portion to the Presbyterian Outreach program for feeding the homeless. Does that satisfy you?"

"Very much." Leaning back, she put her feet on the coffee table, happy she and her dad had finally reached an understanding.

Her father coughed. "Now about your college education...."

"I got my student loan, and I intend to go to law school, after all. That way I can combine the practice of law with helping those who can't afford a regular attorney's fees." Take that however you want. "Galan thinks it's great that I want to become a lawyer and do pro bono work."

"Speaking of needing--if you need more money for tuition, I'll gladly give you whatever is necessary, no strings attached."

"Galan and I are working out the money angle between us, but I appreciate your offer...."

"See you at the wedding," she said after a few minutes of family news, anxious to see everyone again.

* * * *

*Two weeks later.*

"Never thought we'd get away by ourselves," Stevie said on a balmy evening in April, a few hours after the reception. Outside the window of their Miami Beach hotel, the glimmering aqua waters of the Atlantic Ocean lapped up on the shore. An ocean liner bedecked the horizon, a far distant speck on the sea. Their luxurious room with its king sized bed was just about the grandest she'd ever seen and one she'd never forget, for she knew this room would spawn memories to last her the rest of her life.

Tomorrow they'd leave for a tour of Europe--London, Paris, Rome, Vienna, and yes, Prague. Just for the fun of it, they'd decided to visit the manor house she'd lived in during her trip through time. But tonight was all she could think about, all she wanted to think about, this night with Galan.

Her eyes shifted to her new husband. In her white short-sleeved satin wedding gown trimmed with Alencon lace, she fingered Galan's silky tie, smoothing her hands across his broad chest. She focused her gaze on every feature--his dark, curly hair, those angular cheekbones and ebony eyes whose look was only for her.

She slipped her finger under his tie knot, loosening it. "Anyway, I'm glad I got to see my family again and that you had a chance to meet everyone. It was a nice wedding, don't you think?"

Warm hands caressed her shoulders as he eased her closer, and his touch alone was enough to send a rush of desire through her, a need to get in bed with him this very minute.

"A very nice wedding," he said, "and you were the prettiest bride I've ever seen." He kissed the top of her head. "I enjoyed meeting your family, too. But honey, I can think of better things to do than talk about the wedding."

She drew back in mock surprise. "Oh, you don't want to talk? Then what do you want to do?"

Galan returned her to his embrace, murmuring against her hair. "Three guesses."

"One guess is all I need." She wrapped her arms around his neck, pressing her body to his, catching his faint sandalwood aroma, the beat of his heart. "Make me yours," she whispered next to his ear. "Let me show you how much I love you."

"Yes!" He released her to close the draperies, shutting out the world. As he turned away from the window, his gaze settled on her again, his expression leaving no doubt of his intentions.

Stepping behind her, he unzipped her gown, letting it fall in a silky heap at her feet, followed by her slip. He placed a light kiss on her shoulder, then moved in front of her, frowning in concentration as his fingers fumbled with her bra until he finally succeeded in releasing the flimsy bit of fabric.

Without a word, he tossed the bra aside and knelt, his eager hands drifting down to her garter belt and underpants, his fingers sliding along her hip. He slipped the satiny garments down her legs as his fingers caressed her skin in silent adoration. She closed her eyes with dreamy expectancy. A rush of heat traveled over her body, finally settling in her feminine core.

"Stevie, Stevie," he whispered. "I never thought I could be so happy."

"Me, either!"

While he clasped her hands, she stepped out of her dress and underclothes. Standing back, he observed her, his eyes reverently assessing her, as if she were the finest Waterford vase, an exquisite floral bouquet, the Mona Lisa.

"You're lovely," he said. "Beautiful!"

Her cheeks warmed. "It's nice to know I'm appreciated."

Self-conscious at her nudity, she hurried over to a chair and perched on its edge, jerking stockings and shoes off, kicking them to the side.

Thankful for the dim lamplight, she rose from the chair while he reached for her, his voice low and urgent. "Honey, please!"

"Hey, not so fast." Stevie removed his tie, sliding it from his neck and tossing it on a chair, where his jacket already resided. "And your shirt." Her fingers traveled down his hard chest, her movements clumsy with impatience. A tuft of curly black hair peeked over his undershirt, sending her excitement skyrocketing to the stratosphere. After she helped him pull his undershirt off, she moved her hands up his muscled arms and across his broad back, loving the feel and scent of him. Unbuckling his belt, she let her hands linger on his lower abdomen as her fingers inched teasingly downward.

He seized her hands in his own. "You're driving me crazy!"

"I'm driving me crazy."

Within seconds, he got rid of the remainder of his clothes, then tossed them onto the chair. He stood before her, magnificent in his perfection, every line, every angle of his hard-muscled body.

For long, silent moments, she stared at him. "You're beautiful!" Overcome with love for him, she tried to make light of her emotions. "And you're mine!" She swallowed past the lump in her throat. "I love you so much. How did I ever live before I met you?"

"My God, Stevie, you are my life." He drew back to look at her long and fully. "To think you could ever love me, knowing what I was...." He sighed and kissed her forehead. "It's a miracle, sweetheart."

Her embrace tightened. "A miracle we found each other," she whispered in his ear. "And nothing will ever change my love for you."

Tears filled his eyes. Brushing his hand across them, he left her to slide the bedspread back, then returned to wrap his arms around her waist. "What are we waiting for?" he said in a husky voice.

Without effort, he lifted her and placed her on the bed, then lay beside her. Between whispered endearments and his touch that kindled desire in every inch of her, he brought her to the point where she could no more deny him than she could stop her heart from beating.

Desperate for him, she welcomed him inside her, unable to think or say a word, wanting--needing--his kisses, his caresses, the sweet, wonderful reality of his love. She ignored a brief moment of pain, then he led her to heights she'd only read about, to breathtaking pleasures she'd only imagined, to an ecstasy she'd only dreamed of.

"Sweetheart!" she cried while mind-shattering passion burst inside her.

"My dear wife." Long moments passed, then he kissed her softly. "Did I hurt you very much?" he asked as they lay side by side, their breathing returned to normal.

She feathered his face with kisses. "Only for a moment."

"I love you, darling," he murmured, nuzzling her neck. "In case I haven't said that enough lately, I'm telling you now."

Her eyes misted. "Same with me."

"Ah, darling."

As the air conditioning cooled their bodies, she lay in his arms, his heartbeat strong and steady beneath her cheek. She entwined her fingers with his. "That ... what we just did ... was nice," she teased. "We'll have to do that again."

"Um, let me think about it. How about next week?"

She gave him a playful tap and snuggled closer. "You have a hairy chest," she said.

He raised up slightly to look at her. "You don't like hairy chests?"

"If I tell you I like your chest, will you tell me you like mine?" she asked, full of mischief.

His hand closed over her breast. "I don't need to tell you," he said in his low, sensuous voice that already had her craving for more. "There are other ways to show you...."

How can anything be so beautiful? Galan thought as he made love to this exquisite woman, meant only for him, this woman who was all he'd ever wanted, all he'd dreamed of. Throughout the centuries he'd waited for her, never knowing the love of a mortal woman, never making love to a mortal woman. Now ... now, she was his alone, his to love and cherish for the rest of their lives. And he was making love to her. Wonderful, beautiful, glorious love. Passion consumed him, a rainbow of vibrant colors, a medley of every symphony in the world, a burst of happiness greater than anything he'd ever known.

Moments later, he turned onto his back, his wife clasped in his arms, his heart beating with love for her. "Only you, no one else, ever."

Stevie eased closer and placed a light kiss on his chest. "No one else for me, either. How could I ever want another man after I've had you?"

As twilight crept into the room and her lover slept beside her, Stevie gazed on his face, his dark, curly hair, his angular features, his firm mouth and strong jaw. She reached over to brush the hair from his forehead, her fingers light and loving. Turning onto his side, he eased closer and murmured her name.

To think he was her husband now, this man who was once a vampire. Tears flowed down her cheeks, and she swallowed hard, loving him so much she ached with it. She knew she'd never lived until now, knew there'd never be another man for her.

Only Galan, for all time.

THE END

Printed in the United States
54835LVS00004B/4-18